MW00718045

Permanent Reminders

A Jaz Dilan Mystery

Kelsey Anne Lovelady

Tea With Coffee Media

Tea With Coffee Media

Permanent Reminders: A Jaz Dilan Mystery Copyright © 2022 by Kelsey Anne Lovelady

Cover and Internal Design © 2022 by Tea With Coffee Media

Cover Design by Victoria Moxely/Tea With Coffee Media

Cover Images by Dreamstime

Internal Images © Kelsey Anne Lovelady via Canva

Tea With Coffee Media and the colophon are trademarks of Tea With Coffee Media

All rights reserved.

No portion of this book may be reproduced in any form without written permission from the publisher or author, except as permitted by U.S. copyright law.

Published by Tea With Coffee Media

teawithcoffee.media

Cataloging-in-Publication Data is on file with the Library of Congress.

Print ISBN#—978-1-957893-14-3

Ebook ISBN#—978-1-957893-15-0

Published by Tea With Coffee Media

Content Warnings

This book contains:

Manslaughter, murder, past references to rape/child molestation/kidnapping, implied child pornography, implied pedophilia, past and current references to alcohol abuse, light homophobic language, depictions of PTSD and its symptoms, and adult language.

Reader Discretion is advised.

Contents

The Seattle Times

THE CATTLEMAN SENTENCED

Tamie Mariah Zuckerberg

June 8th, 19984

The streets of Seattle are finally free from the tyranny of The Cattleman. Seth Frost, 46, has been convicted of murder, sexual assault, and kidnapping. The judge passed down a life sentence in the Federal Detention Center, Seatac.

Frost's reign of terror began in January of last year. His first victim, Ashley Klinkenhammer, was found dead in *Pigment of Truth*, a tattoo parlor on North Queen Anne Avenue. Three more victims—Cynthia Eriksen, Sara Banks, and Felicia Orman—were found throughout the year in various tattoo parlors around Seattle. The police have yet to explain Frost's moniker or how the victims were connected.

Frost was finally apprehended almost a year ago after his final victim escaped and ran to the home of one Jimmie Kwan. The police acted quickly without sirens and within an hour, Frost was arrested at his home on August 17th, 1997. Kwan has yet to comment on the case.

It has taken almost a year for the trial of Frost to take place. The court had to hold it at Gonzaga Law School in Spokane. This location served two purposes; first, it provided a secret location for the trial until the sentence was passed down. Such secrecy was necessary after a security breach at King County Courtroom's jail. The second purpose of the location was to find the jury. "Every citizen in Seattle proved to be ineligible to serve because they were too biased against Frost", says Police Chief Michael Tennant. Based on our research, over ninety percent of the State of Washington called Frost guilty long before the trial even began. He has truly proven that he is a menace to society.

The state's opinion of Frost is so strong, in fact, that many believe a life sentence in prison was too light. Charles and Laura Klinkenhammer—the parents of Frost's first victim—told the times, "He never should've been born, but since he's already here, the death penalty is the only option. Hopefully, the other monsters in that prison will do the court's job."

When the final victim testified in court, the general public had to leave the courtroom; only the judge, court reporter, attorneys, and jury were present. When we attempted to contact anyone who saw her, all refused to comment or reveal her identity.

In fact, when the anonymous victim went missing, the police did not release that information to the public. Chief Tennant told the Times, "The withholding of the information was to help the victim; Frost only killed his victims after the police made public statements regarding them. We thought that by not releasing a statement, we could buy ourselves and the victim more time. We were correct, thank God." Several people have contacted the Times, claiming to know the final victim. None of these claims coincide and none have been confirmed.

Whether Frost's sentence is enough to heal the people he's harmed, only time will tell.

ALL THAT JAZ

"**I**'M HOME!" JAZ DILAN'S voice echoed around the compact, two-bedroom apartment. As the sun set over the Newark neighborhood, it broke through the dark winter clouds. The blood-orange light illuminated the dining room and eat-in kitchen. The living room, on the other hand, was lit by hand-me-down lamps and the flat-screen TV, which was blasting some women's pro-wrestling program. The hardwood floors didn't look nearly as beat up in the natural light as it did under the fluorescent bulbs. *Just like me* Jaz would always say; she always hated how pale she looked in fluorescent light. She'd lost count of how many times people had compared her to a china doll under artificial lighting. It was only

January--almost February--and she couldn't wait until winter's end; then there would be warmer natural light to bring out the manhattan tan in her skin.

"Hey, Aunt Jaz!" Jaz knew her niece was home before the teenager called to her; the suffocating musk of her Xea body spray completely overwhelmed the calming essential oils Jaz had put in the diffuser that morning.

Jaz waved her hand, trying to get her niece's perfume away from her nose. "Whew. Got a date tonight?" The body spray wasn't the only indication of this; the teenager was wearing her favorite black, tattered dress, and she'd actually bothered to comb the tangles out of her half-curly hair.

Rosamie jumped off the couch. "Yeah, Annie and I are going to the movies after our support group." *Liar.* "But enough about me. How was your day?"

Jaz folded her arms over her graphic-t-shirt-covered chest. "It was okay. Now, what do you want?"

"What?" Rosamie asked.

"You want something. What is it?"

Jaz's niece put her hand to her heart as her brown eyes mimicked that of a puppy's; wide and innocent. "Can't your favorite niece just ask how your day was because she loves and cares for you?"

"*Only* niece," Jaz corrected before saying, "and that bullshit may have worked on your mom, but not with me. Now talk."

Rosamie sighed and ran her hand through her curly, black under-cut. "Okay, so I've *finally* settled on my first tattoo and—"

Jaz dropped her bag on the ground by the door and slipped off her coat. "No way in hell."

Rosamie followed Jaz into the kitchen, whining, "Come on, Aunt Jaz!"

Opening the fridge, Jaz stated, "I am not going to design or give you your first tattoo."

"Why not?"

As Jaz cracked open a diet soda, she explained, "You're too young."

"I'm sixteen! You were sixteen when you got your first tattoo!"

After taking a sip of her soda, Jaz lectured, "Apples and oranges. I had a good reason. You just want to rebel, and I don't have time for your mother to put a hit on me."

Waving Jaz's point off, Rosamie said, "Oh, she's never gonna find out."

"How do you know?"

"Because I'm never seeing or speaking to her again, so how would she find out unless someone snitches? And you would never do that." The look Jaz gave Rosamie made her doubt the statement. "Would you?"

"We'll never know," Jaz said ominously before she became serious again. "You say you'll never speak to her again now, but you never know; it may take a year or ten but you two might patch things up."

Rosamie huffed, "Fat fucking chance," under her breath as she slumped back into the living room and flung herself back onto the couch.

Jaz slumped next to her niece and put an arm around her. As she petted the buzzed side of Rosamie's head, she remembered when Rosamie got the haircut. It had actually taken Jaz by surprise. Rosamie's idolization of her aunt made Jaz think she would do anything to look just like her--down to growing her hair out, straightening it, and getting the carmine highlights put in. So when Rosamie came out with a natural, seal brown undercut, Jaz was surprised. And a bit relieved.

Putting herself back in the moment at hand, Jaz said, "I know things are rough. You're angry and think if you stay angry, your mom will come crawling for forgiveness. I went through the same thing with your lola."

"Are you seriously shrinking me right now?"

Ignoring Rosamie, Jaz continued, "She's just having a hard time coming to terms with the fact that you're growing up."

"And that I'm not the next Stephen Hawking and going to Harvard to become an engineer?"

Jaz shook her head. "You go to Harvard to become a lawyer. You go to MIT to become an engineer. And Stephen Hawking was a physicist, which you go to Stanford for. And she wants you to live your dreams like she never could."

Rosamie argued, "'Cept I don't *want* to become an engineer or a lawyer or a physicist."

In an attempt to calm her niece, Jaz clarified, "She just doesn't want you to go through all her hardships."

"You mean like being a teen mom with a missing, deadbeat baby-daddy, and three part-time jobs at thirty-five?" There was that blunt tone of Rosamie's.

"Exactly."

Rosamie scoffed. "If that happens, it'll be the next immaculate conception."

"You *do* know what 'immaculate' means, right?"

"Impossible."

"No, it means 'pure'," Jaz corrected.

"Oh. So what do you call it when an experienced lesbian winds up pregnant?"

"Suspicious." Jaz cackled when her niece pushed her shoulder playfully. When the laughing fit was over, Jaz put an arm back around

Rosamie's shoulder. "One day, you're going to want your mom in your life."

"Maybe. But right now, I want a tattoo."

With a roll of her eyes, Jaz stood up and started walking towards her room to change. "Then you will be getting it from someone else."

"Come on! You're the best tattoo artist in the city—"

Jaz cut her niece off by correcting, "No, I'm not."

"And you're my aunt!"

"So?"

"So you'd give me a discount!" There was that look again; the one that made uncertainty break Rosamie's face. "Right?"

"With the risk you'd be putting me through? I'd charge you double."

"It's not a crime!"

"Tell that to your mother."

Rosamie pouted. "You would seriously gouge me on the price? You'd do that to your favorite niece?"

"*Only* niece, and absolutely."

"Now that *is* a crime."

"Sue me." Jaz's apartment bell buzzed, signaling that the ladies had a visitor. Pressing the call button, Jaz asked into her intercom, "Yeah?"

Through the crackling interference of the intercom, Jaz heard, "Hey, Jaz! It's Annie!"

Rosamie glimpsed at her phone. "Early as usual."

"Come on up!" Pressing another button, Jaz unlocked the building's front door. "Don't forget, you have work tomorrow."

"Ugh. You sound like mom," was all Rosamie said as she slipped her leather jacket on over her intentionally tattered dress. It hadn't escaped Jaz that Rosamie's leather jacket was very similar to the one that Jaz wore every day. In fact, ever since Rosamie was in middle school, she would try to emulate Jaz in looks, language, and mannerisms. This made Jaz feel somewhat guilty for the friction between Rosamie and her mom; the disrespect that Rosamie had shown Jaz's little sister sounded a little bit like how Jaz sounded in all her stories about dealing with crazy, self-centered New Yorkers. Apparently, Rosamie didn't realize that such attitudes and languages should only be used on rude strangers and not her mother.

When there was a knock, Rosamie opened the door, revealing her girlfriend--a short, round and adorable girl with wispy black hair that had been pulled into a fashionably messy bun. Her chocolate eyes were huge behind her rectangle glasses, and they shined with an excitement that was just as obvious in her perfect smile.

Rosamie gave Annie a peck on her lips, bringing a pink blush to the girl's arabesque skin. "Hey, bae."

As Annie used her pastel-colored shirt to de-fog her pure red glasses, she greeted, "Hey, hon. Hi, Jaz!"

"Good to see you, Annie. Love the shirt."

"Thanks! It's from the Empire Hearts collection!" Jaz nodded like she knew what that was. *Knowing Annie, it's either an anime or a video game.* "You doing anything tonight?"

"Yeah, I'm grabbing dinner with a friend."

Rosamie interjected, "Good. So you won't be waiting up. Come on, Annie." She grabbed Annie's hand and started dragging her down the hall.

Jaz called after them, "Not too late!" Rosamie gave a dismissive wave while Annie gave a respectful "Yes ma'am" as she was being tugged along.

Garrett slumped in the booth, complaining, "Seriously? These guys aren't even that good."

"Then why do you keep watching?", Jaz asked in mock annoyance.

Garrett held up his hands, putting his tattoo sleeves on full display. "Hey, I don't set the channels."

"Yeah, but you keep coming back here on the same night of the week and drag me with you."

"Pfft." The scoff made Garrett's caramel beard and mustache ripple. "'Dragging' my ass. You love the food here."

"True." Jaz had taken the subway to meet her best friend, Garrett Weber, for their monthly meet up at *The Gym Bar and Grille.* Located downtown, the well-kept place wasn't busy like it would be on the weekend, so it was simple for them to get their favorite table; a metal booth with black leather cushions. Bolted-down in the middle was a hundred-pound weight plate that acted as a spinning table tray. It also had the perfect view of the one TV—out of twenty— that was always playing the edgy-arsty cable channel. That night of the week was when new episodes of *Ink Professors* broadcasted. It was Garrett's guilty pleasure; he always complained about it yet watched it religiously. He would even jump into fist fights with the sports crowd if they got rowdy enough to block his view. *Whatever floats his boat, I guess.*

Thank god there's not an important game tonight; watching Jaz's skinny friend start fights with men two or three times his size was embarrassing. It didn't matter how many Viking tattoos he had; Mjolnir wasn't going to stop the meatheads from laughing when Garrett would cuss them out. In fact, the blond undercut and thick beard made his outbursts all the more hilarious. Several people had pointed out that he looked like a prepubescent teen who was trying so hard to grow facial hair so he could look older and tougher.

As a commercial break interrupted *Ink Professors*, Garrett bit into his cheeseburger. "How's work?"

Jaz sighed as she spread more green chili on her own burger. "I'm having to turn *good* customers away. I mean, I appreciate the business, but I'm just one person and there are only twenty-four hours in a day."

With a mouthful of onions and swiss cheese, Garrett asked, "No luck finding an apprentice?"

Jaz sighed "No. I mean, there's no lack of applicants, but no one gets it."

"I didn't know there was something to 'get' in tattooing."

"You know what I mean." As a preview of the next week's *Ink Professors* episode played, Jaz pointed to the TV. "They're like those assholes. They think they can get rich or that they can just do whatever they want. The person paying for the tattoo is just a piece of paper with arms and legs."

Garrett nodded in understanding. "I'll ask my apprentice if she knows anyone looking for a job that she would recommend. She's the best apprentice I've ever had, so hopefully she has friends with similar work ethics."

"Keep me posted."

"Will do." They continued to watch *Ink Professors* until the commercial break that started on a predictable cliff hanger. Garrett asked between bites, "Any new crazy customer stories?"

Jaz chuckled. "Well, punching bag balls has officially been dethroned."

Garrett's face fell. "Aw man, I loved that dude. So who's the new ruler of the insane asylum?"

Jaz cleared her throat dramatically. As she spoke, she spread Jaz hand out in front of her face, as if she was picturing a billboard or marquis that quoted her. "I call him, 'Call of Duty: Butt Ops'."

Garrett coughed as soda burned its way up his nose. "What?!"

"A guy literally asked if I could tattoo a crosshair over his asshole."

Garrett scoffed, "Let me guess; something for his boyfriend?"

"Nope. Girlfriend." More soda went up Garrett's nose as he suffocated from laughter. When he could breathe again, Jaz asked, "What about you?"

Garrett chuckled. "Best I got is I tattooed a pen on the side of this guy's head. Like, it looks like it's tucked behind his ear forever."

"That's it?"

"I've been pawning all my crazy jobs onto my lacky."

Jaz shook her head. "Wow. You're a dick."

"Hey, she has to learn that some clients are coo-coo for cocoa puffs. The only way she's gonna learn is through experience."

"So you just *happen* to benefit from teaching your apprentice how to handle the drunks, crazies, and insensitive assholes the hard way?"

Garrett shrugged. "Happy accident." Jaz kicked him under the table, sending the friends into another fit of laughter.

Their laughter was interrupted by one of the waitresses setting a martini down in front of Jaz. "Compliments of a gentleman at the bar." Jaz and Garrett furrowed their brows at each other before peering around the waitress into the bar area. The drink came from a guy who looked like he was celebrating getting cast on *Jersey Coast*; a fake tan covered his arm tattoos. *He had to be drunk when he got all of those.* He wore his sunglasses on the back of his head, tucked beneath his spiked, frosted tips. His teeth were as shiny as the thick chain around his neck, and the knock-off Rolex on his right wrist. He raised his canned beer to Jaz as he popped his overly-groomed eyebrows.

Jaz handed the martini back to the waitress. "Tell him that if I accepted this, I'd be ruining a twelve-year streak, and he's not worth that."

The waitress was confused until she saw the alcoholics anonymous pin on Jaz's jacket. "Got it." She walked back into the bar. While they couldn't hear or read lips, Jaz and Garrett watched the waitress speak to the party boy. After a moment, the guy gave Jaz a horrified look and ducked out of sight, cheeks glowing beneath his artificial pigment.

Garrett applauded. "Well done. Excellent control."

"It gets easier every year. Besides, I knew you would knock it out of my hand just because of the guy who bought it for me."

"That is pretty ballsy; hitting on a woman who's out eating with another guy."

Jaz scoffed as she drank from her diet soda. "Guys like that don't care. All women are fair game to them."

"Gross. We may have to find you a real boyfriend if this keeps up."

Jaz scoffed again. "You know I've committed myself to spinster-hood."

"Right. Right."

"Have *you* met anyone?" The lively atmosphere stifled. Garrett shrugged with his mouth and stared down at his food. He chugged down his soda, clearly wishing it had been a beer. Even that martini Jaz was given would do the trick. "Sorry. I just worry—"

"Well, don't. I'll get over Jess in my own time and in my own way."

"Right. Sorry."

Silence fell over the table until Garrett chuckled. "Boy, we're pathetic, aren't we?"

"Speak for yourself, and while you do, I gotta piss like a racehorse."

As Jaz slid out of the booth, Garrett chuckled, "Demure as ever."

"You know it." Jaz walked towards the back of the building, passing the *Jersey Coast* wannabe on the way. He was timid as she passed.

The single stall bathroom was the one place that made the pristine, gym-inspired bar look less than pristine; it was covered in writing and carvings. There were initials of couples—the ones with one set of initials scratched out were everlasting reminders of drunk, one-night stands that never went anywhere. There were also numbers; some were helpful like New York's Suicide Prevention Hotline. However, most were numbers advertised for "personal trainers" who would help you "work out and have fun doing it". Beneath those numbers were responses like, "7 secs of cardio won't make me a VS model." Jaz was sure the only reason why there wasn't a glory hole was that the single stall didn't facilitate anonymity.

Once the door was locked, Jaz pulled out her cell and began typing on the pot.

Recipient: Rosamie

Jaz: How's it going?

Rosamie: gre!at! yobu?

She's drunk as hell.

Jaz: Good. When are you gonna be home?

Rosamie: Idk. e12?

She must've realized how drunk she sounded and switched to the abbreviations to avoid getting caught.

Jaz: Okay. Be careful.

Rosamie: y, mmo. :P

"Yes, mom."

Jaz: You gotta come up with a better insult. LOL

Rosamie: :P

By the time the text conversation was over, Jaz was done in the bathroom. When she got back to the booth, it was empty. There was a napkin on her side with writing on it.

Sorry. Got called into work. Emergency. Pay you back tomorrow

- Garrett

"Got called in?" He's the boss; he called himself in.

The waitress came and set the check on the table. However, she was holding a glass of wine in her other hand. "Should I tell this guy the same thing?" She was referring to the out-of-place trust-fund-baby in a polo shirt who was sipping bourbon out of a tumbler. *It's not nearly as classy without the fireplace and smoking jacket.*

"Asshole." Jaz wasn't talking about the trust-fund-baby.

2

WHERE IS THY STING?

J AZ WAS JOSTLED AWAKE, not by her cell phone alarm, but by her cell phone *ringing*. Peaking at the screen, Jaz rolled her eyes. It was Mr. Hong; Rosamie's boss. Jaz was never going to forgive her niece for listing her aunt's personal number on her work application. Jaz didn't even say hello when she answered the phone. "Rosamie! You're late again! Get here now or you're fired! Don't think I won't do it!" Mr. Hong must've had a wall-installed landline; cell phones didn't crack like that when people hung up, even in anger. This was not how Jaz wanted to start her morning.

Jaz threw the covers back and ripped herself out of bed. She yelled, "Rosamie. Get your ass up. You're late again, and Mr. Hong is pissed," as she walked into the eat-in kitchen and turned on the coffee maker. After Jaz popped a few pieces of bread into the toaster, she yelled again, "Rosamie!" as she marched up to her niece's bedroom door and threw it open.

It was impossible to tell if Rosamie had come home the night before; the room was in such disarray that it looked abandoned and lived in at the same time. All Jaz did know was that Rosamie wasn't there, and she obviously wasn't at work.

Jaz scanned her phone. *No new or missed messages.* She went to her contacts, clicked on Rosamie's page, and hit "call". "Hey, weirdo who's calling me in the age of text! It's Rosamie! I don't use my phone to talk to people, so get with it and DM me!" The voicemail had played instantly; Rosamie's phone was off. Jaz scowled as she hung up without leaving a voicemail. *She hasn't done this since her first night in New York. What the fuck?* She jumped back to contacts and scrolled up to Annie's page.

The phone rang four or five times, and Jaz was ready to hear Annie's voicemail when a groggy voice answered, "Hello?"

"Annie?" Jaz asked, uncertain if she had the right number.

"Yeah?"

"It's Jaz."

"Oh, hi Jaz." Annie sounded like she was in serious pain.

"Are you okay?" *Stupid question.*

"Oh, yeah. I just have a really bad headache." *Big surprise.* "What's up?"

"Rosamie's boss just called to yell at her for being late," Jaz did her best to keep the annoyance out of her voice. "She's not in her room, and I don't know if she came home last night. Is she there with you?"

"Yeah. Sorry. We were both so tired after the ba—movie, and we were closer to my apartment, so we came to get some rest. Sorry, I should've called,"

At least she apologizes for not contacting me. "It's okay. Can you just wake her up and tell her to get to work?"

"Sure."

"Oh, and Annie?"

"Yeah?"

"The best cure for *that* kinda 'headache' is a shot of pickle juice. You know, just in case Rosamie also has a 'headache'."

There was a long moment of silence before Annie said, "Thanks. We'll give that a try."

"No problem. Tell Rosamie to text me when she gets to work," It was hard to keep the amusement out of Jaz's voice. *They thought they were so sneaky.*

"I will. Talk to you later, Jaz."

"Later, Annie." Jaz hung up and got back to her coffee.

Right when she was starting to get comfortable, Jaz's cell rang again. Expecting to see Mr. Hong's number again, she furrowed her brows when she saw Annie's name on the caller ID. She answered, asking, "Annie?"

"Jaz?!"

"What's wrong?"

"It's Rosamie! I don't know what happened! I don't know what to do!" Each sentence was broken up by a raspy, high pitched inhale; Annie was panicking so much that she was beginning to hyperventilate.

"Calm down, Annie. Tell me what's wrong."

"SHE'S DEAD!" Every ounce of heat in Jaz's body abandoned her limps and settled into her chest where it felt like it was cooking her heart. Was that why she stopped breathing? Because the burning in her chest was stalling her lungs?

Recognizing this burn that left her breathless, Jaz pulled her left forearm in front of her eyes. She examined the Mandela pattern that had been tattooed into place twenty years ago. Her eyes darted to the open spaces of clear skin between the black outlines as she imagined what colors she would put in each spot. When she was younger, she had physically colored those spots in with her collection of sharpies. After so many years of coping this way, Jaz could just do it in her mind's eye.

Eventually, Jaz's body cooled to a normal temperature, despite the sweat that drenched her brow. She could hear something other than her own heartbeat. It was Annie, yelling "JAZ!" from the other end of the phone. The moment Jaz heard that, she bolted out of her door only stopping to grab her keys and tennis shoes that she put on during the cab ride to Annie's apartment.

She's not dead. She's not. This is some stupid prank she put Annie up to because she's made that I refused to give her a tattoo. She's not dead. She's not dead. She's not dead. These same thoughts repeated in Jaz's head as a yellow cab sped her from Newark to New York, near the area of Annie's college. It was going to be a pricey cab fare, but Jaz couldn't afford to be cheap and take the subway or bus. This was too damn important.

"Uh, lady. I think you might have to walk the rest of the way." Jaz looked over the front passenger seat to see what the driver was talking about. A crowd had gathered around the entrance of Annie's apartment building. Some of the people were in pajamas and sweats, signaling that they were tenants who had been evacuated so that the police could investigate. Others were early morning workers and tourists who were rubbernecking. *Fuck!*

Jaz didn't bother to ask what she owed the driver; she just threw a hundred-dollar bill at him and leapt out of the car, dashing towards the crowd. Jaz pushed her way to the front of the crowd and was only stopped by two police officers who were trying to control the crowd. "Ma'am, you can't go in there," the female police officer warned.

"My niece is in there!" Jaz pleaded desperately.

The other police officer—a man—stepped in, saying, "Ma'am, you need to calm down."

"No! My niece is in the building!" Jaz's desperation was turning into rage as her hands balled into fists and that heat in her chest crawled up her neck to her face and blossomed over her arms.

"Ma'am, I can assure you that we evacuated everyone out of the building. If your niece is here, she's somewhere in the crowd."

"Unless she's dead!"

The woman took over again. "Ma'am, please calm down."

"Fuck you!"

The female police officer seemed to snap in that moment. "Ma'am, if you don't calm down immediately, we will arrest you for disturbing the peace and interfering with a police investigation." The threat stilled and silenced Jaz; *I can't help Rosamie in jail.* The female police officer's partner looked on, just as intimidated as Jaz was. "Why would you think that your niece is in the building and dead?"

"Her girlfriend called me. She told me." Jaz spat with just a little more attitude than the officer appreciated.

The male police officer did his best to diffuse the tension between Jaz and his colleague. He asked, "What's your name, ma'am?"

"Jasmine Dilan."

With a poignant look from his partner, the male officer scrambled to pull out his notepad to write down the information. Meanwhile, the woman asked, "Your niece's name?"

"Rosamie Dylan."

There was another poignant look between the cops. "And the name of your niece's girlfriend?"

"Annie Xun. Stop looking at each other and tell me what happened!"

The cops looked between their notepads and each other one last time. "Wait here." Jaz groaned in frustration as the female cop entered the building, leaving the male cop to watch over Jaz and Jaz's side of the crowd. Jaz fidgeted the entire time but didn't try to push back or talk back to the cop. Jaz could see the pity and concern in his eyes, but she was grateful that the cop didn't try to make conversation. *This is just some big prank. Rosamie is alive and just trying to get back to me. She would absolutely be willing to waste police time for a prank like this. She's alive. She has to be.*

After about five minutes, the lady cop came back out of the building, followed by a man in a suit with pale taupe skin. When the cop pointed to Jaz, the man's deep brown eyes regarded her, taking in her sweaty body that had goosebumps rising from the February chill. The suit suggested he was a superior of the cops—maybe an investigator. "No. No no no. Please no. Please just be a friend of Rosamie's. Please just be a friend of Rosamie's. Please just be a friend of Rosamie's." Had anyone else been in the same situation and thinking the same thing,

Jaz would seriously question why someone Rosamie's age would be friends with a man who looked to be in his thirties. Logic, however, hadn't been present ever since Jaz got the call from Annie.

The man approached Jaz and asked, "Jasmine Dylan?"

"Yes?" She was shaking. Was it her anxiety or the cold?

"I'm Detective Josiah Moore." Detective Moore removed his suit jacket, revealing his badge as he draped the jacket around Jaz's shoulders. "You shouldn't be out in this weather without a coat."

"I came here as quickly as I could. My niece—" Jaz cleared her throat to start over, but the detective interrupted her.

"Monroe told me. Please come in," Turning to both cops, Detective Moore ordered. "Keep an eye on the crowd." The officers did as they were told with nods. Following the detective was the last thing that Jaz wanted to do; she had dealt with enough cops when she was a teenager. But if she wanted answers, she didn't have much of a choice. Josiah led Jaz into the building, but they stayed by the door instead of going up to Annie's apartment. "You said that your niece is named Rosamie Dylan?"

"Yes. Please tell me she's alive. Please tell me this is just some stupid prank she's using to get back at me." It took all of her strength to not grab the detective by the shoulders and shake him. She knew that she already looked crazy in her pajamas, sockless shoes, unmade-up face, uncombed hair, and dear-in-the-headlights wide eyes. She didn't want her actions to make her look any worse.

The detective looked at Jaz in pity. "I'm sorry, Ms. Dylan. But I'm afraid you were told the truth. Your niece has passed away."

Just like when Annie told her, all the heat in Jaz's body rapidly migrated to her chest, leaving her arms and legs colder than they already were. She slumped against the wall as the heat in her body spilled out of her eyes and she struggled to breathe. "What happened?" she gasped out.

"We don't know. Until we can confirm that no foul play is involved, we're treating her as a victim."

Jaz's eyes went wide. *Please, God. No. Not again.* "You think she was murdered?"

"It's just a formality." *Please let that be all it is.* "I know this is all very shocking and that it's a difficult time right now, but would you mind if I asked you some questions."

Jaz didn't hesitate to say, "Yes. Of course."

Josiah pulled out his smartphone, opened an audio recording app, and hit the red button. "Can you please state your name for the record."

"Jasmine Dilan."

"Can you spell that please?"

"J-A-S-M-I-N-E, last name D-I-L-A-N."

The detective eyed her suspiciously. "Interesting. I noticed that the victim spells her surname with a Y."

"That's because her mother chose to take the Americanized version of our name when our parents got divorced. Meanwhile, I took our father's native Filipino spelling." It had been so long since Jaz needed to explain the discrepancy that she had almost completely forgotten about it.

"I see," The detective seemed skeptical. "How did you know to come here, Miss Dilan?"

"Annie called me."

"Annie Xun? The owner of the apartment your niece was found in?"

"Yes." That's when something occurred to Jaz. "Where is Rosamie? Can I see her?"

Josiah shook his head. "I'm sorry, Ms. Dilan, but we're examining the body and the scene right now. We can't risk anything being tampered with. If foul play is involved, that could allow the perpetrator to get away. However, I will ask you to accompany me to the coroner to ID the victim when we're done here."

Jaz didn't know how to feel about his answer. On the one hand, she needed to see it for herself. On the other hand, the moment she saw Rosamie, the horrible situation would become real. "How--" Jaz cleared her throat of the tears that hung there, ready to spill at any time. "How did she die?" *Do I want to know the answer?*

"At this point, we can't be positive of anything. We'll need to wait for the coroner to examine the body." *Even if he could take a guess, he probably can't tell me anything.* "What do you do for a living, Ms. Dilan?"

"I'm a tattoo artist."

If the detective had any thoughts about Jaz's profession, he didn't show it. "Does your niece live in the city?"

"She's living with me, but her mother is her legal guardian, and she's in Seattle."

"And her father?"

Jaz scoffed, "Who knows?"

Josiah nodded in understanding. "Can you tell me why your niece was living with you?"

"She is going through a rebellious phase and her mother was at her wit's end. Rosamie called me after she got kicked out of the house, and I bought her a plane ticket."

"How long ago was this?" Detective Moore sounded skeptical again.

Jaz shrugged. "About a year."

"Have Rosamie and her mother spoken since that time?"

"Not that I know of." *Based on Rosamie's attitude towards her mother, I highly doubt it.*

"When was the last time you saw your niece?"

"Last night."

"What time?"

Jaz rolled her eyes up, thinking back. "About 6:30."

"Did anything happen?"

Jaz furrowed her brows together. "Like what?"

"Was your niece acting strange? Did you two get into a fight? Did she mention having a fight with someone else? You said that you thought this might be a prank to get back at you. Why would she want to get back at you?"

"She wanted me to design a tattoo for her, but I said no."

"Why?"

"One, I think she's too young. Two, her mother is really against the idea, which means that it's completely illegal. Even if it weren't, I don't have the time or patience for that kind of family drama should Ruby ever find out."

Josiah nodded again. "Would her mother ever want to harm Rosamie, or has she harmed her in the past?"

"Not in a million years! They had a rough relationship, sure, but Rosamie was still her daughter." *How could he even think such a thing?*

Josiah raised his hand in a "calm down" gesture. "I have to consider all possibilities, Ms. Dilan. Do you know if your niece had any enemies?"

Jaz shrugged again. "I mean, her boss wasn't too crazy about her."

That statement seemed to pique the detective's interest. "In what way?"

"Rosamie was late to work a lot and she mouthed off when she was there. He found her as disrespectful as her mother did." *I'm surprised she HASN'T been fired yet. Mr. Hong threatens it enough.*

"Where did Rosamie work?"

"A Vietnamese restaurant called *Taste of Nam.*"

Josiah clicked off the recording and put his phone away. "Thank you, Ms. Dilan. That's all the questions I have for now. I'll have one of my officers take you to the station. You can wait there until we get the body to the coroner. If I think of any more questions, I'll ask them at the station. I'll also need your home address so that we can investigate there."

Jaz passed along her home address before asking, "Can I call Rosamie's mother? To tell her?"

Josiah shook his head. "I'm sorry, Ms. Dilan, but I'm afraid I have to make that phone call. It's standard procedure."

Jaz sighed but nodded. At that point, Annie came down the apartment building stairs with a duffle bag and swollen eyes. "Annie."

"Jaz." Annie ran up and threw her arms around Jaz, weeping into her thin tank top. Jaz rubbed the teen's back gently, doing her best to keep herself together and be strong in the situation. "How could this have happened?"

"I don't know, Annie."

Josiah allowed the two to have a quiet moment before saying, "Jenkins and Monroe will take you both to the station. I'll see you both there." Josiah ascended the stairs and disappeared, leaving Jaz and Annie in the care of Officer Jenkins and Officer Monroe.

The officers escorted the ladies out through a back-alley door. When the cops started walking in two different directions, Annie asked, "Aren't we riding together?"

The male officer from before—who had to be Officer Jenkins—answered, "No, ma'am. Standard procedure." Annie and Jaz looked at each other with nervous sorrow.

Jaz tried to be soothing as she comforted Annie. "It's okay. Everything is going to be okay."

"Ma'am?" Annie nodded to Jaz before following Officer Jenkins to his police cruiser.

Jaz followed Officer Monroe to a separate cruiser, where she opened the back door and allowed Jaz to slide onto the leather seats. The caged backseat was disconcerting, but the officer probably couldn't let her in the front seat. *Panicking won't do any good*. She wrapped Detective Moore's jacket tighter around her shoulders.

Shit! Jaz had forgotten to give the jacket back to the detective before they left. He would have to wait until they saw each other at the station. As Jaz and Officer Monroe sped through the city, Jaz kept the black jacket tight around her arms, inhaling the earthy musk that had to be from the detective's cologne. It was oddly soothing. *It smells like home. The woods after a rain. Who would've thought I would ever miss that hell?*

Jaz didn't spend the whole drive to the station staring out the window; sitting there and thinking of nothing eventually gave way to the repetitive negative thoughts that were constantly bombarding her brain. The only thing that stopped those thoughts was the Mandela tattoo; Jaz stared at it, mentally coloring in the image about five times over before Officer Monroe finally pulled the police cruiser into a parking space.

When they arrived at the NYPD station, it was bustling. Reporters were swarming the place to get scoops about crimes that had happened all over the city. As far as Jaz could tell, only a few reporters knew something had happened in Annie's neighborhood, and none of them knew the specifics.

Inside, other officers and detectives were rushing around, talking about their own cases, wrangling petty criminals, and making small talk if they had the time. Nobody paid attention to Jaz as Officer Monroe led her through the station, using codes on pin-locked doors whenever necessary. Monroe asked if any interrogation rooms were available after taking Jaz's fingerprints. None were, so she led Jaz to a locked waiting room where a few other people were. "When a room becomes available, I'll come back and get you. Bathroom is over there. Can I get you something to drink?"

"Do you guys have coffee?"

"Of course. Cream or sugar?"

"No, just black."

"Coming right up." Five minutes later, Jaz saw Monroe with a coffee cup in her hand, but she was debating with Officer Jenkins. *They must be trying to figure out how to keep me and Annie apart until a room opens up.* It took another five minutes for the officers to come to a compromise. By that time, Jaz's coffee was lukewarm.

Half an hour later, an interrogation room opened up. In the meantime, Jaz accessed her calendar through her phone and called her customers to cancel their appointments. She continued to clear her schedule after Monroe escorted her to an interrogation room and refilled her coffee. When she finished with her calendar and clearing her appointments, there was nothing else to do but keep staring at the

Mandela tattoo. *I have to hang on. I have to keep a clear head. I have to keep calm.*

Jaz had been at the station for an hour by the time Detective Moore joined her in the interrogation room. Now that she had calmed down and composed herself, she got a better look at him. It actually surprised her that he was a detective; aside from the fact that he looked too young—he couldn't be much older than her—she was expecting a hard-boiled, Columbo wannabe. This guy had a face for Hollywood, not the NYPD. *Not the real NYPD anyway. More like the NYPD on cable TV.*

"Sorry to keep you waiting, Ms. Dilan. The investigation at your apartment took longer than we anticipated."

"Can I see Rosamie now?"

"Not yet. I still have a few questions for you." Jaz sighed in frustration but didn't argue. Josiah sat down across from Jaz, pulled out his cell, and started a new recording. "You said you saw your niece at 6:30 pm last night?"

"Yes."

"What did you do after that?"

"I went out to eat."

"Alone?"

"No, with my friend Garrett Weber."

"Where did you go to eat?"

"*The Gym Bar and Grille.*"

"How long were you there?"

Jaz cast her mind back, trying to remember what the clock said when she got home. Once she remembered that, she did the math and subtracted the commute time. "Probably an hour? Maybe an hour and a half?"

"What did you do after that?"

Do they think I had something to do with this? "I went home, took a shower, and went to bed."

"With Mr. Weber?"

"God, no! We're just friends." *He thinks I had something to do with this.*

"Can anyone confirm that you went back to your apartment?"

"You mean 'Did I take someone with me'? No." *Maybe he's right.*

"Could any of your neighbors have seen you?"

This is all my fault. Jaz thought for a moment. "No, but my building has security cameras at all the entrances and on every floor. No one gets in or out without being recorded. You could check with the landlady. I should show up around eight last night, and not be seen again until a little after seven this morning."

"I'll keep that in mind. Did your niece tell you what she was doing last night?"

"She and Annie are a part of an LGBTQIA+ teen support group. They meet every Monday night at the Newark LGBTQ Community Center. Rosamie said she and Annie were going to a movie after the meeting."

"You sound like you didn't believe her."

Jaz shrugged with her mouth. "I believe that they went to the meeting, but I'm pretty sure they went to a bar afterward."

"What makes you think that?"

Jaz opened her phone and pulled up her last text messages to Rosamie. Showing the phone to Detective Moore, she said, "I checked in on her shortly before I left *The Gym.*"

Josiah read through the text messages and nodded before handing the phone back to Jaz. Jaz stared at her screen as new tears started crawling down her cheek. *These are her last words to me. And mine to her. I didn't even say goodbye.* "Ms. Dilan?"

Jaz realized that the detective had asked her a question. "What?"

"Can you take a screenshot of that and send it to me?"

"Sure, but why?"

"The timestamps. They'll help us narrow down the time of death." Detective Moore gave Jaz his work cell number and waited for her to text him the screenshots. "Do you have the contact information for your sister and Mr. Weber?" Jaz passed the numbers and addresses to the detective before he stopped recording. "Thank you very much, Ms. Dilan." He passed his business card across the table. "Feel free to call me if you think of anything that might help us."

"Can I see Rosamie now?"

"Yes. Follow me." The detective took Jaz through the station into the freezing building next door. The first room they came to first was an office with a model skeleton, scattered medical books, and strewn files. After peaking in and seeing no one in the room, Detective Moore continued down the hallway to the heavy metal double doors at the end. Opening the doors, he called out, "G'day, Bailey."

"Har har, Moore." *They're definitely Australian.*

"Bails, this is Jasmine Dilan. Ms. Dilan, this is our coroner, Dr. Bailey Martin."

Dr. Martin was a tall, fit person whose lab coat was too tight and short on them. Judging from the tan, they were more at home in places warmer than New York. Bleach dreadlocks were pulled back in a braid that reached their hips. As they offered Jaz a hand, she saw some pacific islander tattoos peeking out from beneath the lab coat sleeve. "Nice to meet you, Ms. Dilan." Jaz nodded but didn't say anything.

"Ms. Dilan is here to ID the minor we brought in earlier."

Dr. Martin's mood took a turn. "Oh. You're her mother?"

"Aunt."

"My condolences. I'm so sorry for your loss." Jaz gave another silent nod. "Are you ready for this?" This nod was hesitant but brave and necessary. "Alright." Dr. Martin took Jaz and the detective over to an operating table with a small, covered form on top of it. The covered body was enough to shoot Jaz up with an unsettling emotional cocktail of sorrow and fear. Her limbs went cold and her chest kept burning. Seeing the look on her face, Dr. Martin hesitated to pull the sheet back until Jaz nodded one last time.

Rosamie's normally glowing, olive skin was pale and dull. Her undercut had been combed through as much as possible, but remnants of a bedhead remained. The way her shoulders were hunched up around her neck made her look so stiff. Thank god her eyes were closed. Jaz wouldn't have been able to handle seeing them devoid of life and sass.

The tears tumbled out of her eyes, but she remained silent. *I shouldn't have let her go out. I should've tried to stop her. I should've been a better aunt. This is all my fault. Why does death follow me like this?*

Detective Moore interrupted Jaz's inner conversation. "Is this your niece, Ms. Dilan?" The question reminded Jaz where she was and what she was there for. She nodded as she wiped the tears away.

Dr. Martin covered Rosamie up, not wanting to overwhelm Jaz. As the teenager's lifeless face disappeared, Jaz was confused. Part of her wanted to reach out and stop the coroner, knowing that it would probably be the last time Jaz ever saw her niece's face. But is this how Jaz wanted to remember Rosamie?

"Ms. Dilan?" Jaz shook her head out of her thoughts and came back to reality, realizing the Dr. Martin had been speaking to her. "I know this is rough and you've already answered a lot of questions, but I do have one more for you. Did your niece have epilepsy or any other medical conditions that would've caused seizures?"

Jaz furrowed her brows. "Not that I know of."

"Would she have told you if she did?"

"Her mother would've." Detective Moore and Dr. Martin looked at each other. "Is that how she died?"

With a sigh, Dr. Martin confirmed, "At first glance, that is how it looks."

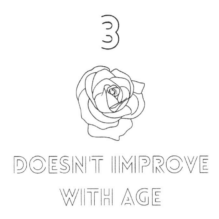

3

DOESN'T IMPROVE
WITH AGE

"WHY DON'T YOU GO take a shower and get comfortable?" Jaz invited Annie to stay with her since the college student's dorm room was still being investigated. When they arrived, Annie looked uncomfortable despite the fact that she had seen the place hundreds of times when she picked up Rosamie for dates or support group meetings.

"Okay. Thank you so much, Jaz." Annie went into the shared bathroom with her overnight bag and started the shower. Before Jaz went into her room, she hit the "heat" button on the coffee maker.

Jaz sat on her bed, flipping her phone back and forth. Jaz had waited around the station until Annie's questioning was done. During the wait, Detective Moore informed her that he was going to contact the Seattle police and request that they contact Rosamie's mother. *She'll call me the moment she finds out. This is going to suck.*

The dreaded ringtone came. Jaz considered letting the phone ring out, but that would make things worse. She had to answer.

Jaz didn't even get a word out after she answered the phone before Rubylyne was yelling, "WHAT HAPPENED?!"

"Ruby—" The mother's weeping cut Jaz off. What could she say? *This whole situation is so fucked up.* Jaz's tears weren't far behind her sister's.

After the fifteen minutes of the sisters crying into each other's ears, Ruby was calm enough to speak again. "I knew it. I just knew it."

Jaz sniffled. "Knew what?"

"I knew Rosa was going to get herself shot! I tried to tell her that her attitude and lack of respect and punk friends were going to kill her, but she just wouldn't listen."

Jaz furrowed her brows as she listened to her sister rave about guns. "Rubylyne, did the cops tell you that Rosamie got shot?"

"They said she was dead!"

"Rosamie wasn't shot."

"Then what happened?!"

"The police didn't tell you?"

"WOULD I ASK IF THEY HAD?!"

They probably did tell her, but she was too upset to hear. I can hardly blame her though. "The coroner thinks it was a seizure, though they can't be positive yet."

"That's impossible! Rosa didn't have epilepsy!"

So I was right. "Ruby, she was found in her girlfriend's apartment. Annie is all about gun control. I don't think she would allow a gun anywhere near the place. Neither would the campus security."

"A criminal could've broken in and shot her, then left with the gun."

Jaz shook her head even though Rubylyne couldn't see her. "Then why did no one hear the gunshot?"

"They make silencers for guns! And New York is full of those mob bosses who would use them to kill anyone."

Spoken like a woman who has never traveled outside of Seattle. "Then why didn't these mob bosses shoot Annie too?"

"She could've hired them to do the job."

Where is all of this talk about mob bosses and hired killers coming from? "Why would Annie hire a mercenary to kill the woman she loved?" Ruby was silent on the other end. "The police are investigating right now to make sure no foul play was involved. When they know more, they will tell us."

"So someone did kill her!"

"We don't know that yet."

"Why else would the police be investigating if they didn't?"

"They said it's standard procedure."

Rubylyne sighed on the other end of the phone. "How am I ever gonna pay for the funeral?"

The words and the despair in them renewed Jaz's tears. "Don't worry about that. I have an emergency fund. I'll do whatever I can to help."

"I never should've kicked her out. She would still be alive if it weren't for me."

Misplaced guilt was something that seemed to run in Jaz's family. "Ruby, you can't blame yourself for this."

"Then who *can* I blame?" Jaz didn't answer. She pursed her lips as she listened to her sister cry for another hour.

Jaz ended her conversation when Ruby was composed enough to say goodbye without sniffling. Jaz knew that she would be crying again immediately after they hung up. Had it been anyone else, Jaz would've tried to keep her on the phone, but Ruby needed her alone-time to handle everything. They were alike in that respect.

When the phone call was done, Jaz thought, *I should probably call Mr. Hong and let him know.* Going back through her old calls, Jaz found the number Mr. Hong called her from and hit the "call" button.

An anxiety-laced teenaged voice answered, "Taste of Nam. Can I take your order?"

"Actually, may I speak with Mr. Hong?"

"Hang on!" Jaz could hear the teen yell for her boss over the sound of dining patrons.

"Mr. Hong. Who is this?"

"Mr. Hong, this is Jasmine Dilan, Rosamie's aunt—"

"Where is Rosamie?! She's hours late! We're understaffed because of her laziness! You tell her she's fired!"

"Mr. Hong, she passed away today!"

"Good. Waste of space and waste of a paycheck. Bring her uniform back by tomorrow and pick up her stuff. Otherwise, it's all going in the trash, and you're getting a hundred dollar fine!" Before Jaz could respond, Mr. Hong had hung up.

4

THE ONLY LOVE
THAT LASTS

J AZ HAD TO TAKE thirty minutes to calm down after the unpleasant phone call with Mr. Hong. The heartless reaction of Rosamie's old boss was infuriating enough for Jaz to throw her phone against the far wall of her bedroom. Thank god she had invested in that phone case; it may have been expensive, but not nearly as expensive as it would've been to buy a new phone or replace the screen. She had taken some time to debate whether she should let Detective Moore know about Mr. Hong's cold nature—surely, he would find it interesting. She ultimately decided to let the detective make his own discoveries, even if it wouldn't be as satisfying for her.

When Jaz came out of her room, she found Annie on the couch in the living room. The girl had changed into some comfortable sweats after a shower and was scrolling on her phone. She was looking for something; what that thing was, Jaz would never know. *Maybe it's just a distraction.*

"How are you doing, kiddo?" Stupid question.

"I'm okay." No, she wasn't.

"Do you want some coffee?"

"No, thanks." Annie sucked on her vape pen and blew smoke into the air. Durian fruit flavored. "Oh, sorry! I didn't even ask if I could smoke."

"Oh, you're fine." *Mental note: stock up air fresheners.* "Can I get you anything?"

"I'm good. Thank you, Jaz." Jaz couldn't tell if Annie was trying to be strong for her own sake or for the sake of not overstaying her welcome. They were going to have to talk.

Jaz sat down next to Annie, looking straight on. "How are you really doing?" Annie couldn't even get the words out; her lips were quivering too hard as she tried to fight back the sounds bubbling up in her throat. Jaz didn't hesitate to pull the child into her arms. The moment she was embarrassed, Annie buried her face in Jaz's lap and started weeping. Jaz pet the girl's hair and rubbed her back, allowing her to cry. The only reason why Jaz didn't join her was because the phone call with Ruby had drained her of all the free water in her body.

After a few more minutes, Annie's sobs had calmed enough for her to ask, "How could this have happened?"

"I don't know, Annie. Did anything happen at the meeting?"

"Not really. We came together for the initial meeting to talk about upcoming events and news stories. Then we split off into our groups, talked about experiences. Everything was normal." That was the truth; Jaz could see it in Annie's eyes.

"Where did you guys go afterwards? And don't tell me you went to the movies. I know that was bullshit."

Annie's face went red. "We went to a bar."

Jaz rolled her eyes. "Well, duh. I figured that out when you were hungover this morning. How are you feeling by the way?"

"Well, you were right about the pickle juice. It just sucked going down."

Jaz nodded. "It always does." She spoke from experience. "Which bar did you go to?"

"A place called *The Ace of Clubs*. I've never been there before last night." Another truth from Annie.

"Did anything happen there?"

"Well, Rosamie did get into a fight."

Jaz straightened up at those words. "With who?"

Annie shook her head. "This really nasty woman. Rosamie accidentally bumped into her while we were dancing, and she started saying shitty things that I'll probably talk about at the next support group meeting. Rosamie didn't like that so things got ugly really fast."

That's not surprising. "How ugly?"

"Rosamie had just smashed a bottle and was ready to lunge when the bouncer broke it up. We all got kicked out after that. We were taken out the front entrance while the bitch was taken out the back."

Jaz pinched the bridge of her nose, cringing at the thought that Rosamie could've been a murderer than night instead of being murdered herself. "Did you guys go home after that?"

"No."

"Where did you go after the bar?"

"Well, Rosamie *really* wanted to get a tattoo—"

You can't be serious. "You got tattoos while you guys were drunk?!"

"Why are you freaking out? You've had a lot of drunk customers."

"Just because lots of people do it doesn't mean that it's a good idea. Aside from that fact that you're not in control of your shit, it makes the process more painful and could result in a *bad* tattoo that is painful as shit." Annie dropped her head into her hands. "It's alright. You didn't know."

"That's the shitty part; I *did* know, but Rosamie was so persuasive." *Meaning "demanding".*

"So you and Rosamie went and got tattoos—"

"No, just Rosamie."

Odd. "Okay. What happened then?"

"Rosamie was in a lot of pain, so I took her back to my place so that she could sleep off the pain and alcohol."

"Did anything else happen in the night?"

"Well, obviously. The question is what? I just didn't hear anything. I don't think I did, anyways. I didn't wake up in the middle of the night. Fuck, why did I drink so much?! If I'd just stuck with water, maybe I would've heard her, and she would still be here." That threw Annie into another round of crying.

Right when Jaz went to put her arms back around Annie, the front door buzzer went off. With an annoyed sigh, Jaz got up and spoke into the intercom. "Hello?"

"Hi. I'm looking for Annie Xun?"

Jaz gave a look to Annie, who nodded. "Come on up." Once Jaz has opened the building, she asked, "Who's this?"

"Isa. She's the lesbian head rep at the support group. I texted her about Rosamie and she insisted on coming. I know I should've asked first, but—"

"Don't worry, Annie. You need your friends right now. I get it." There was a knock on the door. When Jaz opened it, she found a very pretty girl in an oversized sweater. Judging from how red her cameo skin was, Jaz determined that the sweater was doing little to keep the girl guarded from the February temperatures. Her brown eyes were big, even without her wide-lensed glasses. Her silky black hair had been thrown up into a bun. A fashion statement or the mark of a woman on the go with little time to focus on appearance? Jaz couldn't really tell.

"Hi. Is Annie there?"

Before Jaz could answer, Annie stepped into view of the door. "Hey, Isa." Isa pushed her way into the apartment without invitation and threw her arms around Annie. Jaz stood by the door, awkward as the teens hugged each other for a long time. When they finally broke away, Annie wiped her tears and said, "Jaz, this is Isa. Isa this is Rosamie's aunt, Jaz."

Isa turned her pitying look to Jaz and stuck her hand out. "It's nice to meet you, Jaz, though I wish the circumstances were different."

Jaz shook Isa's hand firmly. "Both feelings are mutual."

"You have my deepest condolences."

"Thank you."

"I should be thanking you; you're being so kind to Annie and she means a lot to us." As Isa put a hand around Annie, Jaz's left eyebrow slid up her head.

"Of course. She means a lot to me as well. After all, she was the most important person to my niece." Sensing Jaz's tone, Isa removed her hand from Annie's shoulder.

Isa cleared her throat. "I do have a question for you. It's tradition for the group to hold a memorial whenever a member passes away.

The circumstances are different than normal, but may we have your permission to maintain that tradition for Rosamie?"

"Yes, of course."

"Thank you. We would love it if you could join us. I'll let Annie know when it's happening. She can keep you posted."

Jaz nodded. "I appreciate that."

Annie interjected, "Let me grab my coat so we can talk."

Jaz asked, "Are you two going somewhere?"

Annie answered on both hers and Isa's behalf. "Just for a walk and maybe a cup of coffee. We won't even leave the neighborhood."

"Are you two gonna be okay?" She was more worried about Annie, but Jaz figured that she shouldn't be so obvious in her feelings.

"I'll be fine. Isa will take care of me."

Isa took the opportunity to put her arm back around Annie. "Don't worry, Ms. Dilan. I'll have her back by ten." Jaz gave Isa another quirked eyebrow look, showing that she wasn't amused by Isa's subtle joke or her second attempt at getting close to Annie. Isa took the subtle hint and removed her arm again. "Are you ready, Annie?"

"Yeah. I'll be back soon, Jaz."

"You sure you both will be okay?"

Annie nodded. "I'll call you if we need help."

"Okay. Be safe."

"We will," Isa answered as she pulled the apartment door closed behind her.

5

PERMANENT
REMINDERS

"**M**A'AM, I'VE ALREADY TOLD you—"

"I don't care if your niece is dead! You should do your fucking job that I paid you to do!"

"Ma'am, you haven't paid me anything yet, and I'm not telling you I won't do the job. I'm just asking to reschedule."

"Fuck you, you scamming bitch! I'm going to tear you apart on Yelp, take your ass to court, and watch you burn in the electric chair!" With that, the final customer Jaz had to call hung up.

Jaz sighed, "Good fucking riddance, Karen," under her breath as she deleted the name out of her calendar. Jaz had decided to clear her calendar for a few weeks in preparation for Rosamie's funeral. It was a perk of being her own boss; she could take as much time off as she wanted whenever she wanted at her own discretion. Unfortunately, half of the names that had been on Jaz's schedule didn't have rescheduled appointments; so many people couldn't understand why Jaz's life didn't revolve around them and the single tattoo they wanted. Everyone of those assholes said they were going to write horrible reviews about her and her tattoo parlor, *Inksignia*. Jaz couldn't worry about those petty people; she had too many things to worry about already. Besides, she didn't want asshole customers like that. In a weird way, this tragedy had allowed her to dodge dozens of bullets.

Jaz looked at her phone; calling all these customers had taken two hours. No wonder she was so fucking hungry. Jaz grabbed her laptop, thinking about all of the take-out places that either had their own delivery service or used delivery apps like PostDash.

The apartment building buzzer got Jaz's attention. *Annie must be back. I should get her a key soon.* Jaz went to her intercom and called out, "Annie?"

"No, Ms. Dilan. It's Detective Moore. May I come in?"

"Uh, sure." Jaz allowed the detective into the building, and a few moments later, heard a knock at her door. Open the door, Jaz asked, "Detective Moore. Is everything okay?"

"Everything's fine, Ms. Dilan. I just wanted to ask you a few more questions. May I come in?"

"Of course." Jaz allowed the detective to enter her apartment and offered him a seat on the living room couch. Josiah sat but didn't remove his coat. Jaz sat down next to him.

Pulling out his phone, Josiah started a new recording. "Ms. Dilan, there's been a development in your niece's case, and I think you'll be able to help fill in some blanks."

Jaz shrugged. "Sure, I'll do what I can."

"You mentioned Rosamie wanted a tattoo. Did she have any pre-existing ones?"

Jaz furrowed her brows. "Not that I know of? Annie told me that Rosamie got one last night, but what does that have anything to do with the case?"

"Ms. Xun told you that Rosamie got a tattoo."

"Yeah. Didn't she tell you that?"

"No. No, she didn't." *Fuck. I hope I didn't just get Annie in trouble.* "Do you know what tattoo Rosamie got?"

"I never asked. If her mother found out, I wanted plausible deniability. Why?"

Josiah passed a manila folder over to Jaz. "You're going to want to see this." With furrowed brows, Jaz took the folder and opened it.

Her heart seized with heat the moment she laid eyes on the first picture, but it wasn't because of her niece's pale back. It was the dark, upside-down S and F surrounded by swollen flesh.

"Ms. Dilan? Are you alright?" Detective Moore sounded like he was speaking to her from outside a cave that Jaz was trapped in. She could barely hear him over the pounding heartbeat and heavy breath in her ears. Her eyes darted back and forth, struggling to focus. Thank God she was sitting down; she would've collapsed if she had been standing.

When the detective rested a hand on Jaz's arm, she moved so fast that she didn't even register what she was doing. It was like she was watching a video of some social media influencer's vlog; running up to her door with a shaky camera while the audio was completely dominated by heavy breathing near the mic. She couldn't hear the bolt lock slam into place, or Detective Moore asking a question over that breathing. In fact, she barely saw the detective as she darted past him and into the bathroom, slamming the door shut and turning the weak knob lock into place.

A hand grabbed the locked knob, trying to turn it. The door didn't give way, but just the sound of it rattling was enough to ratchet Jaz's heartbeat up even further. She crawled into the shower tub and curled up into the fetal position. "Ms. Dilan? What's wrong? Please open the door." The detective kept knocking on the door and turning the knob, hoping that it would suddenly give away. Every time the door didn't open for her, the detective kept trying to talk to her using every tone of voice to get Jaz to open the door. Jaz tried to block out the noise with her hands and even by turning on the shower, letting ice-cold water cascade down onto her until it warmed to scalding temperatures. Even that wasn't enough to block out the sound of the detective doing his best to reach her.

The sound of breaking and crashing made Jaz jump in the shower puddle she laid in. The detective had taken it upon himself to force his way into the bathroom by slamming his shoulder against the door. It came open easily due to the short screws that the landlord had used to install the door plates; half an inch screws made it easy for any burglar to kick in a door with those screws. Jaz knew this when she moved in and replaced the screws for her apartment door plate with stronger, four-inch long screws. She never imagined that she would need to do the same thing with her bathroom door.

Jaz didn't let the detective get a word in edgewise before she started screaming, "GET OUT! GET OUT! GET OUT OF MY HOME!" When the detective tried to help her out of the shower, she crawled away from him and kept screaming that she wanted him to leave. Eventually, the detective held his hands up and backed out of the bathroom, pulling the door closed behind him. It wasn't long after that that Jaz heard her apartment door open and close again.

Jaz had completely lost track of time as she stared at her Mandela tattoo; she had no clue how long she stayed in the tub with the shower running. What she did know, was that it had to be long enough to completely soak her clothes, cover the bathroom mirror in steamed condensation, and for her to mentally color in her Mandela tattoo so many times that she lost count. She felt exhausted and her throat was dry and hoarse. She remembered every action she took after the detective showed her those photographs, but they didn't feel real; more like they were elements of a very realistic bad dream.

When she finally came back to herself, Jaz turned off the water before stripping out of her clothes, leaving them hanging on the shower's curtain rod. She didn't dry herself with a towel—at least, not effectively. Rather than running it over her hair and body, she just wrapped it around herself like little kids did when they got out of the community pool on the colder days of summer.

Still dripping wet, Jaz walked out of the bathroom and into her bedroom, hunting for some dry pajamas. They didn't stay dry for long; the clothes got wet spots from her hair and wet skin the moment she put them on. She considered just sucking it up, but the wet spots would be too cold and uncomfortable for her to deal with for the rest of the night. Jaz stripped again and properly dried herself before slipping into a pair of sweats that needed to be washed. *They'll do for a night.* She also threw her hair up into a hasty bun so that it didn't drip water everywhere.

As Jaz walked back into the living room, her phone was the first thing she saw. *I'm sure the detective is worried and wants an explanation.* But did she have the emotional strength to give him one?

Better get it over with. Jaz picked up her phone and rummaged through her coat, searching for the business card Josiah had given her while she was at the station. Once she found the card, she dialed the number on there. She hoped that this wasn't going to be as bad as she thought it was going to be.

"This is Detective Moore," Josiah answered.

"Um, it's Jaz," she said with hesitance.

"Hello, Ms. Dilan. How are you?" The detective was acting like absolutely nothing had happened. *But why?*

"I'm," Jaz paused, not knowing the best way to answer without lying. "I'm here." There was a long pause, showing that neither one of them knew what to say. "I feel like I owe you an explanation."

"You don't, Ms. Dilan. You owe me nothing. I, on the other hand, owe you an apology. I should've approached this subject with more delicacy."

"It's fine, Detective." Not even Jaz believed her own words. "You were just doing your job."

"My job is to find out the truth of serious crimes, not cause distress for those who are already grieving. From the bottom of my heart, I apologize profusely."

"I appreciate that, Detective." And she really did. "Do you think that what I have to tell you will help solve Rosamie's case."

"It might fill in some blanks, but only if you're comfortable with talking to me about it."

"I think I'm okay now."

"I'll be up in a few minutes. The PostDash with our dinner is almost here."

Jaz shook her head. "Now there *has* to be some rule about you buying a suspect dinner."

Josiah shrugged. "It doesn't count. I'm, technically, off duty."

"I don't think your boss will care about that technicality."

"Then don't tell him." Finally, there was a buzz at the front door of Jaz's apartment building. There was a PostDash delivery girl asking for entry. Jaz let her in. A few moments later, the delivery girl was at her door with a bag from *The Lucky Pagoda Chinese Bistro*. Detective Moore opened the door, paid the girl, and took the food. Setting the take-out boxes on the coffee table, he asked, "What's on your mind, Miss Dilan?"

"If you're off duty, do you have to call me 'Miss. Dilan'?"

Josiah looked at her, questioning. "I don't know. Do I?"

"No."

"Okay. What's on your mind, *Jaz*?"

"You're taking an awful lot of risks: sharing evidence; buying me dinner. You could get fired."

"Why does that worry you?"

Jaz shook her head. "I don't understand why you're taking such a huge risk. What's in it for you?"

"Hopefully, what's in it for me is figuring out exactly what happened to your niece."

Jaz narrowed her eyes at Josiah. "What if I'm responsible?"

"Is that a confession?"

"No! I just don't understand how you know you can trust me."

"Well, in the first place, we still haven't confirmed that foul play was involved. There's a chance that Rosamie just had a seizure in the night and suffocated by accident."

"Isn't it suspicious that she had a seizure when she'd never had one before?"

"So you confirmed that she didn't have epilepsy or any other medical condition?" Jaz shook her head. "Not necessarily. According to Bails, it can take a person up to twenty-five years to have their first seizure if they are prone to any. Even if she didn't have epilepsy, seizures are still possible. Though, it may be difficult to pinpoint what triggered the seizure."

"Okay, but what if foul play *is* involved? How do you know you can trust me?"

Josiah looked Jaz in the eye. "Jaz, do you know what happens when you've worked in the police force for twenty-five years?"

"Can't say I do."

"You gain a sixth sense to be able to tell when people are bullshitting you. In the entirety of our conversations, my bullshit-dar hasn't blipped even once. You're honest, almost to a fault. Aside from which, I can't find any motive you would have. I highly doubt you had an opportunity, and I get the sense that you had no means to cause a seizure." Jaz gave the detective a long stare before tucking into her shrimp. "Are those good enough reasons for you?"

"Well, I understand a bit better."

"Good, 'cause I still need some answers."

Jaz froze mid-bite with her kung pao chicken. "You seem to know everything."

"Not everything."

"Aren't you going to record the conversation?"

"Should I?"

Jaz sighed and shook her head. "It's not going to matter to the case."

"Why not? Why would Rosamie *want* to get the signature of Seth Frost—the serial killer who kidnapped and raped you—on her back?"

Jaz admitted, "I don't know. I don't even know how she found out about what happened." She shook her head in frustration. "She was just a stupid kid who was desperate to look like a badass. What looks more badass than a mark from a serial rapist and murderer? She was just a little shit."

"Unfortunately, this suggests that there was more to it than that." Josiah passed a letter to Jaz.

Dr. Hann L. Thompson
Chief Psychiatrist – Federal Detention Center, SeaTac
2425 S 200th St
Seattle, WA 98198

January 15, 2018

Rosamie Dylan
4335 Maiden Lane #5
New York City, NY 10038

Dear Miss Rosamie Dylan,

    As the chief psychiatrist at the Federal Detention Center, SeaTac, it is my job to rehabilitate the inmates to the best of my ability. In order to do this, I have complete access to prisoner's mail and it is up to me to determine if any letter would be harmful to the process.

Your letters caught my attention partly because of the recipient. The contents within them disturb me greatly, even more so now that I have discovered your connection to one Seth Frost.

I have determined that your letters would completely undo what little progress I have made with Mr. Frost over the last twenty-one years. I must ask you to cease and desist your attempts to contact him. All letters from you will be returned to you and if the attempts continue, we will be forced to contact your parent/guardian for your own safety as well as everyone else's.

Sincerely,

Dr. Hann L. Thompson

"We found that in the trash can in Rosamie's room. We've already contacted Dr. Thompson to confirm it." Jaz didn't know what to think other than *there was something wrong with that kid.* "You didn't know she was trying to contact him, did you?"

Jaz shook her head. "Did you have the Seattle police tell Rubylyn?"

"I wanted to speak to you first. We want to keep her informed, but there are some pieces of information that are unnecessary and cause more harm than good." Jaz nodded, understanding. "Do you think we should tell her?"

"No. At least, not yet. I need to think about this and figure out if it should come from me."

"I understand."

"Thank you for bringing this to my attention, Detective. I don't know how much it will matter to the case, though."

"You're sure Frost has no connection to Rosamie or her death?"

Jaz gave the detective a look. "I think we'd both know if a guy who's supposed to be serving a life-sentence in Seattle were in New York."

Josiah nodded. Silence fell over the two. Jaz could tell he felt like he should say something, but didn't know what. "I'm sorry you were his victim."

"I'm not his victim. I'm his survivor." Jaz gave Josiah a long hard stare, punctuating her point before stuffing her face with shrimp.

After a pause, Josiah asked, "I understand if the answer is 'no', but would you mind letting me see *your* tattoo."

"I can show you, but you won't see it. I got it covered the moment I had the opportunity."

"I don't blame you. Then can you tell me anything else about the photo I showed you?"

"I didn't really get a look at anything else. What else do you want to know anyway?"

"Well, swelling is to be expected after death, but that area was a bit more swollen than the rest of the body."

"She could've been allergic to the tattoo ink. I'm sure the booze has something to do with that, too."

"She'd been drinking?"

Shit. I did it again. "Annie didn't tell you?"

Josiah's brows furrowed back together. "No." Josiah pulled out his phone and started a new recording. "Can you tell me everything Ms. Xun disclosed to you about the night in question, Miss Dilan?"

"Uh, she told me that she and Rosamie went to a club after their LGBTQIA+ support group."

Josiah nodded. "Just as you suspected. Which club?"

"Uh, something to do with cards. *Ace of Spades*? Something like that."

"They both drank?"

"Yeah."

"Did she tell you about anything unusual?"

"Annie said that Rosamie got into a bar fight with some homophobic bitch, and they all got kicked out."

Josiah's interest piqued at that tid-bit. "Where did they go after that?"

"She said Rosamie got her tattoo and then they went back to Annie's place."

"Where did Rosamie get her tattoo done?"

Jaz shook her head. "I don't know. I didn't ask and Annie didn't tell me."

"Did she say that anything happened during or after the tattoo?"

"All Annie said was that Rosamie was drunk and in a lot of pain."

"Do you find that odd?"

Jaz shrugged. "No. Tattoos can be pretty painful, especially when you throw alcohol into the mix." Jaz furrowed her own eyebrows. "Although the location of the tat is not usually very painful."

"Thank you, Ms. Dilan." Josiah clicked off the phone.

"Did I just get Annie in trouble?"

"Ms. Xun got herself in trouble, Jaz. She should've known better than to lie to the police. Now the question is, why did she lie?"

"Well, she and Rosamie were underage. Maybe she just didn't want to get in trouble for underage drinking?"

"And the tattoo? Why did she lie about that?"

"I can't answer that one."

Josiah closed his take-out and stood up. "Goodnight, Ms. Dilan."

Jaz didn't take the time to wonder why the detective left in such a hurry; there was too much on her mind to worry about the actions of others. Those thoughts on her mind pushed her to stand up and make her way to the bathroom turning on the light, Jaz ripped off her tank top and turned her back to the mirror. Looking over her shoulder, Jaz caught a glimpse of the black dragon wings that took up most of the space, from the top of her shoulder blades to the small of her back. It relieved her to see that those wings were still there, but as she looked at them, she could see the initials SF hidden in the folds and veins of the wings. Another person wouldn't see them because they wouldn't know to look for them. But Jaz did.

The apartment intercom buzzed again. *Busy night,* Jaz thought as she put her tank top back on. Rushing to the intercom, Jaz realized that Annie and Isa had returned. She allowed the young girls into the building and let them into her apartment when they knocked. Jaz could tell that Annie was tired from the events of the day, but Isa just wouldn't leave.

Jaz finally had to say, "Well, I appreciate you looking after her, but I'm sure your parents are worried sick. You'd better get home."

"Actually, my parents—" Jaz stepped closer, standing over Isa with dark eyes. "Right. Well," As Isa stood up and grabbed her coat, she mumbled, "Sorry to bother you," as she rushed out of the apartment. If Annie was unhappy with Jaz's treatment of her friend, she didn't say anything.

Once the door was locked behind Isa, Jaz said goodnight to Annie and went to bed herself. She tossed and turned for fifteen minutes before she grabbed her phone from her nightstand charger. A web search took her to the Federal Bureau of Prisons website. The "Inmates" tab dropped down into a menu, and the first option was "Find an Inmate". With a tap of her finger, Jaz was taken to a page that said, "Locate the whereabouts of a federal inmate incarcerated from 1982 to the present". Jaz typed in all the information she had—doing the math of the age—and hit "search".

One result popped up with no matching mugshot. *That's probably for the better.*

SETH ASHLEY FROST
Register Number: 18369-219
Age: 67
Race: White
Sex: Male
Located at: SeaTac FDC
Release Date: UNKNOWN

The Klinkenhammer's must be disappointed. Jaz was about to click off her phone when she saw the list of related links next to the info card. Those links included methods of contacting inmates. With furrowed brows, Jaz tapped the "Call or Email" tab. Jumping down to the email section, Jaz read:

Electronic messaging has become a standard form of communication within most American homes and businesses, and it can now be used to help inmates stay connected to their families. The Trust Fund Limited Inmate Computer System

(TRULINCS) application enables electronic messages to be exchanged between inmates and the general public in a secured manner. With the inmate's eventual release, maintaining family ties will improve the likelihood of a successful reentry into the community, thus reducing the potential for recidivism.

After more info about restrictions, monitoring, and funding, there was a link to learn more about TRULINCS. The link had another blurb about funding, but it also had a page indicating that all BOP facilities had TRULINCS access.

The one thing that brought Jaz comfort was that inmates could only correspond with people on their approved contact list. Even though Frost could request to add people to that list, he had to know that they existed and how to reach them first.

With a relieved and exhausted sigh, Jaz clicked off her phone, put it back on the nightstand, and pulled the covers over herself.

6

STRAIGHT-LACED

J AZ WOKE UP ON the cold, checkered-tile floor of *Inksignia*. It was
dark and quiet outside. It had to be super late. When did she fall
asleep?

The fluorescent lights flickered, and the sound of a tattoo pen filled
Jaz's ears. She stepped into the back to see a man in a dark shirt sitting
on a rolling stool. He was leaning over a dark-haired female, tattooing
something into her back. Jaz rolled her left shoulder, trying to shake
off a soreness.

"Who the fuck are you?" The man didn't answer. "Hey!" He didn't
budge. "I'm talking to you!" *What is this guy's deal?* "HEY!" Jaz

slammed her hand on the man's shoulder, gaining enough of his attention to warrant a spin in the stool.

The moment his black eyes met Jaz's, she had to fight to not be consumed by the soullessness in them. His smile was menacing with the surrounding stubble on his tanned, strong chin. "I knew you'd come back to me, Jasmine." His voice was gentle like a grandfather's, but that gentility sent a shiver down Jaz's rigid spine.

The lights flickered as Jaz stepped back. Desperate crying filled Jaz's ears. The client was handcuffed to the tattoo chair, naked and shivering. The skinny teen bruised her wrists as she fought against the cuffs. When did Jaz's parlor turn into a basement? This dark, cold place that belonged in a horror movie was the stuff of her real-life nightmares. It felt like the uninsulated walls were closing in around her.

"Sh. Sh. There, there, kitten. Nothing to be afraid of." Jaz felt an itch by her ear as the man patted the crying teen's head. "Yes, it's going to hurt, but it will be worth it. You'll be mine forever." The man picked the tattoo pen back up and started scraping it along the skin of the naked girl.

White, hot, pain scraped its way across Jaz's shoulder blade. Who was screaming? Jaz? The teen? Both? The scream deafened Jaz, making it impossible to tell the difference.

Jaz snapped her eyes open but froze. The room was dark except for the streetlights spilling past the blinds. Every cover was on the floor. Jaz looked at her phone. 1:27 am. The sight of the secure apartment made Jaz release her breath. She gathered her blankets and cocooned herself before laying back down.

Jaz tossed for an hour until her blankets slipped back to the floor. "Fuck," she whispered as she crawled out of bed and turned on the lamp. She grabbed her favorite mechanical pencil and her current sketchbook—a Christmas gift from Garrett. Sitting crisscross on her bed, Jaz flipped to the first clean page in the sketchbook.

At first, she just started automatic drawing—scribbling on the page at random for five minutes to warm up her wrist and cleanse the emotions out of her body. Once that was done, Jaz started a new page, but paused her pen over the parchment. *What should I draw?*

Draw a tattoo for me. Jaz wasn't sure if it was normal for people's thoughts to take on the voice of those recently passed. Nevertheless, it was Rosamie's voice ringing in her head.

After what you did? Why would I want to draw anything for you?

Because you still love me. And you miss me. Jaz didn't react to the mental retort before her pencil started scratching across the paper. Normally, she would've pulled up reference photos for what she was drawing, but she had drawn so many roses in her time that it was muscle memory to her. Less than fifteen minutes later, the entire page was covered in roses of all shapes and sizes from all different angles. None of them made her happy to look at.

Sighing in frustration, Jaz crawled out of bed. After a stop at the bathroom, Jaz put on some sweats and her tennis shoes. She snuck past Annie and out of the apartment. Jaz made her way down to the street. The brisk winter air chilled her through her sweatshirt. The sound of the city nightlife provided some comfort. She didn't get halfway around the block, however, when she heard footsteps behind her. She tried to do the subtle head turn, but it was too dark for her to see if anyone was following her. After three more head turns with no sign of who the footsteps were coming from, Jaz whipped around to look her stalker in the face.

No one was there. Jaz was the single soul walking the neighborhood that night. Not even a dumpster-diving raccoon was around.

The moment Jaz took a tentative step, she heard another footstep. She had been spooked by her own footsteps echoing off the brick walls and concrete sidewalk.

"Fucking dumbass." Even as she cursed herself, Jaz rushed back the way she came. As she hurried, she fought to not allow her footsteps to play any more tricks on her mind. She was flipping her own mind the middle finger from within the pocket of her coat. She ran into her building, fumbled to unlock her door, threw it open, and slammed it behind her.

The noise startled Annie, making her roll off the couch. "Wh-what's going on?! Who's there?!"

"Shut up!" It was Jaz's lower-floor neighbor; the one who seemed to throw parties every night and had a weird work schedule. Word around the building was that the landlady was working on evicting him A.S.A.P. *Hypocrite.*

"It's just me, Annie. Sorry, I woke you."

"Jaz? What're you doing?"

"I'm just going for a walk."

"Are you okay? You sound like you just ran a marathon."

"Yeah. I'm fine. The sound spooked me too."

"Oh. Right." The two strange roommates sat in dark silence, unsure of what to say or do. "Well, goodnight."

"Goodnight." Jaz hurried back out of the apartment. She couldn't sleep and wandering around proved useless and unsettling. There was only one option. After waiting for five minutes, Jaz tiptoed back into the apartment and quietly took Annie's keys.

It was a little past three when Jaz arrived at Annie's apartment building. Once the building was in sight, Jaz saw a cop guarding the door. She gripped Annie's ID lanyard, hoping that would be enough for this guy. As she approached, the cop turned to her. "Good morning ma'am."

"Good morning, officer."

"Coming home awfully late, aren't you?"

Jaz scoffed, "The joy of working the graveyard shift."

"Well, I hear ya there."

"Is there anything wrong, officer?"

"Just some extra security, ma'am."

"Nothing's happened, has it?"

"Everything is just fine, ma'am. This is just a precaution we're taking because of some recent activity in the area. Do you mind showing me proof of your residency here?"

Jaz pulled out the lanyard and used the ID to swipe in, taking care to cover the photo with her hand. The door light changed from red to green, and a gentle beep sounded loud enough for Jaz and the policeman to hear. "Does that work?"

The cop nodded. "Do you live on the third floor, ma'am?"

"No, officer."

"Okay. You have a good night, ma'am."

"You too, officer. Thank you." Jaz slipped into the building. She kept her eyes forward until she was out of sight and in the stairway.

Even though the building seemed quiet, Jaz moved cautiously to the third floor. The floor had been completely cleared out so that none of Annie's neighbors would tamper with the evidence. Annie's door was still taped off, so Jaz carefully reached around the tape to insert the key into the doorknob. Once the door was unlocked, Jaz quickly ducked under the tape into the apartment, quietly but hastily closing the door behind her.

Jaz stood in the dark for a moment before she decided that it was too creepy. She clicked on the lights. *Annie must've watched a lot of IKEA porn when she moved in*. Not a single square-foot of this university-owned studio apartment was cluttered or wasted. There had to be at least a dozen hidden nooks and crannies that the cops missed.

The bed frame was missing a mattress, which had to have been taken in for evidence. Either that or disposed of; *I'm sure neither Annie nor any other future tenants would want to sleep on a mattress that someone died on*. However, there was a blanket and pillow folded and stacked in the corner of the apartment. The sight took Jaz back to Annie's phone conversation the morning before. It hadn't occurred to her at the time, but the conversation indicated that Annie and Rosamie weren't sleeping together. *I suppose not all teenagers are fucking each other*. But even Rosamie called herself "experienced". *I can't think Annie would've taken the floor if they got into a fight. It's her fucking apartment; she could've just told Rosamie to leave, and Rosamie would've done it*. Jaz knew this fact from experiencing a handful of fights with her niece herself. But why had Annie slept on the floor?

Jaz got down on her knees and peeked under the bed. Annie had taken full advantage of the space. Jaz reached and pulled out the first thing she grabbed. It was a heavy, aluminum briefcase that was locked. *Where would Annie keep the key?* Jaz scanned the room until her eyes fell on an Empire Hearts funky figurine. When Jaz picked it up, she felt it was hollow and something was sliding around inside. A twist of the plastic hairpiece revealed a tiny key hidden in the head.

Opening the case, Jaz found the most underwhelming thing to keep locked out of sight; paper. Not even legal paper, but simple bank statements. Jaz was about to close the safe in disappointment when she saw the account's balance. $7,004.94.

Jaz furrowed her brows. She knew that Annie's family of engineers and lawyers had paid for her entire education—including her living costs. Even then, the girl still applied for every scholarship available to her. She also knew that Annie didn't even have a part-time job; she was a freelance artist, but between her prices and the infrequency of commissions she talked about, there was no way that she would be making that much money. Other statements indicated that she also had over a thousand in a retirement fund. *Why does a seventeen-year-old need a retirement fund?* Annie had opened the Roth IRA a month after meeting Rosamie. She also had a little over two thousand in another account, the statements for which were labeled "EMERGENCY". *I appreciate how responsible she is, but where is all this money coming from?*

Once the safe had been closed, locked, and pushed back under the bed, Jaz turned her attention to Annie's laptop. This seventeen-inch, ten-pound monstrosity was made for gaming and was about six months old. Jaz opened it and was greeted with the sign-in screen. Jaz couldn't find anything written down, and the four passwords she could think of off the top of her head failed. Jaz didn't want to risk alerting Annie to her actions by entering too many wrong passwords, so she closed the laptop.

There weren't any more obvious hiding places that Jaz could see. She took a chance and went to the bookshelf that held a huge collection of manga, a ton of art textbooks, and at least ten sketchbooks.

Pulling a random sketchbook, Jaz found it full of portraits of a single woman, along with several practice sketches of roses. The undercut hair and septum piercing made it easy to recognize Rosamie. Jaz understood how Annie had earned the title of "prodigy" looking at these pictures. Jaz looked at the pictures with a forlorn expression written all over her face.

Out of nowhere, the sketchbook ended, and it was clear that the pages had been ripped out. Jaz found the trash bin beneath the card table that acted as Annie's drawing desk. It was full of paper balls and snack wrappers. When Jaz uncrumpled the paper, she found more portraits of Rosamie. Some may have warranted being thrown away, but others were some of the best work in the book. There were some that Jaz couldn't tell if they were good or not; they had been scribbled out or torn apart. *So a love-hate thing. Got it.*

As Jaz was returning the sketchbook to the shelf, she noticed a dictionary hidden among the manga. When Jaz pulled it out, she found a combination lock on the pages' side and heard a clunking from within. It was a book safe. *Anal much on the security, Annie?*

What would the combo be? Jaz went back to the Empire Hearts figurine, but there was no three-digit number to be found. She tried Annie's birthday again, as well as Rosamie's. She also tried their anniversary. Nothing worked. Jaz pulled out every sketchbook and every piece of scratch or loose-leaf paper. What few numbers she found proved useless.

When Jaz went to look through the manga, the *Thorns of the Rose* series caught her eye; it was the only incomplete series on the shelf, and each book was out of order. With Annie being so organized, there was no way that was an accident. Jaz turned back to the dictionary safe and entered the numbers as they appeared on the shelf; 213.

The book safe popped open, revealing a pocket notebook. Flipping through the pages, Jaz found it was the closest thing Annie had to a diary; it was full of a bunch of ideas for big tattoos and graphic novel stories.

The last entry was written about ten days before:

· *New idea for original manga. Straight girl gets into relationship with gay girl to rebel against parents. Gay girl falls tragically in love with straight girl while straight girl uses and abuses gay girl*

· *Don't know how it ends yet. Maybe I'll get an idea tonight. Maybe it will be therapeutic*

· *Title Ideas*

1. *Scared Straight*
2. *Straight and Narrow*
3. ***Straight Laced***
4. *Damn Straight*
5. *Straight to the Point*
6. *Give it to me Straight*
7. *Straight Face*
8. *Straight Shooter*
9. *Straight Up*
10. *Put Her Straight*

Seeing the underlined title "Straight Laced" jogged Jaz's short-term memory; she pulled a few of the sketchbooks back out and flipped through them until she found the manga-style art piece with "Straight Laced" written in fancy calligraphy. What Jaz had assumed was a couple piece with Rosamie and Annie in corsets had been a concept for the cover of this manga idea. *That means Rosamie is straight?!*

"Ahem." Jaz jumped and fumbled for her pepper spray. "You know, the 'DO NOT CROSS' on the tape isn't a suggestion." It was Detective Josiah Moore.

"Isn't it a little late to be working the beat? Or early? Either way, shouldn't you be in bed?"

"I could say the same thing to you, and unlike you, Ms. Dilan, it's my *job* to investigate, which requires me to be available 24/7 as needed." The detective was in no mood for games; that much was obvious in his tone.

Jaz shrugged. "So what are you investigating?"

"That's confidential information, and *this* is a crime scene. What are you doing here, Ms. Dilan?"

Jaz scoffed. "I would think that would be obvious."

"Ms. Dilan, I could arrest you for interference. You're not in a good position to give me sass. I'll ask you one more time; what are you doing here?" *Yep, definitely not in the mood for anything other than business.*

Jaz sighed, "I couldn't sleep. I needed to do something. I need answers, so I came here."

Josiah's stern look softened. "I understand how you must be feeling in this difficult time, Ms. Dilan, but you can't just go around, trespassing on crime scenes. It's a criminal offense and it won't help anyone." Jaz sighed again. Josiah gave his own sigh in response as he rubbed her forehead. "Okay, look. If you show me everything you found, I'll take you home and we'll never speak of this again."

Jaz furrowed her brows together. "I thought you already searched the place."

"We did, but you and I have different definitions of 'interesting items'. I'm curious to see what you thought was suspicious."

"Why are you offering to let me off the hook?"

Josiah crossed his arms over his coated chest. "Are you going to take the deal or not? I'd like to get some sleep tonight, so make a choice."

Jaz was silent for a moment before kneeling and pulling the aluminum case out from under the bed. Opening it back up, she showed the detective the bank statements. "Isn't it a little weird that a college student with no consistent job is making this much money?"

Josiah shrugged. "Well, this could just be gifts and allowances. Still, I'll check into it. What else?" Jaz picked up Annie's journal and showed the detective the "Straight-Laced" entry. "So?"

Jaz picked up the sketchbook that was still open to the cover concept-sketch. "I think the story idea came from her relationship with Rosamie?"

"So, which one is the one that's not gay?"

"Based on the sketch and the ideas that's in the journal, I think it's Rosamie."

"Rosamie wasn't gay?"

Jaz shrugged, "Annie must have some reason to think so."

"And what do *you* think?"

Jaz sighed. "I don't know. I mean, I never saw anything weird, but Rosamie was charismatic. If I'm honest, she could be manipulative. Maybe there was something Annie saw, heard or felt that I didn't."

Josiah took the journal and the sketchbook along with the most recent bank statements. "Anything else?"

"Not really. I couldn't figure out the password to her laptop."

"I'll take it to our tech guy if we find any reason to confiscate it. I can't take it without a warrant and probable cause yet. Is that everything?" Jaz nodded. "Good. Time to take you home."

As Jaz and Detective Moore exited the building, Detective Moore whispered to the guarding cop, "Never let this woman back in the building again unless she is with me."

"Yes, sir." The guard gave Jaz a glare as she passed by. *He must've gotten quite a tongue-lashing from Josiah before he caught me.*

Most of the drive back to Jaz's apartment was quiet. *Please let the early morning lull in traffic hurry this up so that I can get the fuck out before he feels the need to make small talk.*

"Why couldn't you sleep?"

"Hm?"

"You said you came to Annie's apartment because you couldn't sleep. What was on your mind?" *Bullshit small talk is sounding pretty good right now.* "Well, let's see. I just found out today that my niece is dead, there's a chance that it was murder, her girlfriend—who is staying at my apartment—is the most likely suspect at the moment, some chick is already trying to un-friend-zone herself for said girlfriend, and niece got a tattoo that is a horrible reminder of the worst time in my life shortly before she died. I don't know. Why do you think I can't sleep?"

Josiah shook his head. "If her being in your apartment worries you so much, why don't you ask her to leave? It's your lease; you have the right to invite or uninvite whoever you want. No one would say you're a bad person for not wanting a suspect in your home."

Jaz rolled her eyes. "I don't actually think that Annie did it. It's just the stress of the whole situation."

Josiah nodded. "I'm sorry. Believe it or not, I know what you're going through—"

Jaz couldn't keep the indignation out of her eyes and voice. "How could you? You're always the investigator; never the victim or the victim's family. Rosamie is just a job to you. They all are."

"Not all of them." Something in the way Josiah said this caught Jaz's attention.

"What does that mean?"

Josiah shook his head again. "It's nothing. What did you mean about a chick being friend-zoned by Annie?"

What's he hiding? "One of the heads from the LGBTQIA+ Support Group came over to check on Annie last night; that's why Annie wasn't there when you came by. This chick was being a little clingy before they left to go grab coffee or something."

Josiah shrugged, "Maybe she's just worried about her friend."

Jaz shook her head. "You didn't see how she acted."

"Well, how did she act?"

"She was putting her arms around Annie, and she didn't seem to want to leave when she brought Annie back."

Josiah shrugged again. "Still sounds like a friend trying to support someone through a dark time."

Jaz let out an exasperated sigh. "Look, I know what it looks like when someone takes advantage of a bad situation to make them look like a hero."

"And how do you know what it looks like?"

"You don't think half of the guys at my high school didn't do the exact same thing after," Jaz trailed off, unable to finish the sentence

Josiah didn't need her to. "Did they know?"

Jaz shook her head as she looked down at her lap. "Not the specific truth. The police and court kept as much information locked down as they could. They kept my name out of every public statement and only necessary people were present when I testified in court. But the whole school knew something had happened because I hadn't shown for two weeks, and when I came back, my attitude matched my new clothes—dark, grungey, and heavy. Different rumors passed around, ranging anywhere from simple rebellion to daddy issues to post-abortion depression. None of them were accurate, but those dumbasses still believed them and started going for me."

Josiah shook his head. "I'm sorry. That was probably the last thing you needed after what you had been through."

"It was. That's why I put one of them in the hospital. They all left me alone after I did." In fact, everyone left Jaz alone after that. Even the people she needed and trusted.

"You should've put them all in the hospital."

Jaz furrowed her brow as she looked over at Josiah. "Most people look at me like I'm insane for just beating up the one guy."

"So?"

"I would just think a cop would feel the same way."

Josiah shook his head. "Nope. You went through something no one should ever have to go through, certainly not a fifteen-year-old girl. Anyone who takes advantage of that kinda trauma is sick and deserves to get their ass kicked."

"Some people defend them because they didn't know the whole story." Jaz remembered how the mother of the boy she beat up called her "pyscho" for attacking her "precious angel who was a perfect gentlemen". It still pissed her off to think about. Jaz had thought she had taken all her anger for the boy and his mom out when she slashed three of the four tires on each of their cars and taken a metal baseball bat to everything. That was the incident that made the court say that Jaz had to go to therapy.

"Fuck them. No one should take advantage of *anyone* who went through *any* kind of trauma. Even if they didn't know the specifics, they had an idea that something bad had happened to you and they tried to use it to their advantage. That's fucked up no matter how you slice it." Jaz stared at Josiah. No one had ever understood Jaz or what she'd been through. That's why she rarely told anyone anything. Even if someone saw her when the anxiety got the best of her, all she would say was that she had anxiety; she would never reveal the source of it, and people rarely asked for it. Josiah *had* to know the truth because of the situation. *Why is he different?* "So who is this girl?"

"Huh?"

"The girl. The one you said was hitting on Annie. What's her name?"

"Oh, uh. I think Annie called her Isa. I didn't catch a full name."

"Might be something to ask Annie about."

"You think Isa might've killed Rosamie?"

Josiah shook his head. "No, I was thinking that she would've been another motive for Annie. Her relationship with Rosamie could've been rocky. A little attention from a third party can and has been enough to spark a fire."

Jaz shook her own head at the theory. "I still don't think Annie did it."

"After everything you found, how are you still unconvinced?"

Jaz shrugged. "She just seems too nice."

"They said the same thing about Ted Bundy." Jaz didn't have a response to that, and she didn't have the time to think of one. "We're here." Sure enough, Jaz's apartment was right outside her door. The sky was starting to lighten with the rising sun.

Jaz unbuckled herself as she said, "Thanks for the ride. And for not arresting me."

"It was a one-time thing. Next time, I can't be so nice. But there won't be a 'next time', will there Ms. Dilan.?" Josiah looked Jaz dead in the eye as he asked the loaded question.

Jaz took a moment to digest the thinly-veiled warning before answering, "No, Detective Moore."

The detective nodded. "Go get some rest. I'll let you know when we make any discoveries or developments."

"Thank you, Detective."

"Goodnight, Ms. Dilan." *Fat chance.* Jaz opened the door, slid out of the car, and walked into her building. Josiah didn't leave until he saw that Jaz had made it inside.

7

ARRESTED DEVELOPMENT

AFTER TOSSING AND TURNING and drawing for an hour, Jaz did manage to get some light sleep that did nothing to rejuvenate her. By the time she woke up, it was late in the morning. Annie had already left a note behind:

Good morning, Jaz!

I'm off to class and my internship has me working this afternoon. I won't get done until about 7. I'll grab my own dinner and see you around 8.

Annie

P.S. I made coffee. Hope it's not too strong.

Bless you, my child. Jaz poured herself a cup and tried to enjoy it before pulling Rosamie's uniform out of the dryer. She ironed and folded it as best as she could before heading out to *Taste of Nam*, hoping to get there before the lunch rush and before Mr. Hong decided to Marie Kondo Rosamie's stuff.

Taste of Nam was a small restaurant, which surprised Jaz; Rosamie said the food was so good that the place was packed all the time. Jaz would've thought that Mr. Hong had invested in a bigger place to maximize profits. Instead, the restaurant looked like a refurbished bodega. Where Mr. Hong could fit a kitchen or tables was beyond Jaz. The popularity of the place had to have come from word of mouth; the boring awning and exterior design didn't catch any eyes or pique any one's interest. Most people wouldn't have known what kind of restaurant it was if it weren't for the Vietnam flag on the awning.

When Jaz tried the front door, it was locked. She had to knock a few times to get someone's attention. Could this really be Mr. Hong? His head was perfectly shaved, and his thin eyebrows were permanently drawn together around his wire-rimmed glasses. Anyone else would've had wrinkles from frowning so much, but he still looked like he was in his mid-thirties. Jaz knew he had to be older; Rosamie said his favorite way to lecture her was to point out that she had it easy because she didn't have to try to survive the end of the war like he did. That had to make him, at least, sixty.

Mr. Hong's lips were set in a frown beneath his thin mustache. He pointed to the sign that said "CLOSED". Jaz held up Rosamie's uniform, which made Mr. Hong say, "Oh," and hold up a finger. Jaz waited as Mr. Hong disappeared to the back of the restaurant. About two minutes later, Mr. Hong opened the restaurant door.

"Hi, Mr. Hong. I'm Jasmine Dilan, Rosamie's aunt? We've not met yet." Jaz put her hand out to offer a shake, but Mr. Hong just glared between her face and her hand. He took moments to snarl especially at any tattoos and piercings that were visible. Putting her hand away, Jaz said, "I'm just returning Rosamie's uniform and picking up her stuff." Without saying a word, Mr. Hong took the uniform and passed an open cardboard box to Jaz. Once the box was in her arms, Mr. Hong closed and locked the door, returning to his morning prep routine.

"You're welcome, ya dick." Looking into the box, there wasn't much that was worth keeping; just Jaz's old phone that she let Rosamie use when she lost hers. Everything else went in the nearest dumpster. *What a waste.*

Jaz thought about spending her day-off at the apartment, but she knew she wouldn't be able to enjoy it; she was too restless. She needed to get out and be with a friend. An hour before noon, she put in an order for two gyros and two frappes with PostDash. She met the delivery guy right outside *Venom Art*—Garrett's tattoo parlor. After paying the delivery boy, Jaz entered the parlor.

Venom Art looked like it had been a biker bar, and Garrett must've kept everything save for the actual bar; in it's place were tattoo chairs and tables. He also could've installed more lights to dampen the dive atmosphere. Garrett must've even kept the biker bar's music selection and heavy base amplifiers. Garrett's pet scorpion, Koki, was in her tank next to the front desk, scurrying around; she hadn't been fed yet. *I keep telling him that she scares away customers, but does he ever listen? No.* Even so, Jaz passed by the tank and greeted the arachnid with a wave.

From the back of the parlor, Garrett yelled, "Closed for lunch!"

"I know that, ya dick!"

Jaz's voice pulled Garrett to the front of the parlor. "Hey!" Garrett gave Jaz a quick hug before asking, "What are you doing here?" Jaz held up the frappe tray and the delivery bag. "Don't I still owe you for Monday night."

Jaz shrugged. "Yeah, but I need to talk to someone, and it seems rude to collect before dumping the world's problems on you."

"Uh, oh. What's up?"

"Food first." Jaz and Garrett sat down around the front desk after Garrett dropped a few crickets into Koki's tank. Jaz passed out the gyros and the coffee before Garrett asked again, "What's up?"

"Um, you know my niece?"

"Rosamie? Yeah. What'd she do now?"

"She, um," Jaz didn't know how to tell the truth.

"Jaz? What's wrong?"

"She passed away." Garrett choked on his gyro. "Don't die." *Fucking word choice.* Once Garett was able to breathe again, Jaz asked, "Are you okay?"

"'Am *I* okay'? Are *you* okay?"

"I'm," Jaz couldn't finish the sentence, lest she cry. As the tears started to prick the corner of her eyes, she shrugged. Garrett walked around the desk to wrap his arms around his friend. The warm embrace unleashed the tears. Garrett didn't loosen his hug until Jaz could take a breath without sniffling or trembling. By that time, the gyros had gone lukewarm, and the frappes were starting to melt.

Garrett was hesitant to ask, "What happened?"

"I still don't completely know. The police are investigating."

"Oh, shit! Is it that serious?"

Jaz shook her head. "Standard procedure. The coroner said that the going theory is that she had a seizure."

Garrett ran a hand through his blond undercut. "Fuck me. That's horrible."

"Yeah, it is."

"I'm so sorry. Is there anything I can do?"

"Just tell me a good, funny story. Any crazies? Oh, wait. You pawn them onto your apprentice."

Garrett sighed out a laugh. "Actually, she didn't come into work yesterday, so of course, the coo-coos came out of the woodwork."

"Oh yeah? What happened"

Once Garrett had taken a sip of his frappe, he said, "Well, first there was the girl who wanted the 'Come-N-Go Burger' logo in the pubic area, sans the 'burger'."

Jaz chuckled. "Clever girl. I like her."

"Then there was the guy who wanted 'glory' and 'hole' tattooed on the bottom of his feet."

Jaz winced, not so much at the idea but at the pain that would be involved. "Why?"

"Apparently, his foot jobs are 'to die for'."

"Jesus."

Garrett rushed through the next sip of his drink, eager to get to the cringiest part of his story. "Oh, but the best one."

"Oh, shit."

"One person wanted me to tattoo 'GERBILS ONLY' around their asshole."

Jaz gave a clueless cringe. "Why?"

"You've never heard of people doing that?"

"What? Sticking gerbils up there? Yeah, but I thought it was a joke."

Garrett shook his head. "Nope. People actually do that."

"Why?!"

"Apparently, there's a g-spot up there that only live critters can hit."

Jaz rubbed her temples, trying to comprehend the stories. "Has sex always been this fucking weird?"

"Yeah, but nobody knew about the shit they didn't do. Once the internet became a thing, all bets were off."

Jaz giggled. "So why didn't your apprentice come into work?"

"She said that there was a tragedy and she needed a day to deal. She's coming back in today after lunch."

"I can't wait to meet her."

Garrett nodded. "You can ask if any of her friends would make good apprentices."

"I'll just have her make a list and email it to me. I'm taking a hiatus until after the funeral."

"I get that."

Silence fell over the friends as they ate their lunch. "So, any more interesting stories? Any good news? Any bad news? Can you believe the weather?"

Garrett gave Jaz a look. "The woman who hates small talk is trying to make it?"

"I just want to talk about anything other than," Jaz trailed off.

"Okay. Uh, Jess got engaged."

It was Jaz's turn to cough on her lunch. "Ohhhhh. I'm sorry, man."

Garrett shrugged. "Hey, it's nothing compared to what you're going through."

"How'd you find out?"

"She changed her relationship status on FaceSpace."

"I'm sorry, dude."

Garrett scoffed. "The ring's as big as he is."

"Yeah?"

"Yeah. He's obviously rich. He's gotta be as dumb as a brick."

Jaz nodded. "That's usually how it plays out. You can't be rich, buff, and smart. Unless you're a psycho."

"Should we hope he's psycho?"

"Up to you, man."

Garrett stopped making jokes to cover up his pain at that point. "What the fuck does she see in him?"

"Dollar signs. She's a gold-digger, Garrett. She always has been. They probably deserve each other."

"I guess," Garrett admitted, begrudgingly. He had never wanted to admit that Jaz had been right about Jess, but he couldn't really deny her anymore. "He'll abandon her one way or another."

Jaz nodded in agreement. "And she'll take him for everything he has."

"Maybe he'll make her sign a prenup."

"Hopefully karma is just that much of a bitch." The friends cheered their frappes at the statement.

The bell at the parlor door rang, drawing the tattoo artist's attention. Detective Josiah Moore was flanked by Officers Jenkins and Monroe. Jaz stood up. "Detective Moore?"

Garrett looked over at Jaz with wide eyes and a pale face. "You know him?"

Josiah answered for Jaz. "I'm the lead investigator on her niece's case." Turning to Jaz, Josiah nodded. "Good to see you again, Ms. Dilan." His eyes were narrowed in suspicion, however.

Jaz nodded back. "I was just having lunch with Garrett."

"So I see." Josiah turned his suspicious face to Garrett. "Mr. Weber, I have a few questions for you regarding the evening of Monday the twenty-eighth."

Garrett shrugged, but Jaz could still see his nerves. "I don't know what I could tell you. I have never met Jaz's niece."

Josiah looked at Jaz before asking, "Is there somewhere more private we could go, Mr. Weber?"

Garrett looked over at Jaz, too. When she nodded, Garrett looked back at the detective. "Uh, sure. We could go to my storage room."

"Good." Turning to Jenkins, Josiah ordered. "Have a look around."

This caught Garrett's attention. "Uh, do you have a search warrant to do that?"

"Do you have something to hide, Mr. Weber?"

"Nothing that would matter to you or your case, but I know my rights and I'm entitled to my privacy."

Josiah pulled a folded piece of paper out of his coat pocket. "No need to worry, Mr. Weber. Nothing we find will be disclosed if it has nothing to do with the case." Rather than waiting for Garrett to react, Josiah turned to Jaz. "Would you mind waiting here until I'm done with Mr. Weber? There are things we need to discuss."

What now? Don't you think you put me through enough yesterday? "Of course, Detective."

Turning to Monroe, Josiah ordered, "Keep an eye on her," before he and Officer Jenkins followed Garrett into the back of the parlor.

The interview didn't take as long as she had expected; only thirty minutes at most. In the meantime, Officer Monroe tried to make small talk with Jaz. The whole experience was painful and Jaz just wanted to know what the hell was going on.

"Hey, Garrett! Sorry about—" Annie trailed off when she saw Jaz and Officer Monroe. "Jaz."

"Annie? What are you doing here?"

"Ah, Miss Xun. Good of you to finally join us." Detective Moore finally returned with Garrett behind him.

Garrett looked at Jaz with a furrowed brow. "You know her?"

Jaz nodded. "She's Rosamie's girlfriend."

Garrett's eyes went wide. "She's my apprentice."

Josiah interrupted, "And she's my number one suspect." Before anyone could ask any questions, Officer Jenkins interrupted and handed Josiah a baggy and whispered into his ear. After looking at the contents of the bag, Josiah mused, "Well, Miss Xun. It seems you left out a few details in your statement." Josiah turned the baggy around. Inside was a piece of tracing paper with Rosamie's tattoo sketched on it. "Annie Xun, I'm placing you under arrest for suspicion of the murder of Rosamie Dylan."

"What do you mean 'it was clearly murder'?!" Jaz had followed Detective Moore when he took Annie away in handcuffs. Garrett was taken to the station as well to be fingerprinted. Jaz had to take the subway because Josiah was with Annie, Officer Jenkins was with Garrett, and Officer Monroe was transporting evidence. This included everything from Annie's trashcan, every empty ink cartridge that was in the building, and whatever records they thought were necessary to the case.

Josiah explained. "Bails is confident that Rosamie suffocated when a seizure was induced."

"How is that Annie's fault?"

"We believe she induced the seizure."

Jaz scoffed, "How is that even possible?"

"The benefit of having a coroner from the outback is that they can recognize venom poisoning by sight."

"Venom? Like a snake bite?"

"Yeah, but there are no bite marks."

"So what? Did she eat it?"

Josiah shook his head. "Venom doesn't have the same effects when it's ingested. It had to be injected into the bloodstream."

Jaz's eyebrows popped up in surprised realization. "You think Annie put the poison in the tattoo ink."

"It would explain the red swelling around the tattoo,"

"But Annie wouldn't--"

"Ms. Dilan," Josiah interrupted. "I understand that you care for the girl, but you have to face the facts. She had motive and opportunity."

"What about means? Where would Annie get venom from anyway?"

"Well, she has that snake tattoo around her ankle, right?" *That's right! I always thought that was out of place with her other nerdy tattoos.* "If she's interested in snakes, she could have a lot of knowledge when it comes to finding and obtaining venom. We'll be able to determine where it came from once we figure out what kind of venom it is."

Jaz sighed, "How long will that take?"

"Six to eight weeks." Josiah didn't miss the look of shock on Jaz's face. "You can't rush a toxicology report, Ms. Dilan."

"Can't Dr. Martin tell what kind of venom it was by sight?"

Josiah shook his head. "Apparently, several venoms have similar symptoms, even if they came from different kinds of animals and insects. We can't get specific until the report comes in."

"Is the tattoo really the only place where the venom could've gotten in? Annie said Rosamie got into a fight. There had to be scratches."

"There are, but why would the woman at the club want to poison Rosamie with venom?"

"She was homophobic, right?"

Josiah shook his head again. "Hate crimes tend to be spur of the moment, which is why they're usually done through battery and assault. Poisoning suggests pre-meditation. Unless she's been stalking Rosamie, there's no way this woman could've known that Rosamie was gay and that they would run into each other that night."

"Well, maybe she *was* stalking Rosamie."

"We haven't found or heard anything to suggest that, and unless and until we do, we can't pursue that path. Besides, how would she inject the venom by just scratching Rosamie."

"Maybe she painted the venom on her nails."

"Like Sigourney Weaver did in that movie?"

Jaz looked at the detective blankly. "I don't think I saw that one."

Josiah lectured, "Ms. Dilan, this is all just speculation."

"So is your theory."

"Yes, but ours is based on fact—not feelings—and, therefore, is more plausible." Before Jaz could protest and open the discussion back up, Josiah cut her off. "Ms. Dilan. I assure you that as the case develops, we will keep you informed. For now, I have work to do."

When Jaz started following the detective, Garrett—who had just gotten fingerprinted—grabbed her and said, "Jaz, there's nothing you can do now."

"But—"

Garrett cut off his friend's protests. "We'll figure this out, but you can't argue with a cop, especially not the one who's trying to figure out what the fuck happened. Let's sleep on it and decide what to do next." Jaz didn't respond, but she allowed Garrett to walk her towards the door. Right as they passed the front desk. She stopped in her tracks. "Jaz?"

"Just give me a sec. Wait for me outside. I'll be right there." Garrett hesitated, "I'm not gonna go tear the detective a new asshole. Just go.

I'll be right there." Garrett did as Jaz asked, but he still seemed unsure based on the look he threw over his shoulder. Once he was out the door, Jaz stepped up to the front desk. "Excuse me. How do I visit someone in the county jail?"

THIS IS SOME FREDDY KRUEGER SHIT

GARRETT AND JAZ HAD just gotten to Garrett's apartment. He had offered to let Jaz stay with him after Annie was arrested. Given everything that was coming to light, Jaz didn't want to be alone in her apartment with her niece's possessions waiting to be a constant reminder of everything. Jaz took Garret up on the offer, hoping that it wouldn't be too weird.

How can he afford this place? Business was good enough to earn Garret quite the bachelor pad at Edgewater. The building was built at the start of the millennium and came with luxuries like fireplaces in every apartment and an in-house dry-cleaner. Jaz had helped Garrett move in, and the sight of the whole place still made her jaw drop.

Garrett suddenly stopped in his tracks as they entered the apartment. "Fuck."

"What's wrong?" Garrett looked at Jaz in horror before looking into the eat-in kitchen. Jaz followed his eyes to the liquor cabinet, filled to the brim with every alcohol Jaz could imagine; there was even stuff that Garrett never drank and only kept around for bragging purposes. "Oh." Silence fell over the friends. *What the hell are we going to do?*

Jaz's cell rang on cue. Looking at the screen she saw it was her sister. Jaz set her duffle bag down and said, "I'll take this out in the hall. You know, so you can," Jaz gestured to the liquor cabinet.

"Right. Sorry."

"It's fine," was the last thing Jaz said before stepping back out into the hall. Careful to keep her voice down so as not to disturb the other residents, Jaz answered her phone. "Hello?"

"I told you that little bitch killed Rosa!" Jaz had to hold the phone away from her ear to avoid going deaf.

"That's just the police's theory right now."

"Theory? They arrested her!"

Jaz pinched the bridge of her nose. "Yeah, but they don't have all the evidence they need to convict Annie."

"She killed Rosa, Jaz! Why are you defending her?!"

"Because I have a reason to believe that she didn't kill her."

Rubylyne was silent on the other end. "You know something."

"What?"

"You know something. Something the police didn't tell me." *Fuck.* "What is it? What did they tell you?"

"Ruby, it's nothing."

"No, it isn't. Something is wrong."

"I don't know anything you don't know."

"Jasmine Lee Dylan, I am Rosamie's mother and I deserve to know what happened to her. Now tell me right now!"

She's not even my mother; the middle name shouldn't work on me! Jaz took a moment before she confessed, "I think *he* has something to do with this."

"Who?"

"*Him.* You know."

"No, I don't know."

Jaz sighed. "Seth Frost." Rubylyn was silent for so long that Jaz had to ask, "Hello?"

"Jaz, I understand that this has brought up some traumatizing memories. For that, I'm sorry. You worked so hard to heal from everything, and this just enflamed the scars. But I promise you that he's still in prison and he won't get out."

"But he can still get mail."

"What does that have to do with—"

"Rosamie was trying to contact him." Another long period of silence. "The police found a letter from the staff at SeaTac, telling her to stop trying to contact him because they thought it would be detrimental." Rubylyne remained silent. *I shouldn't have told her.*

"Wh—Ho—But why would she—"

"I don't know." *I can't tell her about the tattoo. That will break her.*

"What was she trying to talk to him about?"

"I don't know that either. The letter from SeaTac didn't go into detail. They just said stop."

"Why didn't the police tell me?! Isn't that an important detail?"

"Who contacted you?" *Play dumb. It will just hurt her more to know that I'm why she was never told about this.*

"The Seattle Police Department. They said the NYPD contacted them and requested they contact me."

"Maybe the NYPD didn't tell the SPD?"

"Maybe. Are you in contact with them?"

"The NYPD? Yeah. Why?"

"Do you think you could find out what Rosamie was trying to talk to him about?"

"I don't know. They're pretty convinced Annie did it, so they may not have even bothered to look into it. Even if they have, they may not tell me."

"Can you, at least, try?"

Guilt rippled throughout Jaz's body as she said, "Yeah, of course."

"I'll try to contact SeaTac too. Hopefully, we'll get some answers."

"Hopefully." *But do we want the answers?*

Garrett was putting a pile of blankets and pillow on his couch when Jaz came back into the apartment after she hung up with her sister. She passed a glance over to the liquor cabinet. The liquor was still there, but there was a huge padlock wrapped around the handles. Part of Jaz's mind breathed a sigh of relief while the other part cursed.

"Hey, is everything okay?" Garrett paused before correcting, "Sorry. Stupid question."

"I know what you meant. The police told Ruby that they arrested Annie."

"How'd she take it?"

She wanted Annie's head on a platter. "She's having a hard time."

"I'm sorry, hon." That's when Garrett's intercom buzzed. With a hit of a button, he got a security camera view of the building entrance. Garrett didn't even ask why the girl with the red baseball cap wanted to come in. "Come on up."

"Who is it?"

"Pizza."

"Bless you, my son." Garrett laughed as he opened the door to greet the pizza girl. When he came back, there were two extra-large pizza boxes, a two liter of diet soda, a platter of garlic breadsticks, and a chocolate chip cookie pizza. "Why the fuck did you order for the last supper?"

"Because you have already had the shittiest week on the planet, and I would rather you eat your feelings than drink your feelings."

Jaz understood that the comment was meant to be a good-natured ribbing, and a week ago, she would've probably laughed. Given how she was feeling in the moment, however, it felt insensitive. Nevertheless, she joined the joke. "I can't tell if that makes you a good friend or a bad one."

"I paid for the whole thing and I'm *still* gonna pay you back for Monday night and lunch."

"Good friend it is."

"Do we want to even bother with plates, or should I just bring the boxes?"

"What gets the food in my mouth faster?"

"Boxes it is." Keeping the delivery in a stack, Garrett migrated to the couch. He put one pizza—plain cheese—in front of him and the other pizza—peppers with onions and siracha—in front of Jaz.

"You ordered one for each of us?"

"I'm not letting your spawn-of-the-devil taste buds kill me."

"Pussy."

"I'm not a pussy! I'm Norwegian! Our diet is ham, fish, and butter."

"So you're bland."

"At least *my* pizza is fit for human consumption."

"Whatever." Garrett clicked on the TV and started flipping through the channels as the friends tucked into their dinner. They finally settled on *Dragged*, a reality competition that paired drag queens with drag kings for a chance to headline in Vegas. The friends sat in silence, and passed the soda, breadsticks, and cookie pizza between them until the commercial break. "I still can't believe it," Jaz sighed.

"I know. She seemed like such a sweet girl."

"No, I mean it. I can't believe that she did it."

"That cop seems pretty convinced, and I *highly* doubt he would tell you anything less than the truth."

"Well, that's his job."

"Yeah, but even if it wasn't, I'm pretty sure he'd bend over backwards for you."

Jaz furrowed her brow. "Why do you say that?"

"Oh, come on. Jaz. Don't tell me you didn't see the way he looked at you."

"What the fuck are you talking about? He was looking at me like someone who just lost a family member."

"Jaz, I'm telling you. He would totally ask you out if it weren't for the circumstances."

Jaz shook her head. "Bullshit."

"Does that mean you're not interested?"

"You're talking to the committed spinster, remember?"

"Yeah, but that was before you met him."

"Why would he change my mind."

"Jaz, I'm a straight dude, and *I* know he's fucking attractive."

"Then you can have him."

"Should I tell him you said that next time I see him?" Instead of answering, Jaz shot the deadliest glare towards her friend. Garrett chuckled, unintimidated.

"Shut up and get your shit together before you pee, asshole."

"Jaz and—what's his name?"

Jaz gave an irritated sigh. "Josiah, you cocksucker."

"Jaz and Josiah, taking NYC. F-U-C-K-I-N—" Jaz shoved a slice of her spicy pizza into Garrett's open mouth. He instantly spit the slice out and stuck his tongue out, groaning in pain. Jaz chuckled as her friend bolted into his kitchen, threw the fridge open, and started chugging the two-percent milk.

"That'll teach you to keep your damn mouth shut." It was Garrett's turn to glare at Jaz.

The commercial break ended, and the friends silently ate as the drag partners walked the runway. When the top and bottom looks had been weeded out, a new commercial break started, giving leave for the conversation to start up again. "It just doesn't make sense."

Garrett sighed. "Jaz, why is this bothering you so much?" Jaz never told Garret about Seth Frost. By the time they had met, she had Frost's mark covered up. The story seemed too long to tell. *Now that Rosamie's dead, it's even longer.* "Okay, look. I have a friend who might be able to put this to rest."

"How?"

"They might be able to figure out what the police know and aren't telling you."

"Do they work for the police?"

"Not exactly."

"Are they a private investigator?"

Garrett shrugged. "In a way," he said before stuffing his face with his bland pizza.

"They're a hacker, aren't they?"

"White-hat!"

"Hacking into police records doesn't sound very 'white-hat' to me."

"Okay, they do a few less than 'white-hat' things on the side, but they can probably figure out what in your gut is saying Annie's innocent,"

"I appreciate the thought, but I don't think INCOGNITO will want to help little old me." The hacker group Jaz spoke of had been in business for about ten years by that point. No one could agree whether they were heroes or terrorists, but everyone knew full well you did everything in your power not to piss them off.

"You never know. They've been talking about getting a huge tattoo. I was gonna design it for them, but if you offer them a discount with a six-pack of energy drinks, they could probably get you EVERY file in the NYPD's database."

"I'll keep that in mind." *Anything to get him to shut up with this.*

Jaz woke up in the middle of the night. She thought it was nature calling until she heard the buzzing that had stirred her. *It's coming from Garrett's room. What the hell could he be doing in there? I know he misses Jess, but I didn't think he missed her* this *much.* Jaz tried to block out the noise with her pillow, but it felt like the couch was shaking with the noise.

Jaz threw the blankets back and got off the couch. Padding across the carpet, she threw Garrett's door open. "What the hell are you—"

Jaz stopped with her heart when she found Garrett on his back with a running tattoo pen buried and thumping in his chest. *Is that red ink or blood?* The sheets were pooling with crimson as Garrett's green eyes stared at the ceiling.

Jaz's legs gave out and she collapsed as she stared at the horrific sight. Her throat strained with hysterical screaming, but there was no sound coming out.

"Tit for tat, kitten." Looking over her shoulder, Jaz saw those void-like eyes trying to devour her. He wasn't smiling this time; he was snarling. His white dress shirt and khaki suit pants were stained with a waterfall of scarlet. The blood came from the tattoo pen sticking out of his chest.

The buzzing became louder when Jaz realized that there was a third tattoo pen in his hand. Jaz scrambled across the floor as he grew a foot taller and advanced on her. She was trapped against the wall as he raised the tattoo pen over his head. His snarl turned rabid.

"Jaz!" Garrett was stroking Jaz's hair as he knelt over her with concern written all over his face. The moment her eyes snapped open, he lowered his voice. "You're okay. You're okay. You're good. I'm here."

Garrett stayed on the floor with Jaz as she caught her breath. Once her heart rate got back to normal, Jaz realized that she had tangled herself up in her sheets. Garrett helped her out of her DIY straight jacket and gave her a once over. "It doesn't look like you hurt yourself, so that's good. Do you think you can get back to sleep?"

"Not likely."

"Do you *want* to go back to sleep?"

"That's a complicated question. I'm tired but," Jaz trailed off, leaving the sentence open-ended.

"I get it. Would it help if you slept in my bed with me?"

"We could try." Garrett took Jaz into his room, grabbing her pillow. He promised to stay with Jaz until she fell asleep, but he drifted off while she laid awake all night.

9

NOT THE
RELATIONSHIPS

"HOW ARE YOU DOING?" *Stupid question.*

Annie shrugged. "I could be better." *That's an underestimation and a half.*

Jaz got a call from the NYPD in the morning. Her application to visit Annie in jail had gone through. She headed straight to the station, and in an hour, she was sitting on the one side of bullet proof class, talking to Annie through a phone. They had thirty minutes to talk. *I gotta make this count.*

"Have you spoken to a lawyer?" Jaz asked.

"I called my brother. He's talking to his friends and colleagues. He wanted to represent me himself, but he knows it would look a certain way in court."

"I hope he finds someone good."

"Me too." Annie fell silent for a moment, debating if she should ask that question that was on her mind. "Why are you here, Jaz?"

"Because I don't think you did it."

"Why?"

Long story. "Call it intuition."

Annie scoffed. "I wish that was enough to convince the detective."

You and me both. "What did the detective say?"

Annie's face went red. "There's a lot you don't know about my relationship with Rosamie."

Less than you think. "What do you mean?"

"I don't think Rosamie was gay."

Jaz shot her eyebrows out of their furrowed state and into her forehead, feigning surprise as best she could. "Why do you say that?"

"When she came to her first meeting, she said she was there because she was unsure of herself and looking to explore. A month later, she invited me out to dinner after the meeting. She made me an offer."

This time, genuine uncertainty knitted Jaz's eyebrows back together. "What kind of offer?"

It took a long time for her to say it, but eventually Annie admitted, "She wanted to pay me to be her girlfriend."

"Like a sugar-baby deal?"

"No. Like I was there for public appearances at meetings and pride events. When we weren't out in public, we," Annie hesitated. "I don't know what we were."

"Why did she pay you?"

"To be honest, I don't know. Every time I'd ask, she'd say she didn't pay me to ask questions. I feel like Isa had something to do with it, but I could just be making assumptions."

Doubt it. "Why do you think Isa's involved?"

Rosamie sighed. "I'll be honest with you; everyone in the group feels like a family. We've only had a few incidences of people not getting along, and it's usually resolved. Rarely do people ask for someone to be booted from the group. But Rosamie," Annie trailed off. "Everyone in the group had something about Rosamie they didn't like: 'she's an attention whore'; 'she's rude'; 'she's shady'; 'she wouldn't listen to anyone else's issues'. Everyone thought these things, but Isa was the only one to voice the issues. That's part of her job as one of the heads; when there's a recurring issue within one of the sub-groups, the head of that sub-group needs to talk to the person or people who are causing issues. I think Rosamie took it personally when Isa called her out and she wanted to get back at her. Though, why she used me to do that, I still don't know."

Annie must be blind. "Did you share the group's feelings?"

"I mean, she got a little bit on my nerves, but I thought she was just having a hard time adjusting. She'd just been thrown out of her home, and her mother refused to accept her—"

"What?" Jaz interrupted.

"Rosamie's mother was homophobic. That's why she threw her out."

"Is that what she told you?"

"It's what she told everyone. Why?"

Jaz shook her head. "My sister threw Rosamie out because she was skipping school, sneaking out, drinking, flirting with drugs, talking back, ignoring her chores, and treating my sister like shit. She didn't even *know* Rosamie was gay until I told her about the support group. And she was thrilled that that's all it was."

Annie looked like she just got knocked over the head. "But why would she lie about her family like that?"

"Good question. Maybe she actually believed that's what had happened. Maybe she was trying to get back at her mother. Maybe it was to help sew the narrative that you think she was trying to push."

"The group's really not gonna like this. Especially Isa."

"Why?"

"Isa actually *did* get thrown out for being a lesbian. Her family's Catholic. You know how it is."

"Right. That's horrible." *That's probably what she was trying to say when I told her to go home. God, I'm a dick.* "You said Rosamie was paying you, but she only had a part-time, minimum-wage job. It couldn't have been that much."

"Actually, it was consistently between eight and nine-hundred bucks a month."

Jaz's brows un-knitted themselves and shot up her head. "Where did she get that kinda money?"

"I don't know. When I asked, she said what she always said. 'I don't pay you to ask questions'."

Wow, I know Rosamie was a shit, but this is abusive. "Why did you agree to take the money?"

Annie shrugged. "My dad always said that it's never too late to save for the future. I don't have to pay rent now, but I will eventually. I wanted to have a nest egg for when I graduated."

"How did you feel throughout this 'arrangement'?"

Annie looked down at her lap with the distinct emotion of shame written all over her face. "At first, it was fine."

"Then you caught feelings."

Annie nodded. "I don't even know why. When we weren't around you and the group, she was barely a friend."

"How many girlfriends have you had before her? Real girlfriends."

"None. Not even fake girlfriends. She was my first."

"Maybe that's why, hon. You wouldn't be the first person who tolerated bullshit because someone, finally, acknowledged that she existed."

"But it was still stupid."

Jaz wished that she could reach through the glass to take Annie's hand. "You're seventeen. You're not supposed to have it all figured out. You learn. You go forward, knowing how you *want* and *deserve* to be treated. You won't make the same mistake twice. Especially since I won't let you."

Annie smiled for the first time that day. It was a small one with a twinge of sadness to it, but Jaz was relieved to see that she still could smile. "What did the detective tell you?"

"What did he tell *you*?"

"Nothing really. He just asked if I was hurt by Rosamie, and then he weaved a narrative where I committed a crime of passion."

"Did he imply how you killed her?"

"No, but he kept going back to her tattoo. Does that have something to do with it?"

Jaz looked around to make sure none of the security guards weren't listening in. "They think you put venom in the tattoo ink."

"WHAT?!" The outburst caught everyone's attention. The security guard's hand fell to her nightstick. She didn't draw it, but only because Jaz lifted her hand and repeatedly apologized, saying that everything was fine and there was just bad news from home. Once Annie apologized, the guard relaxed, and the other visitors and prisoners went back to their private conversations. "Why would they think that?" Annie whispered.

"The coroner could recognize venom poisoning by sight and the tattoo is the most likely point of entry."

"Where would I even *get* venom from?"

"Well, you like snakes, right?"

"I hate them!"

"Then what's with the snake tattoo on your ankle?"

Annie looked down at the tattoo in question. Jaz couldn't see it, but she imagined that it peaked out from beneath the pant leg of Annie's orange jumpsuit. "I got that because I read an article about a guy who got over his fear of spiders by getting a bunch of tattoos of them. I thought it would work for me, but it didn't. I've even talked to Garrett about getting it covered."

I knew it couldn't be that easy. "Annie. About the tattoo you gave Rosamie. Do you know what it is?"

Annie furrowed her brows. "Rosamie said it was some symbol from her favorite thriller show. Is that a lie?"

"I don't know. I just have never seen it before." *She doesn't need to know. Not yet at least.*

A buzzer went off, signaling that visitations were over. Annie quickly said, "Oh! The memorial is today at lunch at the library where the group meets. Sorry, I forgot to tell you."

"Shit happens," Jaz said, gesturing to the environment. "I can still make it."

"Say goodbye for me."

"I will." With that, Annie was escorted back to her cell, and Jaz was escorted to the NYPD waiting room.

Right as Jaz was leaving, Josiah Moore was coming in. "Can't stay away, can you?"

Jaz didn't look up as she was signing out. She said coldly, "I just came to check on Annie."

"Sure you didn't talk to her about the case?"

Jaz shrugged. "We didn't know each other very well before this. There wasn't much else to talk about."

"I hope you didn't tell her my trade secrets for my case against her."

"Actually, I let her do all the talking and pretended like I knew nothing." *It's kinda true.*

Josiah gave Jaz a suspicious look. "Now, I have to seriously wonder if you've done that to me."

"You're the detective; you know more than I do."

"I'm not so sure about that."

Jaz brushed past the detective, saying, "I have a memorial to get to."

The Newark Public Library was kind enough to allow the support group to use their entire auditorium for the memorial service rather than keeping them confined to the center within the library. The place was decorated with rainbows, with special emphasis on pinks, reds, purples, and whites. Some of the attendees wore black while others matched the decorations. *They went to all this trouble for someone they didn't get along with. They really stick together.*

"It looks like everyone came," Garrett guessed—he was kind enough to take the day off to accompany Jaz to the event. "You're going to need someone you know there." He was right—not just about Jaz, but about the whole support group being present. Members ranged from thirteen to seventeen in age. Isa and the other heads of the group were the only adults, and they were all under the age of twenty-one. The only thing that indicated that everyone didn't like Rosamie was that no one was crying.

Jaz and Garrett managed to arrive five minutes before opening words were set to start. The moment they walked in, Isa walked up with a young man whose black, fade hair-cut matched his tailored suit. "Ms. Dilan. Thank you so much for coming. Hector, this is Rosamie's aunt, Jasmine Dilan. Ms. Dilan, this is Hector Yuen, the president of the group."

Offering a hand, Hector said, "It's a pleasure to meet you, Ms. Dilan. Though I wish it was under better circumstances."

Jaz returned the handshake. "So do I, Mr. Yuen."

"Please, call me Hector."

"In that case, you both can call me Jaz." Jaz caught Isa's taken aback look out of the corner of her eye. "This is my friend, Garrett Weber." Jas allowed handshakes to be exchanged before she asked, "Is it okay that I brought a plus one?" She didn't even think about the idea that this could be a closed ceremony with limited RSVPs.

"Of course, Miss Dilan," Hector assured. "We always encourage our guests who have lost loved one in our group to bring whoever they need for support, so long as they don't cause any trouble."

Garrett joked before Jaz could stop him. "Well, fine. I know when I'm not wanted." Hector and Isa hesitate briefly, not knowing it was okay to laugh until Jaz gave a little chuckle that briefly broke her grief. *That's why I asked him to come. Sometimes, I just need him to take me out of the funk for a moment.*

As Garrett's joke died down, Hector took over the conversation. "Rosamie spoke highly of you at our meetings, Miss Dilan. It was good of you to open your home to her when she had nowhere else to turn to." Jaz bit her cheek. *Now is not the time to set the record straight.*

Isa interjected, "We have a seat reserved for you at the front. Would you like to say anything during the service?" Jaz's initial gut reaction was to say no; *I hate public speaking and I hate lying.* The thing that made her change her mind was remembering that Rosamie didn't have many friends. *I don't like what she did, but I don't think she was a bad person.* Jaz nodded.

The service was delayed by five minutes, and it wasn't just because they needed to grab another chair for Garrett to sit right next to Jaz. Jaz looked around and saw Isa by the door.

"What's up?" Garrett asked after he noticed Jaz looking towards the door.

Nodding in Isa's direction, she said, "She's looking for someone."

"Who?" Garrett asked.

"I don't know for sure, but I do have a hunch." *Surely, she knows that Annie was arrested.*

After five minutes passed, Hector came to speak to Isa. She looked disappointed but she followed him to the front of the seats. The service began with Hector greeting and thanking everyone for coming. Once every person lit the candles they were given, Hector spoke about Rosamie and her time in the group. *He's being pretty vague. Still, at least no one's scoffing or snickering.*

After Hector read a poem, Isa spoke on her experiences with Rosamie, also being vague. She also read a poem before saying, "We are honored to have Rosamie's aunt, Jasmine Dilan, join us today. She would like to say a few words."

Fuck. I should've thought this through. Garrett squeezed Jaz's hand, using their long-time-best-friend sense to tell that she was nervous. "You'll be fine," he whispered in her ear.

When Jaz stepped up to the podium and looked out into the crowd of strangers, her mind drew a blank. *What the fuck do I say?* "Hello." *Idiot.* "I am Rosamie's aunt." *No shit. Isa just said that.* "I'm not the best at making speeches, so please forgive me." The gentle nods from a few attendees were reassuring that they would be patient with her.

"Rosamie came to live with me a little over a year ago." *They already know that, dumbass.* "I don't think I could've imagined being here at that time.

"I was there the day Rosamie was born; with her father missing, I had to help her every chance I could. I never felt the call of motherhood, and I probably never will, but believe me when I say that I wanted to protect her from all the horrible things in the world." *Obviously, I failed.*

"Rosamie was the feistiest smartass I ever met, and that's saying something, because people have said the same thing about me my whole life. If she didn't like someone or something, she let the whole world know. If someone attacked her, she fought back. If she was hurt, she would use the pain as inspiration and energy. Once she got an idea in her head, you couldn't talk her out of it. Is there any wonder why I saw so much of myself in her?

"When Rosamie told me that she had joined this amazing group, I was so happy for her; she was going through a rough time in a strange, huge place, and I hoped that she could make friends to help her in ways I couldn't. I hope you all know that this group meant a lot to her, even if she didn't do the best job at showing it.

"Thank you all for coming and allowing me to speak." *Now sit the fuck down before you keep lying through your teeth.*

Hector closed the ceremony, inviting everyone to take part in refreshments after the service. Candles were snuffed and half of the audience left. The other half gave Jaz their condolences between bites of cookies and sips of coffee.

It got to be too much and Jaz had to step out of the auditorium for some air. "Jaz? Jaz Dilan?" *Fuck. Thank god Garrett's in the bathroom. Seeing her now would kill him.*

Garrett's ex-girlfriend was the first thing everyone thought of when they heard the term "gold-digger". Bleach blonde hair tumbled over her obvious boob job. Her fake tan was way too dark, and she never heard the accessory rule from any of the fashion magazines she read religiously. *It's late February, freezing out, and this girl will risk her health just to wear a crop top.* "Jess. Hi!"

"OMG, it's been forever!" Jess threw her arms around Jaz, catching her off guard. Jaz had to fight to not cough on the heavy rose perfume that covered Jess's body. *Does she sweat the stuff?*

"How have you been?" Jaz asked, trying so hard to sound interested.

"Well," Jess coyly brought her left hand to her chin in mock contemplation. "Mock" because her ring finger was wiggling in every direction possible, making the enormous pink diamond catch the light.

"Oh, yeah. I heard you got engaged. Congratulations."

"Thanks! Frank is, like, the greatest man I've ever met." *Meaning "the richest".* "It's never too early to start planning the perfect wedding, so I'm picking up some research material." Jess held up the pile of bridal magazines that she had just borrowed from the library. *Well, I hardly thought you were here to read something that requires a brain to understand.*

"Do you already have a date?"

"Absolutely! June 21st of next year! It's, like, the perfect day to get married in the Bahamas." *Of course they're the destination wedding assholes.*

"Well, congratulations again," Jaz nodded with a fake smile plastered all over her face.

"Thank you! I better get home! I have a lot of work to do! See ya!" Jess skipped off out of the library before Jaz could say goodbye. *So long, Malibu Barbie.*

"Who was that?" Jaz turned around to see Isa.

"Oh, just Garrett's ex. Glad he wasn't here to run into her. How much did you hear?"

"Just the destination wedding bit. She's very," Isa struggled to find the right word. "colorful."

"That's one way to put it." The two stood in the hall in silence, unsure of what to say. "How are you doing?"

Isa nodded with that exhausted nod everyone used when they were lying about how they were actually feeling. "I'm holding up. How are you doing?"

"I'm alive." Which was always Jaz's way of saying "everything is going to shit and it's a wonder I'm not dead from stress and anxiety".

Isa nodded. "Yeah, that makes sense. Thank you for coming. That was a wonderful speech."

Jaz shook her head. "It really wasn't but thank you for inviting me and for allowing me to speak."

"Of course." Isa kept turning her head, searching for something at each end of the hall.

"Who are you looking for?"

"Oh, sorry. I was just wondering where Annie is. I thought she'd be here?"

Jaz furrowed her brows at Isa. *So she doesn't know.* "Isa, Annie was arrested yesterday."

Isa's face froze in horror. "WHAT?!"

"The police think she killed Rosa—Isa!" The teen ran off in tears before Jaz could stop her. *How can Annie not see why Rosamie would use her to get back at Isa?*

"Is everything okay?" Hector had poked his head out of the auditorium doors to see why there was yelling in the hallway.

"I just told Isa that Annie was arrested yesterday." Hector's dark eyes widened in shock. "The police think she has something to do with Rosamie's death."

"Oh, fuck. I better go after her."

"Hector." The president of the LGBTQIA+ Teen Support Group stopped in his tracks and looked back at Jaz. "Is Isa in love with Annie?"

Even though Hector's face was saying "yes", his mouth was saying, "That's Isa's story to tell. Not mine."

10

PLAYING WITH SNAKES

"ARE YOU SURE YOU want to do this now?" Garrett asked. "You know, there's no rush. No one will blame you for taking your time."

"I want to be able to come home and not dread this place all over again." Jaz's apartment was dark and cold from being untouched for about a day. That day of abandonment made the apartment even more disturbing than it already was. It took several deep breaths before Jaz could enter Rosamie's room. A few things were missing—Rosamie's laptop being the big one—but the police had left as much as they could undisturbed. A layer of dust was already collecting on the mess. The room belonged in a haunted mansion, not a New York apartment.

"Besides, maybe the police missed something," Jaz justified as she sat on the floor. She picked up every piece of clothing, smelled the ones that weren't underwear, stained, or ripped, and separated them into "clean" and "dirty" piles. The ripped and stained clothes went into a "trash" pile with the used panties. The clean clothes were folded to be donated. The dirty clothes would get washed, and eventually donated as well. Interspersed between the clothes were junk food wrappers and soda cans. *If I have to call a fucking exterminator.*

The moment Garrett saw a dirty pair of the teenager's panties, he held his hands up in a "I'm-not-touching-that" manner. "How about I focus on the trash, papers, and donations list for your taxes?"

Jaz nodded. Garrett was already going above and beyond, helping her do this cleanse after the funeral. She was hardly going to ask him to go through her nieces dirty clothes, nor was she gonna make him stay there any longer than he wanted to.

The friends didn't know how long they had been cleaning when Garrett suddenly spoke up. "Hey, should we keep any of these papers?"

"Let me take a look." Jaz groaned as she climbed off the floor and walked over to Garrett. She peered at the pile of fliers and pamphlets in his hands. The top flier was for the LGBTQIA+ Support Group. Jaz had never heard anything of the other fliers.

ANARCHY: The Mother Of Order. Essex County College. TR, 1:20-2:35, CR 1004. Teacher: Polanksi

SEX: IT'S NORMAL! New York City Housing Authority Pink Houses Community Center. Wednesdays @ 5 pm.
Harley La Croix

Feminists Unite. YWCA-NYC. Tuesdays @ 3. Karla Bronx

The Spice Garden. Emporium for all your Wiccan Needs: Healing Crystals; Ritual Candles; Incense; Herbal Teas; Tarot/Astrology/Palm Readings; and more. 424 E 9ᵗʰ St.

Those were just the fliers with the dates and locations highlighted; there were several others—ranging everywhere from Buddhism to Study Abroad Programs. "Huh," Jaz said, pondering. "Rosamie would go out almost every single day and night during her first week here. I wonder if she was going to all of these classes and groups.

"I'll look through them later more thoroughly. You can just set them on the kitchen counter."

"You got it, boss." Garrett saluted before following his orders and stepping out to the kitchen. Jaz made a mental note to look into the groups later, when Garrett couldn't stop her.

After another hour, the clothes were all sorted and most of the garbage was cleaned up. Jaz picked up the dirty clothes pile and was about to drop them—or what could fit—in the washer. As she walked past the coffee table in the living room, the phone she had retrieved from Mr. Hong caught her eye. *I wonder what she has hidden in there.*

Jaz picked up her old phone. It wasn't locked, so she could look through the whole thing. It seemed relatively the same as it was when she passed it down to Rosamie; no new apps, no new photos or videos. Not even new texts between Rosamie and Annie. *The how the fuck did they stay in communication?* Right when Jaz was about to shut the phone down, she noticed a new note called "Accounts". It held usernames and passwords for different online accounts, including Rosamie's debit card account that she had opened after she got her job at *Taste of Nam.*

Jaz went to her laptop, prompting Garrett to ask his friend, "What's up?"

"Just checking something," she mumbled as she jumped onto her web browser. Jaz searched for the bank Rosamie used, and when she found the bank's site, she logged into Rosamie's account.

Garrett had clearly seen the look of intent on Jaz's face and came to stand over her shoulder, watching her work on the computer. "I'm not sure it's legal for you to take a dead person's money," he jabbed.

Jaz rolled her eyes. "Annie told me that Rosamie paid her a lot of money to act as her girlfriend."

Garrett held his hands up as his face went a little red. "Whoa! TMI!"

"She's not a prostitute, Garrett."

"Pretty sure when you pay someone to hang out with you and pretend to be interested in you, it's either prostitution or a sugar relationship. So, which one was it for them?"

"I don't know. Neither does Annie really, and honestly, I don't care right now. Right now, I want to know where Rosamie got the money to pay Annie. She sure as hell didn't get it from her job. I thought maybe the bank could tell me where the money was coming from."

"Are you sure you want to go down this rabbit hole, Jaz?" Garrett asked with uncertainty. "You might not like what you find."

"Garrett," Jaz said with exasperation. "Too many things don't add up. I need some answers, no matter how bad they are. Otherwise, I'm always going to wonder and I'll never be able to move on."

"Okay. Okay. I hear you," Garrett conceded.

Jaz clicked over to the "Tranfers" page of Rosamie's bank account site. She scrolled through the transactions looking for specific numbers and names. "Okay. The last time Rosamie paid Annie was on the first of February." True to Annie's word, it was between eight-hundred and nine-hundred dollars, and similar payments were made every month since Annie and Rosamie started dating.

"Jesus! You weren't kidding," Garrett admitted in amazement at the numbers.

But the transactions that caught Jaz's attention always came on the same day as the deposits made to Annie. Around two-thousand dollars were deposited into Rosamie's account every month, and they all came from the same place. PorChive.com; the porn archive website.

The moment the two friends saw the domain in the statements, Jaz slowly turned to look at Garrett. "You know, sometimes I hate it when you're right."

11

TIME-RICH AND CASH-POOR

A SECOND SEARCH THROUGH the account info on Jaz's old phone proved that Rosamie was enrolled at Essex County College. By the time Jaz had gotten up the courage to leave her apartment and get to the campus, it was late afternoon. There was almost no one around to help Jaz find the right building for Professor Polanski's office, which she had written down. She had to find a whole map of the campus and get lost three times before she found the right building. By the time she found the office, the professor was locking up for the evening.

Professor Polanski was one of those professors who tried to connect with his students—most of whom were, at least, two generations younger than him. He had allowed his white, wiry hair to grow long enough to be structured into a man bun. It looked wrong with his blue dress shirt, kahki pants, and loafers. The moment Jaz laid eyes on him, a shiver went up her spine. *Why am I freaking out?* "Excuse me? Professor?"

The professor took one look at Jaz and rolled his eyes. "No, you can't get an extension on your paper. You should've started working on it the day I assigned it, not the day before it's due."

"Uh, no. I'm not one of your students—"

"Then the lady's room is around the corner, second door on the left." The professor pushed past Jaz, making her follow him.

Annoyed, Jaz said flatly, "I believe I'm the guardian to one of your students."

"Your child needs to learn how to fight their own battles if—"

"Was Rosamie Dilan in your class?"

The professor stopped and turned a horrified look to her. "Who wants to know?"

"Her aunt."

"What do you want from me?" *What's he so afraid of?*

"I came to inform you that Rosamie passed away, so she won't be—" Before Jaz could finish, the professor collapsed into one of the armchairs that scattered the hallways. His face looked like a white bedsheet that needed to be washed. His wide eyes were welling up as he struggled to speak. "Are you alright?"

"I-Uh-I'm—What happened?"

"She had a seizure." *Why do I feel like he shouldn't know that the police are investigating?* "Were you close to her?"

The professor quickly wiped his tears away and straightened his clothes. Clearing his throat, he said, "She was one of my best students."

Rosamie hated school and she was the best student he had? How low is that bar? "Do you mind if I ask when you last saw her?"

"Sat—" The professor cleared his throat again. "Uh-um. It was last Thursday. In class." *Lying through his teeth.* "I'm sorry, but I have papers to grade," The professor rushed back to his office, unlocked the door, threw himself inside, and slammed the door behind him. He didn't bother to turn on the lights, and when Jaz listened at the door, she could hear him weeping.

What. The actual. Fuck?

Jaz thought she had gone blind; she was conscious, but her eyes never adjusted to the darkness. The air was cold and unnerving like the atmosphere of a concrete compound. Wherever she was, it made her squirm.

Blue sparks cut through the darkness. They flashed so quickly, Jaz thought her eyes were playing tricks on her. The sting on her skin confirmed that she wasn't hallucinating.

Jaz's eyes kept seeing sparks after they had stopped and darkness had engulfed her again. They pulsed white when the darkness surrendered to bright, white illumination that took the form of a spotlight. Jaz had to cover her eyes and allow them to adjust before she could properly see the horror before her; Annie was slumped and cuffed to a chair, smoke billowing out of her still form. Burns sizzled gaps into her beautiful tattoos. There was a stain on the crotch of her shorts, and liquid dripped down the edge of the chair's seat. Thank god her eyes were taped shut; who knows what they would've looked like open? Assuming they were still intact.

Applause and cheers killed the silence. A velvet curtain closed Annie's body off from sight, and the man with black hole eyes slid into view. He looked like a demented carnival barker. "Welcome one! Welcome all! Wasn't that a wonderful opening act?" The crowd cheered again. "But I know what you're really here for." A stomp started with one person and swept through the crowd. The beat grew to a deafening volume until the ring master cut it off like a drumline conductor. "Have at 'er, boys!"

The crowd sounded like rioting football fans after their team won the NFL. Before she could think, cold steel locked around Jaz's wrists and yanked her onto her back. As the pain wracked her body, her skin raised at the cold air. How did her clothes come off? Dark figures loomed over her, chuckling as their phones flashed from the pictures they were taking. Jaz struggled as she screamed, "Stop!" No sound came from her throat, and the humiliation persisted. One of the chuckles in the crowd grew louder and maniacal. The laugh was coming from Hell's Ring Master, who stood over her like Doctor Frankenstein stood over his waking monster.

Jaz sat up and was blinded by the overhead light in her room. The light did nothing to fight fatigue or bring her comfort. She had to lay back down while her eyes readjusted until they stopped burning. Once she could see again, she grabbed her phone to look at the time. She never saw it; Garrett's waiting text diverted her attention.

Since you won't go to the police about what we saw on Rosmie's laptop, here's my hacker friend's address. Bring energy drinks if you go.

An address with a link to an online map followed the message, but Jaz had to ignore it and put the phone down for the moment. *I need to get them off of me.* Jaz rushed to the bathroom and started the shower.

Jaz looked between Garrett's text and the building in front of her. Once she confirmed that everything matched, she walked up the door and hit the call button for the right apartment number. The voice that answered was tired and irritated, "What?"

"Um, hi. I'm looking for," Jaz peaked at her phone again. "Jude Carmichael."

"What for?"

"I have a job for them?"

"How'd you find this place?"

"Garrett Weber gave me the address?" Rather than responding, the person buzzed Jaz into the building. Jaz climbed six flights of stairs, struggling to lug the two six-packs of "NOCTURN" Energy Drinks in her hands. When she finally reached the seventh floor, Jaz trekked to the corner apartment and took a breather before knocking.

The door creaked open, but it seemed like no one was behind it. Stepping into the studio, Jaz could smell that its tenant hadn't aired the place out since they moved in. The only light came from the four computer screens assembled on the desk. Aside from that, there was no furniture. A single pillow and blanket in the corner acted as a bed. Any clothes this person owned came out of a cardboard box and was collected in a cheap laundry basket—though the smell suggested that the clothes didn't end up in there until they had been worn for three days straight. A mini fridge was next to the computer desk. On top of it was a hull of snacks, but no sign of anything that would make a legitimate or remotely healthy meal.

The door to this cave slammed shut behind Jaz, making her jump. Turning, she found a lithe, bald figure in a sweater and boxer shorts, staring down at her with dark eyes. "Who are you?"

"My name is Jaz Dilan."

The person looked down at the two six-packs of energy drinks. "Must be some job you have,"

"You're Jude?"

"No, I'm their butler. Let me go fetch them from the batcave." Jude yanked the six-packs out of Jaz's hands and took a seat at the computer desk. They cracked a can open and chugged down half of the drink before asking, "What can I do for you?"

Jaz pulled out a piece of paper where she had written Rosamie's PorChive username. "I need you to hack into this PorChive account."

"I don't do cheating husband bullshit."

"I don't have a husband – "

"Or cheating wife bullshit."

"The account belongs to my underage niece who was murdered this week."

Jude gave Jaz a long look before taking the paper. "Well, that's a new one. Are the police involved?"

"Yeah, and they took my niece's laptop."

"What exactly are you hoping I'll find?"

"I want to know where the money she made has been coming from, or who has been paying her the most. I also want to know if she was in contact with anyone specific and whatever you can find out about them."

Jude sucked their teeth. "That's pretty risky, especially since the feds are involved. You're gonna need more than a couple of drinks."

"How about half off a tattoo?"

Jude's eyebrow quirked up. "You're an artist?"

"Garrett and I have been in the business for about the same amount of time, so I'm just as good as him."

"Prove it." Jaz pulled out her phone, opened her tattoo photo gallery, and handed the phone to Jude. The hacker swiped through the photos, not breaking their poker face until they got to the end. "You got a deal." Jude opened Jaz's contacts and put their number in as "Unlisted". "Expect a text from me in the next twenty-four hours."

"You'll be done that soon?"

"I'm very good at what I do." Jude's computer rang out a video call ringtone. The contact name was simply "WH4919". "Now if you'll excuse me, I have another client to tend to." Jude turned their back to Jaz, letting her show herself out. Once Jaz closed the door behind her, she heard the door lock.

Jaz's phone rang when she got back onto the street. It was Detective Josiah Moore. "Hello?"

"Ms. Dilan? You're gonna want to come in. We just got a confession."

Jaz stopped in her tracks. "Annie confessed?"

"Not exactly."

12

ONLY FOOLS RUSH IN

J AZ DIDN'T BOTHER TO stop at the NYPD's front desk; she just rushed to the back and ran right up to Detective Moore, who was just leaving an interrogation room. "Detective Moore, what's going on?" The detective looked over his shoulder into the interrogation room. On the other side of the one-way mirror, Isa sat at the table, twiddling her thumbs and tapping her feet. "Isa?"

"She was waiting for me when I came into work this morning. She said she wanted to confess to the murder of your niece. I just got done interrogating her."

Jaz shook her head. "She couldn't have done it."

Detective Moore quirked an eyebrow up. "You were the one who said I should look into her." Jaz had forgotten how suspicious she was of Isa in the beginning. Ever since she saw the tattoo that killed Rosamie, she had only one suspect in her mind, even though it was, logically speaking, impossible. "She has a great motive."

"To kill or to confess?"

"What do you mean?"

"I went to a memorial service that Rosamie's LGBTQIA+ support group held for her. Isa was looking for Annie, and when I told her that she had been arrested, she flipped out and ran off."

"So you think she confessed to save Annie."

"It's been done before, hasn't it?"

"It has. And luckily we're both thinking the same thing." When Jaz's eyebrows drew together, the detective held up a piece of paper. It was an application to visit a person in jail; the same form Jaz had filled out, but this one had Isa's name and information on it. "The visitor log-book also revealed that Isa had come to visit Annie yesterday. My guess is she got as much case info out of Annie and put together a confession."

"So why is she still here?"

Josiah held up a finger for each of his points. "One, because I can't prove that she's lying yet. Two, because even if she didn't kill Rosamie, she's committing a crime by interfering in an investigation."

"She's just trying to help Annie."

"Who is most likely a murderer."

Rather than opening up that conversation, Jaz thought carefully. "Is there a way for me to ask Annie a quick question." The detective's brow quirked up again. "I just want to ask if Isa has ever been to Garrett's shop."

Detective Moore quirked a brow again before grabbing a sticky note. He quickly scribbled a question down before calling Officer Monroe over. "Give this to Miss Xun in cell three. Wait for an answer." Officer Monroe took the note and went off without asking any questions. Meanwhile, Detective Moore asked, "Coffee?"

Jaz sighed. "Please." The detective walked Jaz over to the coffee bar and grabbed two paper cups, filling each of them with coffee. "Cream or sugar?" Rather than answering Jaz pulled a cup out of the detective's hand and started chugging it down. "I'll take that as a 'no'."

"Sorry. Thank you."

"Refill?" Jaz pressed the cup back into the detective's hand, who refilled it.

"So, why did you call me? I thought you wanted me to stay out of it."

"Part of my job is to keep families up to date when investigating mysterious deaths of their loved ones."

"So what's the off-the-record answer?"

The detective chuckled as he poured cream and sugar into his coffee. "That would actually be it; your perception. You caught on about Isa and her feelings for Annie before I did. I wanted to see if we had the same instincts, despite your original suspicions. Plus, you seem to be cooking up a plan to catch her in a lie, and since you know Annie, Mr. Weber, and the tattoo parlor better than I do, I wanted to see if you could help. Just this once though."

"I figured as much."

Officer Monroe came back, saying, "Miss Xun says 'not that she knows of'."

"Thanks, Monroe." As Officer Monroe went back to work, Detective Moore asked, "What're you thinking?"

"Let me talk to her and you'll see."

"Absolutely not."

"She'll expect you to walk in. The best way to trip her up is to give her what she won't expect. That would be me." The detective still seemed unsure. "You can watch us if you don't trust me."

Detective Moore gave a deep sigh and said, "Just this once." He opened the door to the interrogation room and allowed Jaz to walk in.

Isa looked up from the table and stood the moment she saw Jaz. "Ms. Dilan. Jaz."

Jaz took heavy, shaky breaths through her nose after the detective closed the door behind her. "You killed my niece. You killed Rosamie."

"I-I'm sorry."

"Why? Why would you do this?"

Isa gulped before answering, "I didn't like the way she treated Annie. She wasn't kind to her."

"But it's kind of you to kill her?!"

"Its—"

"Do you have any idea what you've done?! You didn't just kill my niece; you ruined my best friend's business!"

"What do you—"

"Annie's boss is my best friend, and because of you, he's losing customers! Everyone thinks Rosamie died because of him!"

"Why would they—"

"Whenever anyone dies after getting a tattoo, people *always* assume the shop is to blame for lack of hygiene! Someone called animal control on him and they took his pet snake and put it down! They blamed his pet for your actions! He's devastated *and* losing customers!"

"But I—"

"Now he can't afford to get the lock changed on his supply closet, which has been compromised, thanks to *you*!"

"I didn't—"

"No one cares that the security cameras prove that this isn't his fault! He's now under investigation! When I tell him what you did, you're not just going to have jail time to worry about. You'll have a lawsuit for everything you've cost him!"

"I can't afford that!"

"You should've thought about that before you killed my niece!"

As Jaz turned on her heel to leave the interrogation room, Isa called to her, "But I didn't kill Rosamie!" Jaz froze. "I didn't do it."

"Then who did?"

"I don't know, but it wasn't me, and I know it wasn't Annie. That's why I took the blame. I was trying to help her." That was the first sincere statement out of Isa's mouth.

"Why should I believe you?"

"I have an alibi for that night. I was in a council meeting for support group. Everyone else will attest that we were there well past midnight, talking and locking up." Jaz looked over her shoulder into Isa's earnest, tearing eyes before she stormed out of the interrogation room.

As Jaz took a deep breath, wiped the fake tears away, and finger combed her hair, Detective Moore clapped, "Well done. I'm both impressed and worried."

"Worried?"

"Well, I have to wonder if you've played mind games with me."

"Well, have you given me reasons to play mind games with you?"

"You tell me, Ms. Dilan."

Jaz gave him a deadly serious look right in the eyes. "Not yet."

Detective Moore nodded. "Good to know. I hope your significant other hasn't given you reason either. They wouldn't stand a chance."

"That's why I'm single, Detective." *He's not even trying to hide the smile now.* "So what will happen?"

"To Isa?" The detective sighed. "Since she's a minor with no previous charges, the worst the court will do is give her community service. I might as well just let her off with a warning and save ourselves some paperwork."

"Thank you, Detective."

"I won't be as nice next time."

"Of course not." Jaz walked into the waiting room and took a seat.

Half an hour later, Isa was escorted out of the interrogation room to the front desk. Her personal items that had been confiscated were returned to her at the front desk. Before she left, Detective Moore took a moment to talk to her out of Jaz's earshot. *Probably telling her to not lie to the police anymore.*

After the lecture, Isa walked into the waiting room. The moment she saw Jaz, daggers filled her eyes. She stomped past her and out of the NYPD building.

"Isa. Isa, wait. Isa!" Jaz dashed out of the building after the girl. She weaved in and out of the foot traffic as she caught up to Isa, who was power walking ahead of Jaz. Everyone could sense Isa's rage and parted for her, not wanting to become the target of that rage. Jaz never stopped calling to her the whole time.

After the chase had gone on for about a block, Isa whipped around and snapped, "What?!" When Jaz tried to pull her out of the way of pedestrians, Isa yanked away. "Don't fucking touch me!"

That's when Jaz snapped back. "Listen, you little shit. I'm trying to help you."

"I didn't need your help! I needed you to stay the fuck out of this."

"Sacrificing yourself isn't gonna save Annie. The detective didn't believe you for a minute. He felt that you were lying; he just couldn't prove it."

Isa threw her hands to the sky in angry defeat. "Well, we'll never know now, I guess."

"If you really want to help Annie, there's a better way to do it."

Isa crossed her arms over her chest. "Regale me, Sherlock."

"Help me."

"Fuck no." Isa started to turn and walk away, but Jaz circled around to get right into her path, stopping her

"I don't think Annie did it either and I've been doing my own investigation to prove it."

Isa's eyebrows drew together. "How does the detective feel about that?"

"As far as he knows, I've taken his warning to heart and have knocked off the snooping."

Isa crossed her arms again. "So what's you're going theory?"

"I have several that I'm looking into. I've got someone else working on one as we speak." *No need to tell her everything until I absolutely have to.*

"Well, what is it?"

Jaz looked around before whispering, "Rosamie was working as a cam girl."

"What?!"

"Sh!"

Isa looked around to see if anyone was listening to them or were giving her strange looks. Then, she said, "I mean, it's a legit job and nothing to be ashamed of for an adult, but she's a fucking kid!"

"I know."

"Does Annie know?"

"I haven't had a chance to ask, but I don't think so since she indicated that she didn't know where Rosamie got her money from."

"What do you mean?"

Fuck. I did it again. "Rosamie was paying Annie to be her girlfriend."

Isa's jaw dropped to the ground as a flush crawled up her neck and face. "Annie's a prostitute too?!"

"No, she wasn't paying for sex. She was just paying for Annie to hang out with her and make it look romantic. It was more like a sugar mamma/sugar baby."

"How much?"

"Like a thousand a month."

"Fuck me! Why?"

"Appearances, I guess."

Isa whispered, "Do you know what Annie's been doing with the money?"

"Far as I can tell, she's just been saving it."

"So she's not, like, in trouble is she?"

"If you mean 'in debt', I don't think so. The investigation seems to be her biggest problem right now."

Isa shook her head. "What does this have to do with Rosamie's murder?"

"I'm having someone look into Rosamie's viewers to see if she had extended contact with any of them. More specifically to find out if any of them were no longer content with hiding behind a screen.

Isa shivered, but still asked, "How can I help?"

"You and I are going to look into people she had more regular direct contact with. Have you ever been to a restaurant called 'Taste of Nam'?" Isa shook her head. "Good. Rosamie used to work there, and her boss wasn't too crazy about her. He's not too crazy about me either."

"What makes you think he'll like me any better?"

"You have no visible tattoos or piercings that aren't in your ears."

Isa nodded in sudden understanding. "Oh, he's one of *those* bosses."

"Yeah. Go to the restaurant and pretend to be a food blogger who wants to write a food review and an article about the owner, Mr. Hong. If you can ask him about snakes without making it weird, that's what we really need to know about.

"After that, I need you to head to the YWCA and ask to talk to Karla, who leads the feminist group. Rosamie was a part of the group. Just see how she reacts to the news about Rosamie and ask some appropriate questions."

Isa pulled out her phone to take notes and GPS a route to "Taste of Nam". "Should I text or call you?"

"Text. I'm going to be investigating other leads and I don't want to tip anyone off. If we need to discuss further, we'll meet at my place tonight."

"Okay. When will you know about the cam girl stuff?"

Before Jaz could answer, a shrill voice called, "Jaz! What a coincidence?!"

Jaz thought, *What did I do to deserve this?* as she turned to Jessica and the man she was walking with.

"Jessica. Good to see you again."

"Same! And this is Frank Kennedy, my *fiance*."

"Well, of course he is." He had the signature "Kennedy" look: strong, handsome jaw; reddish-brown hair that had been expertly quaffed by a personal family barber; eyes the same color as the money he had too much of. He was six-foot-four, at least, and looked like his job was to do nothing but work out twelve hours a day, seven days a week. He probably hadn't even looked at a carb since he hit puberty. He went to the trouble of making sure his polo-shirt was tight enough to put every chiseled muscle on full display. The raybands were just for "flexing", as Rosamie used to say; they were hardly useful on such a cloudy day. Jaz could also tell that he was wearing those stupid, silicone, overshoe covers that were waterproof. *Probably doesn't want to get any dirt on his Guccis.* "Jasmine Dilan."

"S'up." *Wonder how much his mommy and daddy paid to get him on the Harvard crew team.* His handshake could crush a small mammal, though Jaz could tell that he was holding back a bit. Probably because of the engagement tattoo around his left ring finger. It was a week old, at most. "Nice ink." The compliment was genuine; it was a simple tattoo and hadn't been filled in yet, but it was well done. Whoever did it had as much experience as Jaz. Garrett probably would've even liked it if it hadn't been attached to Jessica's new walking gold mine.

"Thanks."

"OMG, I just had a great idea! What if Jaz finished our tattoos!"

"Oh, you're an artist?" Frank asked.

"Uh, yeah, but I'm taking time off for a while and I have other appointments lined up for when I do so. Yeah, it's gonna be a while."

Jessica whined. "I don't want to wait, but I want it to be really good."

Frank interjected. "Do you have any idea when your next opening is?"

Jaz shrugged. "I mean, worst case scenario, I could be gone for a month. And I had to reschedule a lot of people to make up for it. It could take two months. Maybe even more."

Jessica whined again but stopped the moment Frank pulled out a wad of cash. "Are you sure you can't be persuaded into putting us at the front of the line?"

Typical. "Perhaps we can have a conversation when I get back from my hiatus, but for now, I think you should save that for her beautiful wedding dress." *You'll need every dollar you can spare.*

And with that statement, Jessica's desires turned on a dime. "She has a point, baby. We need to prioritize."

Frank put the wad away. "Whatever you want, baby." *Oh, never say that to her. She will take you up on the offer.* Turning back to Jaz, he asked, "You got a business card?"

"Fresh out. I'm on my way to order more from the printer."

Jessica patted his bulging bicep. "That's okay, baby. I know how to reach her." Jessica winked at Jaz in that "you're-welcome-for-our-valuable-business" way.

Frank shrugged. "Then I guess we'll be calling you in a month if we don't find someone else."

"Great."

Jessica took over. "Anyway, speaking of wedding dresses, we have to go. We have an appointment at *Klienfields.*"

"Oh, very nice." *She's gonna be so disappointed when she hears the TV show that filmed there doesn't exist anymore.* "Well, you two better get going. It was good to meet you, Frank."

"Ditto, Jaz."

Jessica called back, "See ya, girl!" as she sauntered away with her fiancé.

Isa stared after the couple and asked, "Am I invisible or something?"

"Don't worry about them. They're so self-absorbed, the apocalypse could be happening, and they wouldn't notice. Besides, you don't want to know them."

"Why are you going on a hiatus?"

"I was planning on it for the funeral, but there can't be a funeral until the toxicology report comes back."

"That'll take a month?"

"Longer. Six to eight weeks. Of course, I would've told them that, even if the funeral had already happened."

13

NEW-WORLD MONGRELS

J AZ COULD SEE *THE Spice Garden* from a block away; the wiccan shop was framed by private apartments on either side, so the tie-dyed red, black, and blue awning was obvious. There was an iron gate that surrounded the front door and windows. Jaz was sure the gate was just to act as a second layer of security when the shop was closed at night, but others probably took it as a wiccan threat against those who would cause trouble for the store, its employees, and its patrons. The two front display windows were completely decorated with full shrines; one for "The Horned God" and one for "The Triple Goddess".

Stepping into the shop, Jaz was bombarded with scents from herbs, spices, and incense. It didn't smell bad, but it was strong. *At least it smells better than A&F.* One wall was covered in bookshelves overflowing with tomes about psychic abilities, tea making, fortune telling, and every other subject a witch would need to study. Other shelves were filled with those herbs, spices, and incenses that were filling the air. Some were in jars with brewing instructions. Others were hanging from the ceiling to dry. Intermixed with the drying herbs were colorful fabrics and crystals of every shape and size. Rainbow candles with specific instructions were tucked in the back corner, next to a beaded doorway. A bark drew Jaz's attention to the little black pug that stood at her feet. *Well, I guess a black pug is kinda like a black cat.*

"Who's your new friend, Loki?" The gravley voice made Jaz jump as she turned to the speaker. Somehow, this man felt both right at home and out of place at the same time. His undercut flopped on his head in a silky, pink and green mop. His five o'clock shadow seemed to be a result of laziness, but he had such a sweet face, he could get away with it. He and Annie must've shopped at the same stores; his *Empire Hearts* hoodie was unzipped to put his "Goth Uncle" t-shirt on full display. "Sorry to startle you. Can I help you?"

"Hi. Are you the owner?"

"One of them, yes. Name's Merlin." *Of course it is.* What can I do for you?"

"Actually, I have a weird question."

"My favorite kind of question."

Jaz pulled her phone out and pulled up a picture of Rosamie. "Do you recognize this girl?"

Goth Merlin didn't have to take the phone from Jaz before he said, "Ah, yes. She comes in here a lot. Almost once a week. She really likes our tarot readings."

"Did she only come in for the tarot readings?"

"Oh, she occasionally bought some of our products."

"Like what?"

"A bunch of crystals, some books, some candles. The typical stuff that people buy when they start taking an interest in Wicca. Her interest seemed to wane as time went on though."

"When was the last time you saw her?"

Merlin bit his lip as he looked up. "Huh. It's been about a week. Maybe two."

"Do you remember anything about the last time you saw her?"

"Mm. Can't say that I do." His brows drew together. "This sounds like an interrogation. Are you on a witch hunt, so to speak?"

"Oh, no! Nothing like that."

"Are you a police officer?"

"No. I'm this girl's aunt."

"Is she okay?" The look on Jaz's face must've answered the question for her. "Follow me, please." Jaz hesitated until he stood at the beaded doorway. "My partner will be able to help more than I will. Trust me," he pleaded. Jaz didn't need to be told twice and she followed Merlin into the next room.

The backroom must've been dedicated to the shop's tarot readings. A round table in the middle of the room had two chairs. It was covered in what looked like a sacred cloth. The walls were lined with shelves full of tarot decks in their boxes. Jaz couldn't be sure if these decks were for sale or if they all belonged to the baby-faced man, who was sitting at the table, scrolling on his phone. How did this guy and Merlin become business partners? The striped tank top and pink Bermuda shorts contrasted with Goth Uncle's t-shirt and video game hoodie. *This guy is gonna freeze if he goes outside.*

Merlin called, "Hon, we have an emergency!"

Baby Face looked up from his phone and looked between Merlin and Jaz. "What's up?"

Turning to Jaz, Merlin said, "Show him the picture." Jaz shrugged, unlocked her phone again, and turned the screen to Baby Face.

"Oh, yeah. I remember her. Came in here every week or so. What's up?"

"She's dead, Leontes," Merlin said.

"Murdered," Jaz corrected.

"Say no more. Take a seat." Leontes stood up from the table and went to the wall. Lifting a shitty abstract painting, he revealed a metal safe with a bunch of strange symbols drawn on the front with silver sharpie. *Are they witches or mobsters?* Spinning the combination lock, Leontes opened the safe with a rusty creak, and pulled out a wooden box. As he returned to the table, Leontes set the box in front of Jaz. The top of the box had been carved to depict a skull surrounded by pentacles, wands, swords, and cups. With a flick of a manicured finger, Leontes unlatched the box. Inside was a tarot deck. The back of the deck had the same skull designed that was on the box.

Jaz took a tentative seat across from Leontes as he began shuffling. "I may ask you questions about the case. Tell me only the bare minimum I need to know. This is, after all, for you. Not for me."

"Uh, okay."

Leontes laid out three cards between him and Jaz. "Is there already someone in custody?"

"Uh, yeah."

"A Queen of Pentacles?"

"Well, what defines a Queen of Pentacles?"

"A female or feminine energy whose born under an Earth Sign."

"I mean, I don't know when her birthday is."

"Well, is she caring? Or financially independent?"

"Both."

"She didn't do it. She's innocent."

"How can you tell?"

Leontes pointed to the second card which depicted a body with swords rammed into their back. "Ten of Swords. It means she's taking the rap for someone else's actions."

"Like she's protecting someone?"

"I doubt it. The High Priestess is reversed; Someone's got a hidden agenda." Leontes pulled a face when he drew three more cards. "What?"

"What? What is it?"

"There's a hidden agenda.," he repeated. "but I think it was a mistake. Something went wrong."

"Like what?"

"I think she wasn't the target. The killer was trying to kill someone else." *How do you accidentally poison someone when you're trying to poison someone else? If it was ingested, I could see that happening, but it was injected. You can't easily get one person's body confused with another. Unless it's in total fucking darkness or you're drunk as hell... Hm. I wonder how dark that club was that Rosamie went to.* "I think the killer was trying to kill this King of Swords."

"So a man?"

"Or a masculine energy. Specifically, one that's an air sign, or someone who's very authoritative. A cut-and-dry leader type. A natural politician."

"Ok."

"You know anyone like that?"

"No one particularly comes to mind."

"Hm. Well, he's in a pretty serious relationship," Leontes said, pointing to the Lovers card.

"Is that important?"

"I wouldn't know about it if it weren't. I think his relationship is the key as to why he was the target. I think this is a crime of passion or revenge for a lost love." He flipped another card. "He's specifically with a Queen of Wands—a woman or feminine energy who is a fire sign who might be pretty outgoing and bold. She's the motivation for the murder. Anybody like that in your life?"

Jessica. "No one that matters to the case."

"Don't be so sure of that." Leontes drew two more cards and furrowed his brows. "Do you have your own suspicions?" Jaz stayed silent. "Is that why you're investigating? To figure out if your fears are right?" Jaz nodded stiffly as she stared at the Devil card he was pointing to. "You're worrying for nothing. Two of swords means that you're on guard when there's no reason to be. You need to calm down because whoever you're afraid of isn't the killer."

"Then who is?" Jaz didn't mean to sound snappy, but the subject had set her on edge, and she couldn't keep the edge out of her throat.

Leontes reached across the table, offering Jaz the deck. "Only one way to find out." Taking the hint, Jaz tentatively drew a card.

"King of Wands?"

"A man or masculine figure who is a fire sign. Or who knows what he wants and will do whatever it takes to get it."

This is bullshit. "Thanks for the advice."

"Any more questions?"

"I'll let you know if I think of any."

Merlin interjected. "We're more than happy to help in any way we can." Leontes nodded in agreement.

"I appreciate that. What do I owe you for the reading?"

"Oh, for something like this? It's on the house." Leontes put the deck back in the wooden box and returned the box to the wall safe.

Rather than insisting on paying, Jaz was more interested in getting out of there as soon as possible.

She marched out of the back room. Her hand had just fallen on the doorknob of the front door when Merlin called to her, "One more thing, ma'am." *What now?* Goth Uncle walked up to Jaz and handed her a white bag. "This is for you." Jaz could tell by the smell that that bag was full of herbs. *Not the fun kind of herbs either.*

"What's this for?"

"For those nightmares you've been having."

Jaz had to clench her jaw to keep it from dropping to the ground. She took the bag. The clicking, cold lumps in the bag had to be five or six small crystals that were steeping in the herbs. Another strange symbol was embroidered into the bag. "How would one use this if they *were* having nightmares?"

"Very simple. Just put it under your pillow every night and let it recharge in the light of a full-moon every month."

"How much?"

"Compliments of the shop. We just like helping people."

It's a wonder they can stay open. "Thank you."

"You're welcome. Sweet dreams now." *One can hope.* With that, Jaz left *The Spice Garden*, never to return.

As Jaz was rushing down the street, her pocket buzzed.

Isa

You're never gonna believe what I found out.

Tell me.

A picture popped up in the text thread. It was of Mr. Hong, smiling and posing for a magazine article. Behind him was a wall of his restaurant, covered in dozens of framed pictures of plants and animals.

These are all pictures of the flora and fauna of Vietnam. His son is a photographer and takes pictures like these every time he travels there.

So?

Another picture popped up. It was a close-up of one of the framed pictures on the wall. A greenish-black snake with a red head stared back at Jaz.

It's called a red-headed krait.

Not very original.

I guess the biologists thought it sounded more professional than "highly fucking poisonous".

Really?

Yeah. AND MR. HONG ADMITTED THAT HE ACTUAL-LY OWNED ONE.

Like in the past?

NO. RIGHT NOW. AS IN IT'S HIS CURRENT PET.

Good to know. Very Promising.

Did you find out anything on your end?

Nothing useful. Check in later.

Roger that.

14

CONSTANTLY UNDER SIEGE

WHEN JAZ ARRIVED AT the Pink Houses Community Center, it was a little after noon. The one-level center opened into a dingy greeting area of off-white tiles and fluorescent lights. All of the chairs and pool tables were second hand. Either that or they had seen a lot of use since the community center had obtained them. There were a couple of college-aged guys playing pool, but other than them and the bearded hipster at the front desk, the center seemed empty.

Jaz asked the front desk hipster, "Excuse me?"

The hipster looked up from his phone. "Yeah, how can I help you?"

"Does someone name Harley La Roux teach a class here at the center?"

The hipster ran his fingers along a room schedule that was hanging on the wall by his desk. "Yeah, but it's not 'til tomorrow."

"That's okay. I was just wondering if there was a way to contact her."

"Uhhhh... wait here." The hipster stood from the desk and walked through a door to a back room that was blocked off from sight by blinds on the windows. *Oooookay*. Jaz stood around, trying to figure out why the hipster was acting weird. "Hey." The hipster was poking his head out of the back. "Can I ask why you want to talk to Harley?"

"I'm the aunt of Rosamie Dilan, who I think was one of her students. I just have some questions about the class."

"Okay." With that, the hipster was gone again. Jaz rolled her eyes and kept waiting for something to happen. The guys playing pool caught her eye—primarily because they weren't playing pool anymore. They were standing around, leering at her. Jaz glared back at them as she reached into her coat pocket, pulled out her can of pepper spray, and shook it without taking her eyes off of them. The smiles on their faces and the laugh that they shared told Jaz that her silent threat didn't do much to intimidate them.

The hipster returned, sitting back down at his desk. "Harley's back in the gym. If you want to talk to her, you can."

"Thanks." Jaz rushed to the back, eager to get out of sight of the pool players. *I hope this place has a back door.*

The off-white tile, fluorescent lights, and second-hand furniture continued into the small room that was the community center's designated gym. There was a small block of tan half-lockers tucked in the corner, and there was a very attractive young woman. She knew she was attractive too; *only people who know their hot workout in shorts and a sports bra in February.* Her petite body signaled that she had gotten at least one extreme boob job. Jaz couldn't tell if she had traces of other cosmetic surgeries; the heavy, water-proof make-up could've been doing all the work, especially since it was holding up well against the sweat. Between the high, smooth, rose gold ponytail and the "ICONIC" baseball cap, Jaz could tell that the "Queens of Pop" were all Harley's major fashion influences. *I'm not a fan of pubic tats, but whoever wrote that "Surprise" could make a killing doing those calligraphy videos.*

Harley finished chugging down her water bottle, wiped her full lips, and said, "Hey. You're Rosamie's aunt?" Her voice was lower than Jaz was expecting. *She has to be a smoker,* Jaz thought, popping a Nicorette into her mouth.

"Yeah. Jaz Dilan." Jaz stuck her hand out.

Harley's inch-long acrylic nails wrapped around Jaz's hand. "Nice to meet you. You said you wanted to talk about Rosamie?"

"Yeah—"

"I know parents and guardians like to think that kids don't think about sex on their own before they get married, but that's not even remotely true, especially with the internet being so easily accessible to them 24/7. Sex education is super important, and I promise you that I am teaching her how to be safe."

"Oh, I agree, and I thank you for teaching her. I'm not here to say that I have a problem with the class."

Harley narrowed her eyes at Jaz. "Oh. Then I suppose you have a problem with *me* teaching the class."

"What? No. Why would I have a problem with you?"

"You mean you don't know?"

"Know what?"

"Oh," Harley hesitated, scrambling to think. "I'm a stripper. And a lot of people have a problem with sex workers teaching sex education."

That's not what she was talking about. "I didn't know you were a stripper 'til just now, but I don't have a problem with that. If anything, you're probably the best person to teach the class because your job relies on your sexual health. It's a bigger deal for you."

"Well, it's refreshing to meet someone with such a forward way of thinking. But if you're not here to complain about me or the class, why are you here?"

Jaz sighed. "Rosamie passed away earlier this week." Harley gasped and covered her mouth but said nothing. "I'm trying to figure out what happened to her. Do you mind if I ask you some question?"

"Oh, my god. Of course! Let's sit down." Jaz and Harley sat down on the beat-up basketball bench that sat across from the lockers. "How can I help?"

"When was the last time you saw Rosamie?"

"Last week. She never missed a class."

"What was she like during classes?"

"Very enthusiastic to learn."

That's not very comforting to hear, all things considered. "Did she ever talk to you outside of class?"

Harley nodded. "Actually, yeah. She contacted me regularly with questions."

"What kind of questions?"

"She was super interested in sex work and money-based relation-ships?"

Oh, god. "She wanted to be a stripper?"

"Actually, she was more interested in porn and sugar relationships."

I hate it when I'm right sometimes. "Sugar relationships?"

"You know, sugar babies and sugar daddies or sugar mommies. Things like that."

"What did you tell her about both subjects?"

"Well, I *absolutely* told her not to get into either until she was eighteen. Obviously, her doing porn now would be illegal, and committing herself to a transactional relationship requires a level of maturity."

Guess Rosamie never told her that she had already started doing both. "Anything else?"

"I told her that there are pros and cons to both situations; both can make you good money, but if she did porn and then wanted a day job, her porn career could make it hard, and sugar relationships don't *usually* end well if someone catches feelings. Aside from which, some men who would offer to be her sugar daddy are assholes who are either married or think they're entitled to do whatever they want whenever they want. The sugar daddy community is rife with 'nice guys'. You know, those douches with massive victim complexes."

"I know them well. Did she ever talk to you about being a sugar mommy?"

"No. She primarily asked about the sugar baby end of things."

Well that makes no sense "Did she express what kind of porn she wanted to do?"

"Camgirl stuff mostly, which I said had benefits since you're working alone. The downside is that there are a million and one creeps out there, and if she were to ever show her face on camera, she could get a good handful of stalkers and hackers. That's why I prefer stripping in a private club; only certain people see me, I still make good money, and if anyone gets too friendly, I have friends who can take care of the situation." *That's not ominous at all.* "Why are you so curious about Rosamie's sex life?"

"'Cause it seems like she didn't take most of your advice."

"What do you mean?"

"Rosamie was paying her girlfriend to go out with her, and the money was coming from her porn channel."

Harley's face fell into her hands as she moaned, "Oh, god." Looking back up, she begged, "Can you not mention that to anyone else here at the center? They'll blame me for it, even though I told her *not* to do it, and I'm already on thin ice because of bigoted parents."

"I mean, I don't see how any of this is your fault; if you hadn't told her what she wanted to know, she still could've looked it up on the internet, and the outcome would be exactly the same if not worse; Rosamie did what she wanted to do. That's not your fault, so yeah, I can keep it to myself." *But is her job the* only *reason why she wants no one else to know?*

"Thank you. I swear, I didn't know, and I told her over and over again to wait until she was eighteen. Longer, if she could so that she would know what she actually wanted and didn't get herself into an unhappy, or even unsafe, position."

"Okay. I believe you." *I have no reason not to yet.* "Did she ever talk about her girlfriend?"

"I didn't even know she was bi."

"Bi?"

"Well, all of our personal conversations seemed to focus on men, so if she had a girlfriend, she has to be interested in both men and women on some level." Harley furrowed her eyebrows. "Although, come to think of it, when she talked to me about sugar daddies and other men, it was always in the context of sex work; like how to find a sugar daddy or viewers. And she talked about them like they were clients, not partners."

"So what does that mean?"

"Well, it could mean nothing and she was simply bisexual. It could also mean that she was homosexual and views relationships with men as business transactions. Or it could mean that she was only sexually interested in men if/when they had the money to pay her. Maybe she was sexually interested in men, but romantically interested in women. With so many different types of sexualities and qualifiers, there's no real way to know her truth without asking her. Unless she had a personal diary, we may never know."

Jaz sighed through her nose. *More questions than answers.* "Is there anything else you can tell me?"

"I'm afraid not. Outside of class and our limited, personal conversations, I didn't know much about her."

"Okay. Thank you, Harley. Can I contact you if I have any more questions?"

"Sure." The women quickly exchanged numbers before Jaz asked, "Hey. Is there a backdoor out of here?"

"Uh, why?"

"I just really don't want to go out the front door."

"Is something wrong? Should we call the police?"

"No, it's just a couple of douches playing pool."

"Oh. You mean Jason and David?"

"If that's their names, then sure."

"I got you covered. I'll walk with you."

I seriously doubt that will deter them. "Oh. Thanks."

"We *girls* gotta stick together." *Why did she say it like that?* Harley escorted Jaz to the front of the center. The pool-playing creeps had abandoned their game and were flanking the front door. *Fuck.* Jaz shoved her hand into her coat pocket and gripped her mace can with white knuckles. She never needed it; the moment the creeps saw Harley was with Jaz, their smirks fell as embarrassment crept over their necks and up their faces. They looked at the floor and took five steps away from the door. *They look like schoolboys who just got caught spying on the girls' bathroom.*

"Hi, boys," was all Harley said to the creeps as she and Jaz passed by. The boys didn't respond and let the girls go without even a look.

As Jaz stepped out into the winter air, she asked, "What was that all about?"

"Oh, they're your typical boys; all mouths, no balls. If you come back, they shouldn't bother you again. But just to seal the deal, give me a hug. That'll really sell it for them."

"You're the boss." Jaz opened her arms and embraced the tiny girl. Sure enough, Jaz saw the boy's faces in the window, watching her and Harley hug it out. The moment they realized Jaz had seen them, the boys jumped out of sight.

When Jaz released Harley, Harley asked, "Did they see?"

"Yep."

"Then you're good. Now, stay safe and get home. Call me if you need me."

"Thanks, Harley."

"I got you, girl." Jaz nodded and started walking away. When she knew she was out of sight of the community center's windows, she turned around. Harley was still outside the center, waving to her. *She better get inside soon; she's not dressed for winter.*

About a block later, Jaz's pocket buzzed:

Isa

I am never talking to that woman again.

> **Who? The YWCA Feminist Teacher?**

Feminist, my ass. She's only a feminist for the white, straight, cis women.

She said that?

Not in so many words...

What did she say EXACTLY?

When I asked about Rosamie, she called her a bitch.

Did you tell her that Rosamie was dead?

Yeah, and she said, and I quote, "Good riddance. She can scissor other bitches in hell."

Geez. Any idea what her deal is?

Not from her; I was too angry to keep talking to her. I had to leave. As I left, some girl overheard me tell the bitch about Rosamie and started a conversation with me.

What did she say about the situation?

She said that Karla—that's the teacher—decided she didn't like Rosamie from day one.

Just because she was gay? How did she even know?

Apparently, she didn't know for a long time. This girl I talked to thinks that Karla didn't like Rosamie because Rosa was kinda passive aggressive.

What else is new?

That's it?

I guess. The girl said that it was one of those things where two women decided, instantly, that they didn't like each other. She said she never understood why Rosamie kept coming to meetings.

Ok. Head on home and cool down. Thanks so much for your help today. We'll meet up tomorrow and compare notes.

Jaz never got an answer from Isa and she didn't have time to wonder why. A text from an unlisted number distracted her.

Jude here. Got the results. Your niece had a small but very loyal, and apparently, rich following.

Gross.

Define small.

50 pervs.

Define rich.

She was making >2k/month. Wouldn't go far here, but considering she's only been making porn for 10 mo, she could easily make a killing w/o lifting a finger if she kept on the trajectory she was on.

Anyone particularly stand out?

Yeah. Most followers paid $20/mo for exclusive access. But 1 was responsible for 50% of her income.

He was paying 1k a month?!

I said that, didn't I?

Did they ever talk?

Yeah, and let's just say this guy was possessive.

Creepy.

You don't know the ½ of it.

Can you figure out who he is?

Well, his username is "Rich3ater". Mean anything to you?

No. Can you hack his account? Maybe figure out who owns the bank account the money is coming from?

That's way more than what you paid for.

2 more 6 packs and I'll block off an entire day of my schedule for your tattoo session. Meals on me included.

Deal.

15

QUEEN OF SPADES

F OR THE FIRST TIME since Rosamie died, the apartment didn't feel horrible to live in; even the cold, cloudy winter couldn't cut through the light in this home. It was quiet, but it wasn't an unsettling quiet. It was a peaceful quiet. The smell of fresh coffee melded perfectly with the anise and thyme Jaz put in the diffuser. She didn't remember preparing that blend, but it smelled too good for her to complain or question it. Jaz poured herself a fresh cup of coffee and sat at her kitchen bar, enjoying the scents.

A harsh knock on the door shattered the peace. The coffee turned cold as it splashed onto Jaz's hand and the bar when she jumped and the essential oils evaporated, giving way to mildew and wet concrete.

The knocking became more violent, and Jaz was sure the whole building could hear and feel it. So why was nobody yelling or checking to see what was wrong?

Jaz dashed over to the door and made sure all the locks were engaged. They were, but they rattled with every impact against the door. Jaz grabbed every dining room chair and piled them up against the door. They also rattled with every knock.

"It's worse than I thought." The voice caught Jaz by surprise, and she lashed out on instinct. Her fist passed right through Goth Uncle Merlin's head.

"How the fuck did you get in here?"

"Well, I wouldn't be here if you didn't follow my directions and put that bag under your pillow."

"The fuck are you talking about?"

"This is all a dream. I'm not really here. And neither is he. None of this is real."

The knocking was so loud that Jaz could barely hear herself say, "Sounds pretty fucking real to me."

"You've never had a dream that felt so real that, when you woke up, you had to do a reality check?" Jaz shrugged her mouth in admittance. "I promise that none of this is real." The door started to crack down the middle. "But whoever this guy is, he has a stronger hold on you than I was anticipating. You need to come back to the shop. This requires a custom job."

"How does that help me now?!"

"Don't worry. Your alarm should be going off right about—"

BEEP! BEEP! BEEP! BEEP! Jaz's eyes snapped open. She was greeted by the sight of her empty room. After taking a lap around the apartment, Jaz found that she was alone, just as she had been when she set her alarm and laid down for a power nap.

Returning to her room, Jaz took the bag that Merlin gave her from under her pillow. She tossed it in the kitchen trash before pouring herself a cup of coffee and starting dinner. *It's gonna be a long night.*

At nine pm, the line outside *The Ace of Clubs* was halfway down the block. *I should've known people would be starting the weekend here. Oh, well. It means I don't have to go home as soon.* As Jaz looked around her section of the line, she spotted a few men who were either single or didn't care if they got caught looking at other chicks. Jaz never took her hand off her mace, which was still tucked away in her coat pocket.

After about an hour of standing in line, only a few people had been turned away for being under twenty-one. Some of them had tried to get in with fake IDs, flashing, and palming cash to the door guy. None had succeeded, much to the rage of a few of them. At least five people had to be restrained and the cops had to be called in. Jaz kept her hood up and her head down in case she recognized any of the cops. She didn't.

With every shuffle forward, Jaz would scan the line behind her, searching for anyone she recognized or anything to signal that this was a bad idea. She also knocked into the couple in front of her when she caught a glimpse of Isa and Hector about fifteen people behind her.

Yanking her phone out, Jaz typed:

Aren't you two a little young to be going to a club with alcohol?
15 people ahead of you. Hooded leather jacket.

Jaz watched as Isa pulled out her phone, read the message, and showed it to Hector. The teens looked between each other and the text before looking up and finding Jaz looking at them. Isa quickly texted back:

Isa
What are you doing here?

I'm an adult. What's your excuse?

Annie told me this is where they went after the meeting, as well as what happened that night.

You mean the fight?

Yeah. I thought I should check it out, but I thought I needed a legal adult with me, so I brought Hector. He knows what's up.

Well, 18 he may be, but unless you both have excellent fake IDs, you're not getting in.

Can you help us?

No. You two need to go home. We'll talk tomorrow. This is too dangerous.

Wasn't it YOU who asked ME for MY help earlier today? It wasn't "too dangerous" then?

I hate it when they use logic against me.

Stay in line for now. Don't draw attention to yourselves. I'll see if there's a back door or window.

Got it.

"ID, please." Jaz passed her driver's license to the bouncer, who *had* to be on steroids; *no normal gym rat has biceps as big as their heads.* "You're good. Have a goodnight, and please drink responsibly." *He doesn't even believe his own message.*

"Thanks." Jaz took her ID back and descended the stairs, entering the club. It was your typical, millennial-created night club; completely dark, save for the black light that made everyone in neon and white glow like bioluminescent fish. The music was some brand of dubstep that was way too loud, and the bar was full of fancy cocktails and microbrews. Jaz pushed her way through to the back of the club, where the bathrooms were tucked away. The bathrooms were the one place where there was no blacklight, which was probably for the best; Jaz was sure a blacklight would just show that the walls were covered in piss, vomit, and semen. There were already a few girls worshipping at a few of the porcelain altars, while their friends held their hair back and cleaned their face between hoarks. A quick scan showed everyone was too toasted to remember or care that Jaz opened the small window that led to an alley behind the building.

Isa

Get out of the line and go to the back of the club. There's an open window. I'll be there.

Got it.

Not five minutes later, Jaz heard running shoes splashing against puddles and slush as they approached the window. "Jaz?"

"Yeah, I'm here. Do you think you can both shimmy through the window?"

Hector's voice piped up, "I might have a hard time, but I can try."

"I'm tiny so I think I can," Isa said.

"Feet first," Jaz advised. Isa eased down onto her bottom and stuck her feet through the open window. Jaz stood back and prepared to catch Isa if the girl slipped from Hector's grasp as he eased her through the window. By the time Hector couldn't reach any further, there was only a foot drop for Isa to take. Once she had dropped down, she stepped back to let Hector follow her. His longer, ganglier limbs made his trip a bit more laborious but once his torso had squeezed through the window, his feet were able to reach the ground, making the rest of the way a cinch.

When Hector realized they had snuck into the women's bathroom, his face went cherry as he covered his eyes. "Did we have to come in this way? I don't want anyone thinking I'm a peeping tom or a pervert or—"

"It'd be a lot weirder for me to go into the men's room and wait for you there."

Isa scoffed and mumbled, "Wouldn't kill them to have a gender neutral bathroom."

Ignoring Isa, Jaz continued, "Besides, the only thing anyone in here cares about is not dying." Jaz's point was punctuated by a vomiting sound that was enough to make Isa nauseous in sympathy. "Just don't touch anyone or anything. Keep your head down, and let's get out of here." Following Jaz's orders, Isa and Hector filed out behind her. Hector specifically used a hand to cut his line of sight off from the women in the bathroom.

Once they were out, Jaz pointed to an empty standing table in the corner of the club. "Grab that table and keep a low profile."

Isa asked, "Where are you going?"

"I'm going to talk to the bartender and see if I can figure out who Rosamie got into a fight with the night she died. Stay in the corner and have each other's backs." Isa and Hector nodded and grabbed the table Jaz had pointed out.

As Jaz approached an empty section of the bar, she saw that a woman about her age was working it. She was thin and fit with long, red hair with the tips died purple. There were small, simple tattoos dotting her thin arms. Jaz was sure they had some significance to the bartender, but, save for the "typical white girl" infinity symbol, no one would understand the significance. Her tank top had clearly been a t-shirt before the woman took a pair of scissors and DIYed it into her personal style. "What can I get you?" *Sounds like another smoker.*

"Can I get the best bottled beer you have with some info?" Jaz slapped down two twenty-dollar bills.

Reaching below the bar, the bartender grabbed a dewy bottle of some New York based microbrew. Popping the cap off, she slid the bottle over to Jaz. "What do you want to know?"

"Did you work here on Monday night?"

"I work every night. Why?"

"A fight broke out between two women that night. One of them had a black undercut. I need to know who the other woman was."

"Well, I don't know for sure because, honestly, a lot of fights break out here. But if it was between women, I'd guess that Karla was involved."

"Karla who?" *YWCA Karla?*

"Don't know her last name. Just know that when she lets loose, she's an even bigger bitch than when she's sober. And that's saying a lot."

"Did you see her here Monday night?"

"Yeah, but I didn't serve her. After being on the receiving end of her wrath, I've made a point to avoid her if I can."

"Why hasn't she been banned from the club?"

"I don't know for sure, but rumor has it she's got some kind of dirt on my boss."

"Is your boss here tonight?"

The bartender took a moment to look around before answering. "As a matter of fact, he just came in with his fiancé. Can't miss 'em."

Jaz looked through the crowd to see to bright figures by the door. One was glowing purplish blue from his white pants, dress shirt, sneakers, and baseball cap. The small woman next to him was wearing a ripped, neon green body con dress over pink lingerie that match her heels and lipstick. The thing that stood out to Jaz was that the fiancée had full tattoo sleeves of white tattoos. *I guess Jessica started a new trend when she asked Garrett to do that for her. It does look pretty cool in the black light.*

Jaz passed the twenties to the bartender and said, "Thanks. Enjoy the beer." The bartender pocketed one twenty with a nod before taking the other twenty to the cash register.

Pulling her phone out, Jaz typed:

Isa

Keep an eye out for the YWCA bitch.
Got it.

Jaz put her phone away and started making her way over to the beacons of white and green, pushing through the concentrated crowds of dancers, drinkers, and friends. The owner and his fiancée grabbed a table that had a glowing "RESERVED" sign and a glowing, red velvet rope cutting it off from the rest of the club. There was even an extra bouncer to handle the rope and make sure people stayed away. As Jaz approached, the bouncer held up a hand, silently telling her to stop. "Mr. Kennedy is not accepting any visitors tonight." *Kennedy?*

"OMG! Jaz!" *Fuuuuuuuuuuuuuck.* Jessica skipped over to the rope, keeping behind it while she said, "Fancy seeing you here!" *Kill me.* "OMG! It's fucking destiny! But why are you wearing all black? Where's your neon?"

"Oh, I only just recently heard about this place and I didn't get the memo."

"Well, that's why I'm here. Babe, can you call off the guard dog?"

"She's cool, Johnny."

"Yes, sir." Johnny unlatched the velvet rope from one of the poles and stepped aside, allowing Jaz to pass through.

"Oh, don't let me impose on your date."

"Nonsense!" Jessica grabbed Jaz's hand and dragged her into the booth next to her. Digging into her purse, she pulled out her cell phone and seven tubes of neon liquid lipstick. "I always keep my favorite SJ lipsticks in here. What would you like?"

To die. "Blue."

"Good choice. Babe, can you hit the flashlight on my phone and hold it up so I can see what I'm doing?" Without a word, Frank did as Jessica asked and shined the phone light into Jaz's face. "Close your eyes."

"Why?"

"Because I'm gonna put it on your eyes, silly. It's totally safe and if you're going to wear all black, we have to compensate with your make-up." Jaz tried to keep the annoyance out of her sigh as she closed her eyes. "So, what made you want to check this place out? You finally getting back out into the dating world?"

Jaz had never told Jess about her commitment to spinsterhood. All Jess knew was that Jaz wasn't dating anyone while she and Garrett were together. Jess had tried to set up a few double dates, but none of them went anywhere. "You could say that." *Better to lie and get her off my back.*

"This is more of a place for youngins like Frank and me." *Passive aggressive much?* "Are you finally going full cougar? Oh, tell me you're going full cougar."

"Well, what can I say. The younger boys can do it better."

"Yas, girl!" Jess snapped. "Get it now!" Jaz had to tense her whole body to keep from cringing.

Five minutes later, Jaz's lips, eyelids, cheeks, and forehead were covered in neon blue patterns. As Jess took a selfie of them, Jaz thought *I look like a fucking Avatar.* "That's much better. Now, you're ready to party!"

"Thanks, Jess."

"Looking good, babe," Frank complimented. "The internet isn't gonna know what hit it when you start your channel."

"Thank you, baby." Jess turned to Jaz. "After we get married, I'm starting a video channel and becoming a beauty guru and influencer."

"Very cool." *Why the fuck am I not surprised?*

"You should come join me on a video so I can show everyone how to make this look!"

"That sounds like so much fun." *Cancel culture, don't fail me now.*

"Uh, would you two excuse me? I have to go powder my nose." *Subtle. Who even says that anymore?* Jaz allowed Jessica to slip out of the booth. She and Frank both watched her saunter away; Frank watched in lust while Jaz watched in embarrassment.

"So, uh, What have you been up to?" Frank asked. *Great conversationalist.*

Jaz shrugged. "Oh, just trucking on. Enjoying my hiatus. I'm thinking about taking some classes at the YWCA."

Frank froze mid-drink when he heard Jaz mention the YWCA. "What classes?"

"Just a few feminist classes."

"Who would your teacher be?"

"Uh, something with a K. Katrina? Karren?"

"Karla?"

"Yeah, that's it!"

Frank sighed as he put his drink down and ran his hand through his hair. "Okay, listen to me. You need to avoid her at all cost."

"Why? You know her?"

"Know her? I made the mistake of asking her out five years ago. Worst decision I've ever made. She's still haunting me to this day."

"Why? What happened?"

"Honestly, nothing out of the ordinary. We went out. We slept together *once.* I broke up with her after that, and she's been out for my balls ever since. I have to let her keep coming to this place just to get her to stop sending death threats to my work and family, and believe me, she's cost me a lot in physical and emotional damage. I have to have the staff here call me if Karla shows up so that we know to stay away. And if she shows up while we're here, I have to get Jess to go to the bathroom for... you know. Cause you know, she always wants to go home afterwards so we can finish the job--"

"I get it," Jaz cut him off, not wanting any more specifics. "Why not just go to the cops or get a restraining order?"

"Are you kidding me? The scandal would ruin my family." *Sounds like Franky is leaving out some key details.*

"Well, she can't be that bad."

"Honestly, she is. She's terrible to everyone who meets her. I don't know what her problem is, but no one fucking likes her. I had to change my plans and propose to Jess in the park instead of here because Karla was here and going ballistic. Do yourself a favor and stay away from her."

"Thanks for the tip."

"Jess would kill me if she ever found out that I let you go through hell like that. Hell, she'd kill me if she knew anything about the situation with Karla." *So Jess doesn't know. Like I needed more confirmation that she was oblivious.* "Just please keep this between us."

"Sure thing." At this point, Franks phone buzzed with a text. He read through it and his eyes went wide as he sat up straight. He looked over his shoulder to the bar where a woman was causing a ruckus. He looked between Jaz and his phone before he put it down and started twiddling his thumbs. Jaz jerked her head towards the bathroom door and said, "Get going." Without a word, Frank practically leapt out of the booth and dashed into the lady's room on the other side of the club.

Jaz pulled her phone out:

Isa

Any sign of Karla?

Not yet.

> **That's not her at the bar? Red hair.**
Karla didn't have red hair.

> **Could it be a wig?**
Maybe, but without seeing her face, I can't tell.

Jaz pursed her lips at the text before looking back at the woman at the bar. It was difficult to tell much about her from a distance; all Jaz would see was a flash of neon red. She stood up and told the guard, "I'm just going to get another drink." The bouncer nodded and let her leave the reserved booth. She walked the perimeter of the club trying to get a better look of the woman at the bar. Sitting in the middle of the bar, at least three seats on either side of her were open. People were actively avoiding her. Not only did the fire red bob make her stand out, but her outfit did too; she was dressed more for a biker bar or BDSM club rather than a black light dance club; there was a lot of leather, chains, and spikes involved. Based on her movements, she was doing a line of shots by herself.

Jaz approached the bar again after watching for a while. The same bartender from before greeted her again. "Another beer?"

"No. Just some more info, and maybe a drink for someone else." Jaz pulled out another two twenties. "The red head in the middle of the bar. Is that Karla?" The bartender nodded in a "is-it-that-fucking-obvious" way. "What's she drinking?"

"Tequila shots."

"Give her another on me."

The bartender shrugged and said, "Your funeral," before taking the money.

Isa

> **Get ready to get out of here.**

Before she got an answer from Isa, Jaz heard, "What's your deal, lesbo?" Karla had stomped her way towards Jaz after she downed the shot that was bought for her. It smelled like Karla's entire aura was just made of tequila.

"Rosamie Dylan is my deal."

"Ugh. Why does *everyone* want to talk about that cunt?!" *So it is her.*

"Probably because she was murdered."

"She was a bitch. I'm not surprised someone wanted her dead."

"Well, if that's a confession, you just made my investigation a whole lot easier."

Karla's eyes went wide. "You're a nark?" Rather than answering, Jaz popped her eyebrows. "Look, I didn't kill anyone."

"Well, you obviously didn't like her, and I know you two got into a fight the night she died."

"Look, all I did was kick her ass and dent her ego. She and her girlfriend walked away alive."

"Why did you hate her so much?"

"She was just a bitch."

"Sounds like maybe I should be making this a hate crime investigation."

"I didn't kill her!"

"Well, you didn't seem to need a reason to hate her. Yet, you did. Maybe *she's* the one who kicked *your* ass, and that was enough to seal her fate."

"Listen, bitch. I didn't kill the cunt. Now, leave me the fuck alone." Karla pushed Jaz away.

"Don't do that again."

"Or what, bitch?" Karla pushed Jaz again.

16

LET THEM TEACH
YOU

"WHAT THE FUCK WERE you thinking?!" That was all Isa said to Jaz during the subway ride back to her apartment. The fight with Karla didn't last long; the bouncers were at the ready to yank the women apart, but not before Jaz could get a few hits in. Of course, Karla could stay at the club while Jaz had to be escorted out. She wasn't complaining; that was the point. All she had to do was wait for Hector and Isa to get out of the club, and they were on their way. She had tried to tell the teens that their work was done, and they could go home, but they insisted on following her.

"Like I've said a thousand times, I was thinking that we needed to get physical evidence that Karla was the one who got into a fight with Rosamie."

"And *why* did we need physical evidence of that?" Isa hadn't stopped pacing the length of the subway car since they boarded. What few people were there were getting annoyed.

"Because everything we had on her before tonight was circumstantial or based on Annie's account, which won't be enough for the cops or a court."

Hector chimed in, "She's right; now that Jaz has her DNA, we can go to the police and have them pull it from under her nails. If the same DNA was found on Rosamie, they'll have probable cause to bring Karla in and question her."

"Well, we can't take it directly to the cops."

Isa stopped pacing and looked at Jaz wearily. "Why?"

"I've been told to stop investigating on my own—"

Isa started pacing again, saying, "Oh, great. We're disobeying police orders. That's just wonderful."

Hector took over. "Then what *can* we do?"

"We need to collect the DNA ourselves and put it into an uncontaminated baggy. Then one of us needs to take it to the cops anonymously."

Hector nodded. "I can help with getting the DNA; my mom and sisters love getting manicures, and I learned how to do it for them so we could save on some money."

"Thanks, Hector."

Isa sat down on the other side of Jaz. "Okay, but who gets it to the cops? They know what the both of us look like." The moment the words left Isa's mouth, she and Jaz slowly turned to look at Hector.

"Well, I guess I could do that too if it would help. But if I do, then we're going to need some gloves."

Isa furrowed her brows together. "Why?"

Jaz answered for Hector. "To keep his fingerprints and DNA away from the evidence. Otherwise, there could be a horrible mix up." Isa nodded in understanding. "There's a twenty in my wallet. Isa, could you reach into the pocket of my utility belt and grab it? You can buy the gloves from the general store near my apartment while we get inside my place."

Isa indignantly asked, "Why can't you grab it?"

"For the same reason that Hector needs the gloves; contamination." Isa rolled her eyes and got the money out of Jaz's belt.

When they got to Jaz's subway stop, they walked about three blocks to her apartment. Isa broke off to get the gloves while Hector acted as Jaz's hands and got them into her building. They both did their best to not make the situation more awkward as Hector dug into Jaz's pocket and pulled out her keys.

Isa rejoined them about ten minutes later with the gloves. They set up on Jaz's dining room table and brought Hector up to date while he did his job. "So, where do you two stand at this point?"

Isa stated, "Well, I think we can both agree that it had to be Karla who killed Rosamie."

Jaz shook her head. "I'm not so positive yet."

Isa practically fell off the kitchen counter. "What?!"

"She may have gotten into a fight with Rosamie that night, and yeah, they may have had some beef. But that doesn't give her means or opportunity."

Hector looks up from Jaz's nails and asked, "What do you mean?"

"Well, Rosamie was killed by venom being injected into her body. If Karla killed her, where or how did she get the venom?"

Isa scoffed, "Probably her own spit."

Jaz ignored Isa and continued, "And even if she could get venom, how did she manage to get it into her bloodstream?"

Isa posed, "Well, she hated Rosamie's guts, right? She could've followed them after the fight and snuck into the back of the shop and tampered with the supplies. I could see her doing that."

"I can't. It's too secretive, and honestly, too smart. She's louder than that. She would want to do something simple but obvious in front of a group."

Isa cocked her head to the side as she looked up at the ceiling. "That, actually, *does* sound more like her." Silence fell over the group as the thoughts started to set in. "What if the venom didn't get in through the tattoo?"

Hector and Jaz looked at Isa. "What?"

"What if Karla didn't poison Rosamie through the tattoo?"

Jaz shrugged. "Then how else could it have gotten there?"

Isa gestured to Jaz. "Have you seen your arms? You look like you accidentally stumbled onto the set of *CATS* with a cast full of method actors."

Jaz looked down at ther arms to see scabbing scratches. The only reason why there weren't more was because Jaz knew what she was doing when she picked a fight with Karla. "So she scratched me. So what?"

"So, she could've put the venom on her fingernails so that when she scratched Rosamie, it got into the blood stream."

Hector rolled his eyes. "Just because Sigourney Weaver did it in that one movie doesn't mean that it's physically possible in the real world."

Jaz shrugged again. "Must've missed that one."

Hector's jaw practically dropped to the floor. "How have you never seen that movie?! It's amazing!"

Isa clapped. "Focus! We're talking about a murderer here!"

"*Possible* murderer," Jaz corrected. "Let's not schedule her public execution *yet*."

"Switch hands," Hector ordered. "So if you don't think she did it, why did you bait her into fighting you and why am I collecting her skin cells right now?"

"We have to explore all possibilities, even the most unlikely ones. If we don't investigate everything, we could miss something. I'm open to being wrong about Karla, but if I *am* wrong, I wanna know about it."

"Fair enough, I suppose," Hector conceded. "Do you have anyone else at the top of your suspect list?"

"Yeah, I do. I just don't know who he is." When Jaz saw the looks on Isa and Hector's face, she knew she had to explain. Turning to Isa, she asked, "Does he know about Rosamie's 'extracurricular activities'?"

Understanding broke over Isa's face. "Oh. No. I didn't want to tell him without your permission."

"Tell me what?"

Turning back to Hector, Jaz explained, "Rosamie was making money as a cam girl." Hector's jaw dropped again, and the more he thought about the information, the more he shivered and cringed.

Isa asked, "You think her death has something to do with that?"

Jaz nodded. "I hired a tech person to do some in-depth research into her account. Apparently, one of her 'patrons' was covering about half of her monthly income." The word choice made the trio shutter again.

Hector looked up wearily. "Do we *want* to know how much that was?"

"About two k."

Isa and Hector yelled, "He was paying her a thousand bucks a month?!" The shouting pushed the partying neighbor to yell hypocritically again.

Isa jumped off the counter and shook like she had bugs crawling all over her. "That is fucking disgusting."

"That's why I'm having my tech person do some more digging to see if we can get a name in connection with the bank account."

Hector asked, "So by 'tech person'," trailing off in implication.

"Yeah, I mean 'hacker'."

Isa started banging her head against the wall. "Great. Let's just get *more* illegal."

Jaz gave her a condescending look. "You gotta better way to catch this guy?"

"Yes! You call Chris Hansen and let him film a reality show about it!"

Jaz blinked. "You were, like, seven when that show went off the air. How do you even know about it?"

"It's called 'the internet'!"

"Okay, okay. Let's just chill." Hector raised his hands, doing his best to keep the peace from his seated position. "I'm sure the police are on to this guy, too. If we can help get him off the streets, I'm willing to bend the rules." Hector dropped the last speck of skin into a clean baggy and closed it. "That's the last of it."

"Perfect." Jaz stood up and grabbed a sharpie pen and a sticky note. She wrote on the sticky note "KARLA BRONX. COMPARE 2 ROSAMIE DYLAN'S NAILS." Handing the sticky note to Hector, she said, "Put that on the baggy. Can you put this in the NYPD mailbox on your way home?"

"Sure thing." Hector put on some leather winter gloves before taking the note and sticking it to the bag. He put both into his pocket.

"Put your hood up and keep your head down when you do. CCTV shouldn't see you."

"Got it. Do you need anything before we go?"

Jaz shook her head. "No, I'm okay."

"Actually," Isa interjected. "I'm gonna stay here." Jaz and Hector looked at her. "If I'm right about Karla and she put the venom on her nails, you're gonna need someone to keep an eye on you."

"I appreciate your concern Isa, but I can take care of myself."

Hector interrupted, "Actually, I think it's a good idea. Even if the method is improbable, it's much better to be safe than sorry. If you start to have a seizure, having another person would be for the best. Hell, if Karla shows up on your doorstep, at the very least you'll have a witness.

"I assure you both that I'm perfectly capable of calling 911 by myself. I'll just keep my phone nearby."

"I won't take 'no' for an answer." Isa planted herself on the couch.

Hector shrugged. "Once she has an idea in her head, there's no use in trying to talk her out of it. I'll get this to the NYPD and check on you both in the morning." Hector walked out of the apartment, leaving Jaz with Isa. *Fuck. I knew I should've bought that six-pack before going to the club.*

Jaz woke up the next morning, feeling oddly refreshed. The sun was shining through her blinds, and it was twice as bright from the piles of snow it was reflecting off of. Jaz sighed as she grabbed her phone and started her morning routine of scrolling through her social media to see what she missed in the night.

For a while, everything was typical; FaceSpace feed was full of nothing but ads and clickbait videos and "news" stories. "#SoAnd-SoIsOverParty" was trending number one on Chattr. Every single person Jaz followed on Momegraph had updated their stories and it took five minutes to get through all of them. After that, she started scrolling through her main feed, which was mostly made up of tattoo artists' account and hashtags. It was always cool to see new tattoo designs that people got or made.

Jaz dropped her phone when her feed suddenly showed Rosamie's tattoo; the upside-down SF that had sent Jaz into a panic when the detective had shown her the picture. Scrambling to grab the phone again, she read through the photo's description:

masterink Tattoo done by @sf.tattoo.artist.

To submit your work, use the tag #masterink. And don't forget to share our page too!

#tattoo #tattoos #ink

Jaz quickly scrolled past the picture to see it again in the next post with a different description:

fancyuuu Timeless. Come get some when my book comes out!

Scrolling again, there was the picture again:

only.me Beautiful. Done by @sf.tattoo.artist

.

.

.

.

.

#tattoo #tattoos #tats #tattoodesign #tattooideas

Flicking her thumb over the screen, Jaz started scrolling so fast that the app couldn't keep up, and it would take a few seconds for each photo to load. An entire block of the same photo with different descriptions went on for pages and pages.

Unable to take the sight, Jaz launched her phone across the room, threw her covers back, leapt out of bed, and darted for the door.

Yanking the door open Jaz found that her apartment had been completely stripped of furniture. In place of everything was a tattoo chair with a stool and a workstation. "Jaz!" *Isa?* Jaz could barely make out the voice over the buzz of a tattoo pen. But there she was; cuffed to the chair, shirtless. She cried and shrieked as a tattoo artist dragged his pen over her back. The tattoo artist was the man with eyes like black holes. He continued to tattoo Isa's back as he took his eyes away from his work and glared at Jaz.

"I'm always here, Jasmine." With a blink, the man was in front of Jaz, grabbing her arm in a death grip. Jaz's free arm shot out on instinct.

"Ow! What the fuck?!" Jaz snapped her eyes open and sat up. Isa was leaning against the nearest wall, holding her face.

"Oh, fuck. I'm so sorry." Leaping out of bed, Jaz went to Isa. "Are you okay?"

"Ow. I don't know."

"Come on." Taking Isa's hand, Jaz led her to the bathroom in the dark. Both women had to cover their eyes when Jaz turned on the light, but Jaz did her best to push through the sting. "Shit. Your nose is bleeding."

"What?!"

"Sit down." Jaz put the toilet cover down so that Isa could sit as she poked around the nose.

Jaz pinched the bridge of Isa's nose. "Does that hurt?"

"No."

She pinched and wiggled the middle. "What about that?"

"No."

Jaz lightly poked at the tip of Isa's little nose. "Does that hurt?"

"No."

"Well, that's good. It means it's not broken. I just must've whacked you hard enough to give you a bloody nose which is easy enough to fix." Pulling a few sheets of toilet paper, Jaz held the back of Isa's head as she pressed the toilet paper into the girl's nose. "I'm really sorry."

"What the fuck was happening?" Isa's voice had gone hyponasal due to the paper catching the blood.

"It was just a nightmare."

"One hell of a nightmare. You threw your phone across your room."

"I did?"

"That's why I came in to check on you; I heard the thud, so I ran in to see if you were reacting to the venom."

"Oh." Jaz didn't know what else to say. All she could do was keep holding the toilet paper to Isa's nose until the blood dried up. "Okay, I think you're good now. Sorry again."

"It's okay. Jaz, are you gonna be okay? That must've been a pretty gnarly nightmare."

"I'll be fine. Don't worry about me."

"Okay. If you're sure?"

"Girl, which one of us was bleeding just a moment ago? I'll be fine."

"Okay. Goodnight, Jaz."

"Goodnight, Isa." Isa walked out of the bathroom and back to the couch. Jaz grabbed the bottle of mouthwash before returning to bed herself.

17

A SOILED GIFT THAT
NO ONE WANTED
TO OPEN

J AZ WOKE UP LATE the next morning. She did her best to quietly replace the mouthwash when she went to the bathroom, but the pounding headache made it difficult. As she stumbled out into the living room, she found Isa sitting on the couch and looking through her phone. "Hey."

Isa looked up from her phone. "How are you feeling?"

Jaz groaned, "Fine," as she rubbed her temple.

"Are you sure? You look like you're in pain."

"Yeah. It's just a migraine." *Never thought I'd have to use that line again.* "What do you want for breakfast?"

"Oh, you don't have to do that. I can pick something up."

"I'm making my own breakfast anyways. I might as well make yours." Jaz's pounding head made it impossible for her to act enthusiastic about anything.

"Well, what are you having?"

"Peanut butter banana oatmeal."

"That *does* sound really good." Jaz didn't respond as she walked into the kitchen and started putting instant oatmeal in the microwave. "I'm gonna text Hector and let him know you're okay."

"Cool." At that point, Jaz's own cell buzzed with a text message.

Unlisted

Check your email. I sent you info about the pedo.

How'd you get my email?

Hacker, remember? Plus it's on your website.

Oh. Right.

Once two bowls of oatmeal had been cooked up with milk, Jaz chopped up two bananas and stirred in some peanut butter. She took both bowls into the living room, handing one to Isa and setting the other on the coffee table. "Thanks," Isa said, taking the bowl. Jaz didn't respond as she took a seat and opened her laptop. "What's up?" Isa asked.

"My hacker got back to me about the head pedo on Rosamie's PorChive channel."

"Oh, shit." Putting her own bowl down, Isa scooted closer to Jaz and looked over her shoulder.

There was an email waiting for Jaz from an unfamiliar email address; burner153@mail.com. *Has Jude really gone through one-hundred fifty-three burner email accounts?* Jaz waved off the questions as she opened the email and found a zip file waiting for her.

When the file had been unzipped and had dumped its contents onto Jaz's computer, Jaz clicked on the first file. It was a screenshot of what looked like an online bank account statement. The account belonged to someone by the name "Harvey Polanski". "Motherfucker."

"What? What? What?!"

Jaz pointed to the name on the screen. "Rosa was taking a class from him at the community college."

Isa leaned in closer to the screen to read the name. "She was taking a class from Pervy Polanski?!"

Jaz slowly turned to look at Isa. "Pervy Polanski?"

"That's his nickname on campus. Every student who has ever taken a class from him calls him that. He's notorious for grading based on gender and wardrobe. If you wear a skirt to class every day, you're guaranteed to pass. A boy got fed up with him one time and asked, in front of the whole class, if he would get an A if he wore a skirt. Pervy Polanski gave him detention for it." Seeing the look on Jaz's face, Isa tacked on, "At least, that's what I've heard."

"If everyone knows he's a perv, why hasn't he been fired?"

"Tenure; he has to get caught fucking or murdering a student before they would even think about firing him. And even then, it would take a lot of public outrage, boycotting, and a heavy lawsuit before they would pull the trigger."

Jaz looked at Isa. "Say that last part."

"About the public outrage?"

"No, before that."

"Has to be caught fucking or murdering—Oh!" Isa suddenly realized what she had said. "Ohhhhhhhh."

Exiting out of the screenshot, Jaz opened the next file. This was another screen shot, but it showed a chat through PorChive. It was a conversation between Rosamie's account and the account that Jude found interesting; "Rich3ater". *Should've guessed it was him from the name. You typically don't teach a subject like Anarchy unless you believe in it.*

Rich3ater

Shouldn't you be working on your research paper instead of talking with little boys?

Aw. Is someone jealous?

I'm not kidding.

The text was interrupted by a photograph of Rosamie flashing the camera. *Note to self; thank Jude for censoring this before sending it to me.*

That's not gonna work.

Yes, it is. We have a deal, remember? I do WHATEVER you want, you give me good grades, and I don't tell the school about your fetishes.

The conversation continued in the next screenshot.

Let's not forget how much I'm paying you.

You're the one who decided to do that. I didn't MAKE you pay me; I was perfectly happy with the grades. And you're the one who threw the # out.

Oh, well, if that's the case, maybe I should cancel my subscription and find a new girl.

Actually, I'm quite enjoying the money. If I were to lose it now, I'm not sure I could keep my mouth shut.

So you get money and grades you don't deserve along with your little boyfriends. And all I get are some pictures and videos?

And a "Stay Out of Jail" Free Card.

Every time Jaz opened a new screen shot, she shuttered to think what each message would say;

I want to renegotiate.

Well, I don't.

I'm not the only one who will go to jail if you tell; it's also illegal to distribute child pornography, which is what you're doing.

Yeah, but 1. I'm a minor; they'll go easy on me. 2. That's assuming I can't get them to believe you tricked me by lying about your age and then blackmailed me once I found out the truth. I can be VERY persuasive.

And don't even think about deleting your account. I've taken screenshots of everything. I've got receipts for daaaaaays.

There was a break between the conversation, showing it had been a few days since Rosamie and the Professor had spoken. In fact, the most recent message had been sent on the day that Jaz had informed the professor of Rosamie's death.

I'm sorry. I'm so so sorry. I didn't want this to happen. I was so angry after your threats, and I thought terrible things. I wanted terrible things to happen to you. But I didn't mean it. Any of it. I'm sorry, baby. Please don't leave. Please comeback. I love you. I love you so much.

The most recent message had been sent the night before.

I miss you so much, baby.

Isa leapt off the couch, doing the crawly bug shake. "Ew, ew, ew, ew, ew, ew. We have to call the fucking cops."

"I don't think we do."

"He's a fucking pedo! Of course we do!"

"The detective took Rosamie's laptop on the first day of the investigation. I'm sure they're using their own tech person who's been at this longer than Jude has. I'm sure they've seen all of these messages and more. They're onto him and close to arresting his ass if they haven't already."

"But he had to be the one who killed Rosamie!"

"How do you figure?"

Isa gave Jaz a dry look as she pointed to the laptop screen. "Duh! He said himself that he wanted bad things to happen to her! Maybe he just couldn't keep those ideas in his head and decided to act on them."

"That wouldn't make any sense though."

"Makes perfect sense to me!"

"You didn't see him when I told him that Rosamie was dead. He was completely shocked. He ran back into his office and locked the door. I could hear him crying."

"That is so fucking creepy!" Isa kept shaking.

"Yeah, but it proves that he didn't know."

"So?"

"Pretty sure he would know someone was dead if he killed them. Unless he was on some super strong drugs when he did it."

"Maybe he *was* on drugs! He's an anarchist after all; he hates rules! He probably does LSD or bath salts as a way to say, 'Fuck the police'. Or he could've been lying! Sometimes murderers do that, ya know."

"Then he is very selective about what he lies about. Surely, he knows it looks weird when he's crying over a single student, especially given the 'hard-ass' persona he has going."

Isa sighed. "Okay. We're going in circles. You investigate a suspect—going so far as to risk getting arrested if the cops found out. Then, when we find something damning, you say, 'No, it can't be them because of XYZ'. Why are we wasting our time if you're going to shoot everything down?" Jaz couldn't look at Isa or answer her. She could just sit and let Isa storm out of the apartment, saying, "If you won't go to the cops, I will," before she slammed the door.

After Isa left, Jaz picked up her phone.

Unlisted

> **Thanks for the file. It helps a lot. I need 2 more favors.**

You're racking up quite a debt.

> **I can pay.**

What do you need?

1 I need you to find someone in the black market I could buy snake venom from and how I could get in touch with them.

3 more 6-packs.

Fine. 2. I need you to confirm that a prisoner at SeaTac is still there and hasn't escaped or been released.

That's easy. Another 6 pack will do it.

> **Deal.**

18

WITH A BREATH OF KINDNESS

A FTER ISA HAD LEFT, Jaz went back through her emails and found another one from another unfamiliar address.

merlin@thespicegarden.com

I notice you didn't come back to the shop for a more personalized nightmare protection ritual. I understand if this is new and a little unsettling, but I promise that it can and does help, and I'd like to help if I could. Let me know if there's anything I can do.

Merlin

Even though the email unsettled Jaz as much as her first trip to *The Spice Garden* had, after the dream from the night before, Jaz figured she shouldn't be a chooser anymore. She called the shop, spoke with Merlin and an hour later, he was buzzing into Jaz's building.

When Jaz opened the door, she found Merlin in the same sweatshirt he'd been wearing the day she met him. In fact, the only thing that looked different was his t-shirt; instead of saying "Goth Uncle", this one said, "Homesick" below a picture of a cemetery. "Good to see you again, Ms. Dilan."

"Come in." Jaz allowed Merlin to enter the apartment.

As he looked around, Merlin's eyes fell on the diffuser. Pointing to it, he said, "I'm glad you have one of those. It'll help with this ritual."

"Well, that's good."

"Where's you bedroom?"

"In the back."

"Is there anything in there you don't want me to see?"

Jaz thought back, trying to remember if she had put all her dirty clothes in the laundry basket, which was out of sight in the closet. "No."

"Okay. Before I enter, do me a favor." He passed a small, tied off baggy that radiated aromas like the first bag he had given her. "Strip your bed of all the sheets and pillowcases. Throw them into the washer with this and wash 'em as you normally would." Jaz nodded and did as Merlin ordered. Once the sheets were all piled into the washer, Merlin entered the bedroom. He took a look around and inhaled deeply before setting his messenger bag down. He pulled out a white, beeswax candle with a holder, an abalone shell, a large feather, and a large sage smudge stick.

"Cleansing?"

Nodding, Merlin said, "With the nightmares I'm sure you've had recently, we need to get the negative energy out. Besides, I know the young lady lived with you, and even if she didn't pass here, death tends to leave some nastiness behind. Can you do me another favor and open all the windows in the apartment? Also, make sure that every closet, cabinet, and drawer is open; we don't want to give the negative energy a place to hide.

Once Jaz had opened everything, Marlin lit the sage and started walking through the apartment, starting at the front door. As he walked, he used the feather to waft the smoke coming off the sage, which he carried in the shell. As Jaz followed him with the candle in the holder, she could smell a hint of lavender with the burning of the sage. She couldn't deny that it was soothing. He had to relight the sage a few times as the smoke started to lighten up, but eventually the entire apartment had been saged.

"Now, with your permission, I'd like to cleanse you."

*/"What do I need to do"

"Just stay still, breathe deeply, and think positive thoughts." As Jaz stood still, Merlin circled her and waved the smoke onto her, starting at her feet and rising to over her head. He did this until the smudge stick went out.

Returning to the bedroom, Merlin put away the smudging supplies and pulled out a silver ribbon roll. Eyeballing the length, he snipped off a foot-length of ribbon. Putting the roll away, he dug into his pocket and pulled out a penny. "I hope this will work. I use all the larger change for laundry and parking meters." Using a pocketknife, Merlin cut a notch into the candle and wedged the nickel in. He wrapped the ribbon around the candle, taking care to make sure the nickel was still exposed. Tying off the ribbon, Merlin took a step back. Gesturing to the bed, Jaz got the sense that he wanted her to lie down. She laid on her back, despite the discomfort she found in the position. "Palms up. I'm going to be placing some healing crystals throughout your body. I promise I will take the best care not to touch anywhere indecent, but the crystals will be cold, and they may give you a shock, especially when they touch exposed skin. I just wanted to give you fair warning." Jaz nodded, clearing up that she understood and consented to this part of the ritual.

With Jaz's eyes closed, her senses of sound and touch were magnified; every time Merlin place a stone upon her body, she jumped a little at the frigid smoothness. In the end, five stones were placed upon her body; one in the middle of her forehead, two over her eyelids, and one in each palm of her hands.

"Demons of the night, be gone from this home. Let this not be a place for you to roam. From this day on, let this woman be. So I command this, so mote it be." Merlin repeated this chant ten times, each time getting a little louder. By the time the last repetition left his lips, Jaz was sure the next neighborhood could hear him. Yet, no one shouted for him to be quiet. Not even the winter winds tried to speak over him. It was like the world had gone silent for this ritual.

Once Merlin had re-collected his stones in the reverse order that they had been placed, he said, "You can stand up now." Jaz sat up and stretched while Merlin packed up his supplies. "Before you go to bed tonight, put three drops of lavender, two drops of rose, and one drop of vetiver into your diffuser. Make sure it runs while you sleep." He handed her another bag. "You already know what to do with that." Sure enough, it was identical to the bag that Jaz had thrown out. "That ought to do it."

"Thank you, Merlin. What do I owe you?"

"For the time and the resources, fifty dollars." *Oddly cheap, considering he came all this way.* Even so, Jaz didn't argue as she passed him a fifty-dollar bill. "By the way, any sign of that King of Wands?"

"Who?"

"The King of Wands. From your tarot reading. The perpetrator. Have you found him yet?"

"Oh. No." The conversation was interrupted by someone buzzing the apartment. Jaz pressed the intercom button. "Hello?"

"It's Garrett."

What's he doing here? "Come on up." Jaz opened the building's front door for her friend.

"Well," Merlin interrupted. "I hope you find him. Who knows? Maybe that King is closer than you think." Before Jaz could ask what that meant, Merlin was out the door and down the hall, passing Garrett on his way out.

"Who was that?" Garrett asked.

"No one. Just someone who knew Rosamie."

Garrett practically had to drag Jaz out of her apartment after Merlin left. Apparently, he was worried because he hadn't heard from her since the night she stayed with him after Annie was arrested. He wanted to check on her, and make sure she was okay. The wellness check turned into him wanting to grab dinner with his friend. Jaz didn't want to; she wanted to stay inand tidy things up from the sagging of her apartment. When Garrett threw her over his shoulder and carried her out of the apartment, she was too tired to fight back. She just told him to put her down. She would come with him willingly if it meant avoiding some embarrassment.

It was an oddly nice day for the time of year, so Garrett said they should take advantage of the weather. They traveled to Central Park. Even in the midst of February winter, there were a lot of tourists who had come to see the famous park. That's why Jaz's favorite Mexican food truck—Papa Gomes's—always parked there; tourists were the easiest customers to take advantage of, especially since food trucks provided some of the best food for the cheapest price in the city.

When Jaz saw the familiar sight of the food truck, she furrowed her brows at Garrett. The epitome of Scandinavian taste, he always complained that the owner of the truck made everything on the menu too spicy to be consumed. He never went to that truck by choice. So why now? "I thought you didn't like this truck."

Garrett shrugged, "Well, I decided to give it another try."

"Why?"

Garrett held his hands up. "What is this? The Spanish Inquisition? Can't a guy change his mind?"

"Normal guys? Yeah. You? No. Once you decide you don't like something, you won't even entertain the thought of it. And when you find something you do like, you won't ever stray from that choice to try something different." Jaz knew she was right, and Garrett knew it too; he was one of those people who, once he found something he liked at a restaurant, he would order it every time he went back to that same restaurant. He would never entertain trying something new. He was as committed to his favorite meals as he had been to Jessica.

Garrett blew through his lips. "You make me sound so picky."

"If the boot fits, man. Now why are we here?"

"I thought it would cheer you up." This was a rare moment for Garrett; it wasn't often that he was willing to put up with something he hated—especially food—just to make something else happy. Jessica had always been the only exception. *He must really pity me. I don't know if I should be touched or insulted.*

Before Jaz could decide how to feel about the whole situation, it was their turn to order. Jaz put her high school Spanish classes to good use as she ordered a burrito with a diet coke and some chips with salsa. She even ordered on Garrett's behalf, getting him a green chili chicken taco. She caught the cooks muttering something about a "white boy" under their breaths, but she chose not to translate that for Garrett. Soon their order was up and the two friends carried their food to a free picnic table. It was one of the picnic tables that had the least pleasing of the views in the park, but that was to be expected with all the tourists around.

"There's a lot of high schoolers around. Shouldn't they be studying?"

Garrett is acting so fucking weird. Since when does he like small talk. "This is about the time that all the theatre students in the country come into town for their festivals and school trips. That's probably what's going on."

Garrett nodded. "You're probably right." Then, his eyebrows furrowed. "Actually, I think we had this same conversation last year."

"And the year before that. And the year before that. In fact, we've pretty much had this conversation every year ever since we met," Jaz said.

"Have we?" Somehow, Garrett seemed like the person in the conversation whose mind was elsewhere. *What could he be thinking about?*

"You okay?" Jaz asked. He didn't seem to hear her. "Garrett?"

"Huh? Oh! Don't you think I should be asking you that question?"

"Well, yes, but I'm not the one is taking my friend to their favorite restaurant out of pity while I'm distracted the entire time."

"I didn't bring you here out of pity," Garrett almost seemed insulted by the statement.

"So you are distracted." *I didn't need Detective Moore to figure that one out.*

Rather than denying Jaz's accusation, Garrett said, "This isn't about me. This is about you. How are you feeling?"

"I'm fine, Garrett."

"When a woman says she's fine, she's anything but," Garrett lectured.

"Just because your girlfriend was passive aggressive doesn't me that I am," Jaz retorted. The moment the words left her lips, she regretted them. The pained look on Garrett's face showed his hurt as he looked down at the picnic table. "I'm sorry. That was unfair."

Garrett shrugged, "I know you didn't mean it. You're frustrated and taking it out on others. I would probably do the same thing in your shoes."

"That still doesn't make it okay. I'm really sorry."

"It's fine, Jaz."

"So, do men mean it when they say they're fine?" While the question was genuine, it was also an attempt to liven the mood.

A small smile came on Garrett's face as he gave a little laugh. "Touche. What say you we change the subject to something less depressing."

"Sure." Jaz sunk her teeth in her lunch, moaning in pleasure at the burst of spicy flavor that splashed over her tongue. "Seriously, I can't understand how you couldn't like this guy's food."

"Well you may be eating your words soon," Garrett jested as he picked up his green chili chicken taco and bit into it. Almost instantly his eyes went wide as he started making the same moaning sounds that Jaz had made when she tasted her food. "Holy fuck, that's delicious!"

Jaz threw her hands up into the air, triumphantly cheering, "We finally found something you like!"

"Geez, woman. Calm down. People are staring." Garrett was right; anyone who wasn't a native New Yorker stared at Jaz, trying to see if she was okay.

"Ah, fuck 'em. This calls for a celebration."

"Then are you buying tonight?"

Jaz brought her hands down and looked at her friend, confused. "Tonight?"

"Yeah. Tonight. You said we should celebrate. Why not have it be tonight?"

"I mean, I was joking. Besides, I can't."

"Why not?" Garrett asked.

"I have plans." Jaz was being intentionally vague, knowing that he wouldn't approve of what she was planning. Jaz just had to hope that he wasn't perceptive enough to tell.

"What plans?" *Fuck. Of all the times he chooses to be perceptive of other people's feelings, why did he have to choose now? What do I tell him?*

Before Jaz could think anything through, she blurted out, "I have a date."

A silence fell over the friends as the lie Jaz told sunk in. Jaz tried to subtly hold her breath as she waited to see if Garrett believed her. It wasn't looking good if the look he gave her was any indication. "You?"

"Yes."

"Have a date."

"Yes."

"With who?"

Jaz could tell that just saying "some guy" wasn't going to cut it. He wanted a name. A real name; not one made up on the spot. "The detective on Rosamie's case." Again, the words came tumbling out of Jaz's mouth before she could think them through.

"He asked you out?" Garrett was surprised.

"Why is that so surprising?" Jaz asked, trying anything to get the focus off of her and her lies.

"No, no! I'm not saying that. I would just think that his boss would think that's a conflict of interest. You know, a detective going out with a suspect who is involved with a case that he's currently working on. Surely, someone would have an issue with it."

"The detective ruled me out as a suspect early on." *Mostly likely because he talked to the staff at the Gym and saw those security tapes I told him about.*

"And you said yes? When he asked you out, I mean. " Garrett was still in disbelief.

"Again, why is that so surprising?"

Garrett was shocked at Jaz's words. "Um, excuse me, but wasn't it just this last Monday that you were reminding me how you, quote, 'committed yourself to spinsterhood'?"

"Can't a girl change her mind?" *Maybe using his own argument against him will get him off my back.*

"Must be some pretty special guy to get you to change your mind. You're as stubborn as I am, and I've been compared to a mule more than once."

"Cause you're an ass?" Jaz hoped that returning to their usual ribbing of each other would get her out from under the microscope.

"That's a donkey. But thank you for playing." That was the first time the friend had laughed like nothing was wrong. If Jaz has been in the shoes of anyone else in the park who was watching them, she never would've known that a tragic, mysterious death had rocked the world of the friends.

As the laughter died down, Garrett said, "Well. Is the detective picking you up for this date?"

"No. We're meeting at the restaurant. You know; better to come separately than to rely on one another to get us home."

"Damn. I wanted to come over and be cleaning a sawed-off shotgun when he arrived."

Jaz gave her friend an amused head shake. "You're not my dad."

"Someone's gotta look out for you."

Jaz was touched by Garrett's protectiveness of her, even if it took a somewhat weird form for their dynamic. "I can look out for myself, but thank you, Garrett."

"I have no doubt; I've seen you kick an ass or two. But two sets of eyes are always better than one."

"Well, if I need a second pair of eyes, you'll be the first to know." At that point, Jaz's pocket buzzed. Pulling out her phone, she found that she had received a text message:

Recipient: Unknown

Unknown: I got the guy you're looking for. His name is Bruno Griffin, and he has a private room at the Viprus strip club. I know you're planning something, so you're gonna want to come by my place before you head there. Knock 3 times and I'll know it's you. Once I give you the package, head to the club and tell the door man that you're there to feed the mad dog. He should take you to Griffin. I don't think I need to say this, but be fucking careful. If they catch onto you, your ass isn't the only one on the line.

"Who is that?" Garrett asked.

"Oh, it's just the detective confirming the time and place," Jaz lied as she shoved her phone back into her pocket.

19

MODEST AND ARROGANT

J AZ CHECKED HER PHONE to make sure the address Jude gave her was correct. It wasn't that she doubted the hacker's intelligence and skills. It was that the Viprus Strip Club looked like the last place she wanted to walk into. The line to get in was long and full of men who ranged from the ages of forty to sixty. If there had been, at least, a handful of women in the line, Jaz would've felt less uncomfortable. It made her wonder what about the club was so unwelcoming to anyone outside of the obvious audience demographic.

Perhaps it was the almost stereotypical appearance of the place: neon lights in the shape of women in provocative poses; not a single window that gave a peak into the interior of the place; the deep base of music that was sexy is a cringy way. The doorman would even unlatch a velvet rope to let patrons enter. *This place is every teenage boy's wet dream.*

Jaz gripped Jude's package with white knuckles. Following the hacker's instructions, Jaz went to their apartment building and knocked on their door three times. The door opened enough for Jude to pass an aluminum briefcase to Jaz with a warning attached to the handle:

When the door man takes you to Bruno, tell him that you want to buy some of his product and hire someone who works for him to kill the people in these photographs. He will tell you that he doesn't do that killing but he's willing to sell you the product. One of the stacks in the suitcase should be more than enough to buy 3. Once you have the product and he has the money, get out. And don't let the police catch you with this briefcase or with Bruno.

The photos that came with the briefcase were of Annie and Dr. Professor Polansky. *How do they know so much about the case? Oh. Right. Hacker.* It didn't take a genius to figure out what was in the suitcase.

With a deep breath, Jaz walked past the line to the bouncer. Some of the men waiting catcalled her and asked if she would get onstage sometime during the evening. Others shouted derogatory terms that would anger Isa and probably the rest of Rosamie's support group. Jaz ignored them, though her heart was racing as she heard both types of calls.

As Jaz approached the doorman, he gave her a quirked eyebrow of confusion. "Can I help you?"

"I'm here to feed the mad dog," Jaz said plainly, following the order Jude gave her.

The doorman's eyebrows drew together in confusion as he looked Jaz up and down. "I don't think I've ever seen you hear before."

"I was recommended to come her by another client." *Please don't hear my heart beating out of my chest. Please don't hear my heart beating out of my chest. Please don't hear my heart beating of my chest.*

"Wait here." Jaz did as she was told while the doorman ducked into the building, though she hoped he wouldn't take too long. Some of the other patrons who were waiting in line were getting antsy. She was sure the ones who had said the derogatory terms to her would soon take the opportunity to make the national news for hate crimes.

Fortunately, right as the crowd started to get rowdy, the doorman returned. One stern look from him was enough to silence them. "Follow me," he told Jaz.

As the doorman led Jaz through the Viprus, the interior of the building lived up to the expectations she had formed based on the exterior: the only form of illumination came from a bunch of red light with threw off everyone's vision; there were about six poles in the whole building that were occupied by a lot of young, pretty girls, all in various states of undress; six more girls were on the ugly floor, performing personal lap dances for the drunkest and richest men in the house; a handful of other girls were acting as waitresses, handing out beers and shots in their bikinis. Some of the girls were either good actresses or genuinely enjoyed their jobs—if they were disgusted or uncomfortable, no one could tell. In fact, only a few girls looked less than enthusiastic, and most of those girls just looked flat-out bored. The music was so loud that Jaz couldn't even hear her own heart beating. This, however, was a relief to her; if she couldn't hear it, no one else could either.

The doorman led Jaz to the back of the building where a door was marked "PRIVATE". He gave a patterned knock that Jaz couldn't really hear because of the loud base of the music. A few seconds later, two girls rushed out of the room, struggling to put their bikini tops and booty shorts back on as they went back to their typical work. Keeping the door open, the doorman gestured for Jaz to enter.

This private room was lit in a way that was still "seductive" but it was easier to see. Judging from the muffle of the bouncing music in the main part of strip club, Jaz could tell that the room was also soundproof. The coffee table in the middle had two open champagne bottles with several flutes strewn about. Since Jaz hadn't seen another champagne bottle in the building, she had to assume that the owner of the club held it specially for this private guest.

Bruno Griffin was the spitting image of what Jaz imagined a black-market venom dealer would look like. His bleach blonde, spikey fade was clearly died if the brunette stubble on his face was any indication. It was anyone's guess as to whether the designer clothing he was wearing was real or counterfeit. Jaz could imagine that he had entire tattoo sleeves on both of his arms, even though she could only see them from elbows down. Some tattoos on his chest also peaked out from beneath the open top buttons on his shirt. The silver chain around his neck reflected red and purple from the mood lighting. His hazel eyes regarded Jaz intently—he was obviously suspicious of this stranger, as were his two bodyguards, though their suspicious looks were hidden behind black shades. *They aren't gonna be very useful if they can't see.*

"Well, well, well," Bruno said, bringing Jaz's attention back to him. "And who might you be?" Jaz had to try to suppress the shiver that went throughout her body as the purr in Bruno's voice slithered into Jaz's ears.

"Amy Russell". Jaz had spent the commute to the Viprus coming up with a fake name. It was unwise to give him her real name; if he caught onto her game, at least the fake name would throw him off for a while. If the police caught him and he was interrogated, the police would be looking for a chick who never existed rather than her.

"Pleasure to meet you, Amy Russell," Jaz couldn't tell if Bruno was saying her name because he didn't believe her or if it was some weird type of flirting. "I'm curious how you came to find out how to find me and what to say to get an audience with me."

"Well, I had to grease a few palms here or there, but when I seek something—or someone out—I leave no stone unturned." Perhaps playing his own game of vagueness would get Jaz out of there alive with the evidence she needed. *Copy his language and he'll think I'm one of him, right?*

Bruno's poker face didn't budge a bit as he took in Jaz's answer. "I must say, it worries me information about me can be so easily bought." With a snap of his fingers, the two bodyguards that were behind Bruno stepped forward to flank Jaz. "You don't mind if my boy here search you, do you Miss Amy Russel? Can't be too careful in this day and age."

Jaz looked between the bodyguards. She really didn't want to be searched but she needed to cooperate if she was to have a change at getting what she needed and then getting out alive. After a hesitant moment, Jaz set the briefcase down and held her arms out to the side. "So long as they don't cop a feel. Let's keep this professional, shall we?"

Jaz wasn't sure if it was her innuendo or her challenging look that made Bruno chuckle. "My thoughts exactly. Donny, will you do the honors?"

"Yes, sir," the bodyguard to Jaz's right affirmed. He stepped in front of Jaz with an unmoved look behind his shades. "Pardon me, ma'am."

Donny precede to pat Jaz down in a way that showed he had experience as a TSA Agent; using the back of his hand to press against Jaz's more intimate areas to save her embarrassment and discomfort. He was as thorough as a TSA Agent as well—which was to say that it took him a full five minutes to feel over her body before he turned to Burno. "She's clean." Turning back to Jaz, he pardoned himself to her again before stepping back.

"Thank you, Donny. Take a seat, Miss Amy Rusell," Bruno offered, gesturing to the chair directly across from him. Picking her briefcase back up, Jaz accepted the seat. "Can I get you a drink?"

"Thank, Mr. Griffin, but I don't drink while I'm working." *I can't get anymore off the wagon than I already am.*

"A good policy. I really should take after you," Bruno said before grabbing a tumbler full of some dark liquor. He downed the entire glass without even blinking.

Once he had swallowed the alcohol, he dug into his pocket and pulled out what looked like a metal case for those intensely strong breath mints. When Burno opened the case and started pouring white powder onto the coffee table, it didn't take a genius to realize that the powder wasn't crushed-up breath mints. As Burno used a credit card to mold the powder into a line, he asked, "Shall I set one up for you?"

"I'd rather be completely sober for this meeting, Mr. Griffin." *Sweet Jesus, if you exist, get me the fuck out of here alive. Preferably not in handcuffs.*

"Suit yourself," Burno shrugged as he rolled up a crisp, new hundred-dollar bill. As he inhaled the powder, Jaz had to repress her grimace; she may have been an alcoholic at one-time in her life, but she never touched illicit drugs that wasn't marajuana, and one experience with that was enough for her to say "Never again". It simply didn't mix well with her anxiety. Jaz didn't even want to imagine how the powder would affect her.

After a few inhales and sniffles, Bruno turned his attention back to Jaz. "Now, Miss Amy Russell. What can I do for you?"

Jaz tossed the photos of Dr. Polanksy and Annie across the table, along with two pictures that she had printed herself; one of Rosamie, and one of Seth Frost. Jaz kept a close eye on Bruno's face as she said, "I need some people taken care of."

The moment he saw the photos, Burno's eyebrows went up. *Does he recognize someone?* "That's a lot of people. What did they all do to warrant such... ruthlessness?"

Is the amount of photos the only reason why he's surprised? "If I were you, I wouldn't ask, Mr. Griffin. The less you know and all that," Jaz said in her best subtle-warning tone. Creating that tone wasn't easy, however; Jaz kept worrying how much longer she could play Bruno's game without consequences.

"Let me guess; you were the side chick to one of the guys. Maybe even both of them. And they both decided to replace you with the two younger models and you're, rightfully, jaded. Sound about right?"

What the fuck does he mean by "younger models"? Despite her annoyance with this criminal's cocky attitude and rude words, Jaz thought that maybe letting him think that he was right would appeal to his ego and maybe make him underestimate her. "You weren't born yesterday, were you Mr. Griffin?"

With a chuckled, Bruno shook his head. "No, I wasn't, Miss Amy Russell. I'm sorry to say that I can't help you, though."

"I was told that you're the guy to come to if I wanted someone dead," Jaz demanded, trying to sound pissed off when she was feeling nothing but panic. *I have to walk out with something. Some kind of evidence.*

"Whoever told you that greatly exaggerated what I do. I provide... substances that *could* be deadly if that's how you intend on using it. However, I don't concern myself with how it's used, and I certainly don't use it in a deadly way myself. All I do is provide my product. Once my product is in your hand, it's up to you to use it however you. I want no part of whatever you're up to, Miss Russell."

With a frustrated sigh, Jaz said, "Fine. What would four whatevers of your 'product' cost me?"

"Well, obviously that depends on the wait of a person but I'd say." Rather than finishing his sentence, Bruno snapped his fingers. This was a signal to beckon one of the guards into handing him a small briefcase of his own. *It looks like someone's insulin case*, Jaz thought to herself. Opening the case so that Jaz couldn't see inside, Bruno pulled out a bottle reminiscent of one of her essential oil bottles. The one that came with the droppers in the cap. "This should be more than enough to get the job done."

"You're sure?" *That's no way that's enough.*

"This is *very potent*, Miss Amy Russell. One fifth of an ounce is enough to kill a man." *Survey says "bullshit", but it's better than nothing.*

"How much?" Jaz's voice was cynical, expecting a high price tag.

She wasn't disappointed. "Ten k." *For an ounce of venom?! What a rip off!* Jaz didn't voice her opinion, however she simply opened her briefcase—mimicking Bruno's method so that he couldn't see how much money she had—and grabbed ten piles of Ben Franklins. She set the piles out in sections of five before closing the case. "Deal."

"Not yet," Bruno interrupted. "Would you mind if I took a look at one of those bills? One cannot be too careful or suspicious these days." Rather than responding, Jaz gave Bruno a long, hard look before slipping on of the hundreds out of its pile. Passing the bill over to

Bruno, Jaz humored him as he felt it and held it up to the light, trying to determine if it was real or fake. *Please look real. Please look real. Please look real.*

"Excellent," Bruno said. Placing his right hand on top of the bottle of venom, he said, "I'll slide the product over at the same time that you slide the money over. This should go without saying, but no funny business."

"Funny. I was gonna say the same thing to you, Mr. Griffin."

Bruno seemed more amused than insulted by Jaz's retort if his chuckle was any indication. "One. Two. Three." Once the "three" was spoken, Jaz pushed her five thousand dollars across the table with her right hand. Bruno mimicked the move with the bottle of venom. The moment the venom was within reach, Jaz took her hand on the money and snatched up the bottle. She held her hand up afterwards however, showing that she wasn't going to try to run with the money. Bruno seemed content with Jaz's move; he didn't sick his guards on her. He just gathered up the money and put it away in his own briefcase. "Now. Is there anything else I can do for you, Miss Amy Russell?"

"Nothing that I think you're actually willing to do," Jaz said dryly.

Bruno chuckled again. "I am terribly sorry that I couldn't help you on that front. If you really don't want to do the job yourself, I'm sure I could recommend someone to you."

"Oh? Do tell."

"Ah, ah, ah. That information will cost you."

"I think I've spent enough money for one night."

Bruno shrugged. "If you change your mind, you know where to find me. Now that business is over," Again, Bruno didn't finish his sentence; he pulled the mint case back out and held up his drink. "Could I perhaps tempt you with some indulgence?"

"Had you been able to deliver *everything* I wanted, Mr. Griffin, I would've said yes. However, now that I have to do the work myself, I think it would be for the best if I take my leave."

Bruno put the mint case away and took a drink. "Suit yourself. If you have need of my services again, don't hesitate to come back."

"No offense onto you, Mr Griffin, but I sincerely hope I don't have to use your services again." That was the first time that night Jaz was telling the truth, the whole truth, and nothing but the truth.

Again, Bruno laughed, showing that he wasn't insulted. "I understand. Goodnight, Miss Amy Griffin. Boys?"

Initially, the call for Burno's guards made Jaz's heart stop. It started beating again, however, when she realized that they were simply asked to open the door for her. "Goodnight, Mr. Griffin." Jaz pocketed the venom and closed her briefcase before leaving. It was a struggle to not rush out like a guilty, terrified criminal.

Once the private room door closed behind her, Jaz breathed a sigh of relief, knowing no one would hear her over the pounding base of the stripper music. After taking a moment to breath and calm down, Jaz started to head for the door of the club.

She stopped in her tracks, however, when she heard a familiar voice laugh loudly and yell, "Shot ski!" *Oh, fuck no.* Turning to the sound with dread, Jaz saw Jessica's fiancé, Frank, at the VIP table by the front door of the club. He and three other guys who looked like carbon copies of him were doing shots off of a ski. There were about ten other guys who were sitting or standing around the table, egging the shot-drinkers on. *Of all the places for him to have his fucking bachelor party, why did it have to be here and why did it have to be tonight?* There was no way for Jaz to leave the club without walking by Frank, and he wasn't nearly drunk enough to miss her. Jaz needed to get the fuck out of there before Bruno caught on to her, and she got the distinct feeling that it took Frank a fucking long time to get drunk, even if he was doing shots. What was she gonna do?

"Jaz?" This familiar voice wasn't as panic inducing as Franks, but the more people who recognized her at the club, the more trouble she was risking getting into. As Jaz turned, she found Harley, decked out in a hot pink and black lingerie set beneath a studded, hot pink leather jack. The black leather boots went all the way up to her thighs and were laced up with pink. The woman's makeup looked much more natural, though that could've easily been because of the red light of the club. *Well, the "surprise" tattoo makes more sense now.*

"Harley?"

"It's good to see you again!" Harley threw her arms around Jaz, catching the tattoo artist off guard with a hug. During the embrace, Harley whispered, "You look uncomfortable. What's wrong?"

"Oh, n—" Jaz cut herself off from saying "nothing" as the opportunity occurred to her. "Near the door. The rich guy with the bachelor party."

Jaz could feel Harley straining up onto her toes. *She must be trying to get a better look.* "An ex of yours?"

Aiding Harley's assumption, Jaz said, "Yeah, and I REALLY don't want to talk to him."

"I don't blame you. He looks like a jerk. Follow my lead." Releasing Jaz from the hug, Harley took her hand and said, "Of course I'm still gonna give you a tour! You're gonna love it here!" As Harley kept up the charade, she lead Jaz to a set of curtains located behind one of the stages with a pole. No one stopped Harley as she threw the curtains open and dragged Jaz backstage.

Does this place have an HR person? Cause they need one if they don't. Pretty sure this is bullshit working conditions. All of the strippers at the Viprus were cramped into the tiniest backstage area Jaz had probably ever seen. Maybe five people would've been able to fit in there comfortably, but ten to fifteen strippers at a time were struggling. None of them complained, however, as Harley dragged Jaz into the cramped area. They all took one look at the two of them and seemed to understand what was happening. They let Harley help her friend out without raising a stink.

"Back here." Harley kept leading Jaz through the backstage area until they came to a wood door that looked like it was about to fall off the hinges.

When Harley knocked on the door, an annoyed voice called out, "Occupado!"

"Katrina, we got a Code Angel. Let us in."

With a sigh, Katrina called, "It's not locked." Harley threw the door open, revealing a single bathroom with no stall—it was just open like it would be in any private home or apartment. Katrina was a stripper with arabesque skin and dark hair. She was in the middle of trying to style her hair to look like cat ears—she had already gotten one molded into place with pins and an entire bottle of hairspray if the smell was any indication.

Katrina stepped back towards the toilet, allowing Harley to run over, reach up, and unlock the tiny window. "Sorry. We don't have a secondary exit. The owner says it's because he doesn't want some perv sneaking into the backstage area, but we all know it's because he's cheap. It's the best we can do right now." Harley punctuated her point by placing a stool right beneath the window. "Do you want us to call anyone? The police? An uber? A hit man?"

Jaz gave a little laugh and said, "That's okay. I think I'll be okay once I get out of here." *This woman is too good for this world.*

Harley pulled a business card out of her cleavage. "Here's my number. Call me if anything happens."

Taking the card, Jaz said, "Will do." Once the card was pocketed, Jaz stepped up onto the stool and started snaking her way through the small bathroom window. Once she got to her hips, she felt two sets of hands grab her legs. Instead of pulling her back in though, they started trying to help push her out the window. Katrina and Harley were helping her squeeze through. With their help, Jaz managed to get out faster with only half the trouble.

This wasn't the first time the girls had helped someone escape the Viprus; Jaz could tell that much by the crates that had been arranged beneath the window to create stairs. Once her feet has disappeared from sight, Jaz heard Harley call out, "Are you okay?"

"Yeah, I'm fine. Thanks again."

"No problem, girl!" And with that, the window closed, muffling the sound of the Viprus' music. Jaz walked to the end of the alleyway, getting back to the main street before she started making her way home. Right as she arrived at the nearest subway station, Jaz heard police sirens nearby. The sound didn't used to bother her. At that moment, however, she had to wonder what had happened and where and when and to who?

Jaz figured that she needed to get the briefcase back to Jude as soon as possible before the police stopped her. The counterfeit money would get them both into trouble if she were caught. Following Jude's instructions from before, Jaz arrived at Jude's apartment building, walked up to the apartment, and gave the patterned knocked to let

Jude know it was a friend and not whoever Jude was so afraid off. At least, Jaz assumed they were afraid; they didn't become a hermit for nothing.

In the middle of the patterned knock, the door yanked open and Jude's pale, boney hand shot out, gripping Jaz by the wrist and yanking her into the dark room. As Jaz stumbled into the darkness, she yelled, "Ah! What the fuck?!"

"Sh!", Jude hissed as they practically leapt onto Jaz, covering her mouth with the same boney hand. That was the first time Jaz noticed that their hand was also clammy; they were seriously nervous. "Someone is in your apartment."

Jaz's heart stopped with the words, and her own hands turned clammy. She stopped struggling to get Jude's hand off her mouth. The hacker ended up doing that of their own accord. "What do you mean someone's in my apartment?"

"This is what I mean," Jude said, gesturing to one of their screens. Taking a closer look, Jaz realized that it was footage on loop from her apartment building. Two sections of the screen showed the entrance of the building from the outside and the inside. Other sections of the screens showed the first, second, and third floor hallways in sections. The looping footage showed someone hitting a bunch of the call buttons outside the building. Then, the building doors unlocked, allowing the stranger inside. The stranger climbed the stairs until they reached the third floor. They walked to the end of the hallways and turned to Jaz's door. It was difficult to see what they had done, but they managed to pick the lock on the door. They slipped into the apartment building, undetected by anyone else.

"Who the fuck is that?!'" Jaz was sure that Jude wouldn't have an answer; the stranger was wearing a thick, thigh-length parka with the collar popped and zipped up around their lower face. A beanie covered their head to their eyebrows. Aside from this, they kept their head down. Jaz couldn't even tell what gender the person was, let alone who they were. But it had to be someone involved in the case; a petty thief wouldn't do to the trouble of sneaking into a locked building to rob a particular apartment all the way on the third floor.

"We'll find out soon enough." Hitting some buttons, Jude updated their screen to show the current feed from the camera just outside the front door of the building. Three cars pulled up in front of the building, with lights flashing of top. "I took the liberty of calling the police." Jaz and Jude watched about six cops pile out of the cars. They took a moment to hit a call-button—*probably the one to contact the landlady*—before they rushed in. Changing the camera views, Jude showed Jaz the cops climbing the stairs to her apartment. In the light, Jaz managed to recognize Detective Moore among the cops. *He probably thought the same thing I did when he heard it was my address that had been hit.* The cops flanked the doors while the detective knocked hard. He looked like he yelled something and waited for a response. None must've come; Detective Moore nodded to two of the cops, who used a battering ram to bust the door open. All but two rushed inside in the apartment. Those who stayed behind kept their guns trained on the door. That was really the last thing that Jude and Jaz saw before three cops dragged the suspect out of the apartment. The beanie had been ripped off in the struggle, but Jaz was sure his pants and briefs had already been around his ankles when the cops broke down the door; it was Professor Polanksy.

Jude and Jaz both visibly shuddered at the sight of the half-naked professor. Neither one of them wanted to know what he was up to in the apartment, yet their imaginations filled in the blanks against their wills. *But how did he find me? How did he know where we lived?*

"Before you ask," Jude said as they typed on their keyboard, bringing up a new window with a digital file from Essex County College. It was Rosamie's, and she had used Jaz's address to register. Of course, he would have access to her records. *Was this his disgusting, twisted way of paying his respects?*

"Heads up," Jude warned. They had taken the screen back to the live feed from the security cameras. Detective Moore had stepped out of the apartment and he was scrolling on his phone. "I get the distinct feeling you're going to get a phone call." A few seconds later, the detective put his phone to his ear. Less than a second later, Jaz's cell phone rang, and the caller ID read "Detective Moore". "Have a good lie ready," Jude advised.

"Hello?" Jaz answered.

"Miss Dilan?"

"Yes."

"It's Detective Moore. Are you alright? You seem panicked?" *Fuck. Way to make it sound like you're anticipating the call, dumbass.*

"I'm fine. I just assumed you made progress in Rosamie's case." *Hopefully he believes me since he can't see my face.*

"Well, I think we have answered a few questions. Could you come to the station, please? I have some," The detective paused not knowing what to say. "Something has happened."

20

PRISON WITHIN A PRISON

"**Y**OU CAN'T DO THIS! I have my rights! Love is love, you non-believers! Fuck the police!" Professor Polanksy was handcuffed to a table in an NYPD interrogation room. He was pulling on the handcuffs so hard that he was bruising and cutting his wrists. If the table wasn't bolted to the floor, he probably could've swung it right through the one-way mirror with his rantings and ravings.

"He's been screaming about us being 'non-believers' since we arrested him." Jaz, unfortunately, wasn't surprised. There were deranged pedophiles all over the world who insisted that they were part of the LGBTQI+ community, and therefore they shouldn't be persecuted for their "kinks". Rosamie had at least a dozen stories of such people who had tried to connect to the support group or get in on pride events. Such people were quickly shut down.

"Who is he?" Jaz asked, trying to hide her familiar disgust with the professor.

Detective Moore looked to his notes. "According to what we've found, his name is Harvey Polansky. He's a professor at Essex Country College. Your niece was a student there, if I recall correctly." Jaz nodded as her only answer. "That's how he found your apartment; it was in her students records as her home address."

"But why?" Trying to pretend like Jaz didn't already have this knowledge was harder than she thought it would be. She had no clue if the detective was believing her. "Why was he in my apartment?"

"We don't know for sure, but we can take some guesses based on the fact that his pants and underwear were off when he broke in." Again, Jaz visibly shivered. No matter what she knew, the idea of what the professor did in her home was traumatizing to imagine.

"How did you know that he had broken in?"

"We got a call from someone who said that they saw him go into your apartment and that they'd never seen him before. They wanted to make sure it wasn't a burglar." *Jude.* "Since your apartment is part of your niece's investigation, we wanted to make sure that it wasn't the culprit looking to mess up or take some important evidence that we had missed."

"So did he kill her?" Jaz didn't believe her own question. How could anyone else?

"We're investigating now. If my hunches are right, he might've had a motive. It's just a question on whether he had means and opportunity." Josiah sighed, "Unfortunately, it may take a while since he isn't cooperating. We have to get a warrant to search him before we can find anything that holds him long enough."

Jaz furrowed her eyebrows at the detective. "He broke into my home. Isn't that enough?"

"Normally, it would be if he had stolen something; breaking and entering gets absorbed by a burglary charge. As far as we can see, however, he didn't try to take anything. Except for these." Detective Moore held up a plastic bag that held a scrunched-up pair of panties. Jaz didn't recognize them, but based on the thong style, she had to assume they were a pair of Rosamie's that hadn't made it into the last laundry load. The sight of the panties and the idea of the Professor taking them made Jaz want to wretch right there in the middle of the station.

"Surely that's something; isn't there some kind of punishment for stealing a minor's underwear?"

"Oh, there is and it is often considered burglary, sometimes with sexual intent. Moreover, some sex offenders have a pattern of stealing underwear, so it could give us cause to investigate normally. But there's a major issue; the owner of these has passed away. Dead people can't own anything, therefore nothing can be "stolen" from them."

"But didn't he steal from her estate?"

"Considering she was sixteen, I highly doubt she had a will. Even if she did, I also highly doubt she would've mentioned her unmentionables and who was to inherit them. Therefore, the ownership of these could be called into question."

"They were on my property. Doesn't that count for something?" Jaz was getting frustrated.

"It will help, but the lawyer will acknowledge the fact that New York's Personal Property Inheritance Distribution Laws aren't clear. You're not a spouse. You're not even her parent or legal guardian, so you didn't automatically inherit any or all of Rosamie's property. It makes it even more complicated that she wasn't a complete resident of

New York. She was just temporarily staying with family, as far as the state will be concerned. The only person who can honestly fight this is another lawyer."

Josiah sighed. "At this point, we have to hope that this open piece of underwear and his actions are enough for a judge to give us a search warrant into his home. Then we have to hope we find more stolen underwear or something even more damning before his lawyer arrives and starts making things hard for us. That's a lot of hopes that we have to have."

"Well, what happens if you do find more underwear?" Jaz asked in frustration.

"Well, it's dependent on his record—which is practically non-existent save for some arrests because he was protesting in a way that disturbed the peace and the like. That would mean that this is his first burglary attempt. If we tag 'with sexual intent' on the end of that, he could get two years, worst case scenario."

"That's it? That's all stealing panties will get him?"

Josiah nodded with a sigh. "Unfortunately, even if we managed to bump it up to burglary, it still wouldn't be considered a sexual offense."

"But he was fucking my niece!" Jaz yelled loud enough to disturb everyone in the NYPD station. Even the petty criminals and drunk assholes who had been arrested were uncomfortable.

"Miss Dilan, I'm sorry, but we have no proof that they was ever any sexual contact between them," Josiah suddenly got a grim look on his face. "Unless there's something you know that I don't." *Fuck.* "Is there something you want to tell me, Miss Dilan?"

If it means that I can get his ass in jail, then I have to take a chance. "Rosamie had an account on a porn website called PorChive. Aside from making videos and posting pictures, she had conversations with another user about how if he tried to give her a failing grade, she would report him for sexual harassment. The username of who she was talking to was Rich3ater, and Professor Polanksy specifically taught a class on Anarchy that Rosamie was in." Jaz left out the part of Jude hacking for her; *I'm not gonna get other people in trouble for my actions.*

Josiah pinched the bridge of his nose. In an instant, he looked ten years older than he was. Jaz was sure the stress of the whole case had done the same thing to her. "Do you have access to your niece's account?"

"Yes. And I can give you the log-in information," Without saying a word, Josiah passed a notepad and pen to Jaz to write down the information. Once she was done, Josiah said, "Come with me." Judging from his tone, Jaz was in deep trouble.

Josiah ended up taking Jaz to another interrogation room. He didn't even bother to sit down as he pulled out his smart phone and started a recording. *This conversation is gonna be on the investigation's official record.* "Miss Dilan, would you mind telling me where you were this evening when I called you?"

"I was just out. Walking around. Trying to enjoy the night. It's been really depressing lately, so I just needed to out and have fun." *There's no way he's gonna believe this. Hell, I don't believe it.*

"Can anyone vouch for your whereabouts?"

"Garrett." *Surely, that's believable.*

"Excellent. So you won't mind if I give Mr. Weber a call to confirm, won't you?"

"Go ahead." *I'm sorry you have to lie for me Garrett.*

"But before I go call Mr. Weber, can you do one more thing for me, Miss Dilan?" Jaz sat silently, waiting for the detective's request. "Would you mind emptying your pockets for me?"

Fuck me. "On what grounds?"

"On the grounds of the fact that I have warned you about interfering with my investigation and you have chosen to ignore my warning. Furthermore, you seem to have withheld important information that you found." It was difficult for Jaz to argue with the detective. He was right; she didn't listen to him and she didn't tell him these things that he needed to know when she found them out.

"And if I refuse?"

"I have enough grounds to put you in a holding cell for at least twenty-four hours, even if I don't find any evidence against you. And with how crowded our cells are, I'm afraid you'll have to share with the Professor Polansky."

He can't do that, can he? Surely there has to be some *rule about separating prisoners by gender. Or at least a rule about not letting a dangerous guy like him anywhere near someone he can hurt.* Jaz wasn't convincing herself at all. With a huff she stood up and started emptying her pockets. She wasn't carrying much; her wallet with some money in cash, two credit cards, her ID, and a metro card. Her apartment and shop keys. Some feminine products in case of an emergency visit from "Aunt Flow" as Rosamie used to say. When Jaz's had wrapped around the vile from Bruno Griffin, she froze. Risking a glance at the detective, she knew that her panic was written all over her face. She couldn't pretend like it wasn't there anymore. *Maybe he'll believe that it's just an essential oil. He's seen my apartment; he knows I have a diffuser.* Even as Jaz put the vial on the table, she knew that the detective wasn't that stupid.

The moment the detective saw the vial, he picked it out as the item of interest. Ignoring the keys and the wallet, Detective Moore picked up the vial and started unscrewing the top. He took a sniff, but Jaz didn't know what he smell; she herself hadn't smelled the venom when she got it, so she had no idea if that would give her away. "Well, well,

well, Ms. Dilan," the detective said with sour amusement. "You've been very busy." Closing the vial and putting it down, Josiah took on a more authoritative tone. "Jasmine Dilan, you're under arrest for interfering in a police investigation."

"Well, at least it isn't going to be so lonely." Annie tried to make light of the situation as she sat on the floor of the cell that she and Jaz were sharing. Jaz's hunch had been right; even in the county jail, male and female prisoners were separated. Detective Moore had taken advantage of her lack of legal knowledge to trick her. *I bet that's how he's caught most of his perps. He's good; I'll give him that.* Jaz wasn't completely sure if lies and manipulation were an abuse of power when used by the police, but if it wasn't, Jaz would have to keep that in mind when dealing with the detective in the future.

"Are they treating you okay in here?" Jaz asked Annie, more worried that they would both be subjected to less than humane conditions.

"Actually, yeah. They treat you pretty good here, so long as you don't make trouble for them. Now it you yell and scream and fight, they'll act accordingly. But at least they have good books in their library; that keeps me on my best behavior." Annie held up a really beat up copy of some fantasy novel that she was engrossed in. Based on how quickly she read and flipped pages, Jaz could also imagine that reading helped Annie keep her anxiety to a manageable level. *Whatever works.*

"Has your brother gotten you that lawyer?" *And are they willing to take on a second case?*

"Yeah. She came by yesterday and reiterated what Eugene told me," Annie explained, not taking her eyes off her book.

"What's that?"

"Unless the police find some actual physical evidence against me, they have to let me go in a few days. Right now everything they have is circumstantial and hypothetical, which isn't enough to hold me or anyone else."

"That's good. I mean, they aren't going to find anything, right?"

"No," Annie furrowed her brows in uncertainty. "At least, I don't think they will."

"You don't 'think'?"

"Well, if their hunch is right and the venom enter Rosamie's system near where I put the tattoo, then it could've gotten onto anything: the needle; the pen; the table; my hands and supplies. And because I work at the parlor, my fingerprints are practically everywhere in the building. They may find physical evidence to support their case against me just because of the circumstances." Annie snapped her book shut, and Jaz could see the worry all over her face. "I don't want to go to prison."

"And you won't because you're not guilty and they won't find anything to say that you are."

"How can you be so sure?" Jaz's heart broke as she saw the tears prick at the corner of Annie's eyes.

"Something about this whole situation doesn't feel right. The pieces aren't fitting together. Something is missing."

"What?"

"I wish I knew. I have covered every possible option, even the most impossible and even illegal options."

Annie looked at Jaz with cautious worry. "How 'illegal'?"

"Why do you think I'm in here? I bought snake venom from a black market dealer tonight."

"What?!" Annie cried loud enough to disturb the other prisoners in the jail. They yelled at her to shut up and that they were trying to sleep. Judging from the slurring, most of them were nursing hangovers too. Annie took her voice down to ask, "Why?"

"So that I could prove to the detective that you didn't buy venom from him; he didn't recognize you."

"You showed him a picture of me?" Annie was getting more and more worried with every statement Jaz made.

"You and one of Rosamie and one of the Professor." Jaz left out the picture of Seth Frost. "He didn't recognize any of you."

"Well, that's good I guess." Annie didn't seem so sure. "You didn't have to risk you life like that though. Not for me."

"I did it for Rosamie. The real killer needs to be found. You can't take the blame for their actions."

"Just be careful. Please."

"I appreciate your worry, Annie, but I'll be fine."

"Come on! Hurry!" Rosamie was dragging Jaz through the streets of New York. She looked happy and carefree; excited even. It was both comforting and sad to see.

The destination was, apparently, Garrett's tattoo parlor. As Rosamie and Jaz skidded to a stop in front of the shop, Rosamie urged, "Come on! Open it up!" Just as Jaz was asking how she was supposed to do what Rosamie said, she felt a jingling in her right coat pocket. Reaching in, she felt jagged, cold metal against her palm. When she pulled out the item, she found two keys on a scorpion keychain. Jaz recognized one as a typical door key, and one as a grate key. Taking the grate key, Jaz inserted it into the lock on the iron curtain that had been rolled down in front of the shop. Sure enough, the cage unlatched from the ground, allowing Jaz to roll it up. Once the grate was gone, Rosamie pushed Jaz towards the normal door, repeating, "Come on!".

Once the door to the parlor was unlocked, Rosamie took control again, dragging Jaz into the darkness of the closed-up shop. "Come on! Make the stencil," Rosamie urged with delighted excitement. The fluorescent lights burst on, revealing Jaz was standing in front of the stencil-making table. There was already a freshly made stencil in Jaz's hand. She didn't recognize or understand the symbol that the stencil would create, but Rosamie's voice came from one of the private tattoo rooms, urging her to hurry up. That was enough to make Jaz shrug at the stencil.

Jaz didn't remember stepping out of the supply room, but the next thing she knew she was sitting in a rolling stool next to Rosamie, who was lying face down on the tattoo table with her shirt in a hasty pile on the floor. Autopilot completely took over, and Jaz pressed the stencil against the smooth skin of Rosamie's back, white looked china white in the harsh fluorescent glow. After pressing and rubbing, a careful peel revealed that the stencil has transferred to Rosamie's skin perfectly.

Teleporting again, Jaz found herself in the supply room. She knew precisely where everything was and started collecting her supplies: gloves; tattoo pen and hose; fresh, sterile needles; and generic black ink. This particular tattoo would require a bit more ink than was typical for a first tattoo; rather than just an outline, this tattoo was going to be completely black. Grabbing the ink from the cabinet, Jaz started measuring it out, estimating how much ink she would need and giving herself a little extra than that estimation just in case.

"What's going on here?" Garrett's voice made her jump, but when she turned around, her heart completely stopped. Garrett's voice was coming out of the mouth of the ghost of her past; the old man with the black eyes, who was looking like he was ready to grab the tattoo pen off the table and stab it straight into her heart.

"Jaz! Jaz!" Jaz sat straight up and found herself still in the jail cell she was sharing with Annie. Sometime in the night, she had drifted off on the bed, which Annie had forfeited to Jaz when she was put in the cell. Annie was standing over Jaz, looking down at her with worry knitted all over her face. "Are you okay?"

"Yeah," Jaz huffed. "It was just a bad dream."

"Must've been a Blind level of bad dram?"

"What?"

"Blind," Annie answered. When Jaz still looked confused, she clarified, "Sorry. It's the scariest episode of *Professor Who* ever made. I guess the reference wouldn't make sense to anyone who doesn't watch the show themselves."

"Yeah." Jaz trailed off, not knowing how to react.

"I just meant that you were screaming."

"Oh, sorry! I didn't realize." *They're getting worse.*

"Don't apologize. I'm just worried about you. Are you sure you're okay?" Annie asked, sitting next to Jaz on the bed.

"I'll be fine, Annie. Thanks."

"No problem. Let me know if you need something. I mean, within reason, " Annie said, gesturing to the bars that trapped them in the cell. "Oh, by the way. I thought about something while you were asleep."

"What's that?"

Annie looked around for any cops or other prisoners who would eavesdrop on their conversation. Leaning into Jaz's ear, Annie whispered, "Garrett keeps a spare key right outside the parlor. It's in the base of the little scorpion statue. It's not exactly the cleverest hiding space; anyone could've figured it out if they watched him long enough."

"What are you trying to tell me, Annie?"

"Well, Garrett is a great boss, but I can kinda tell that he rubs some people the wrong way."

Jaz knew exactly what Annie meant; Garrett didn't get involved with all of those fights at *The Gym* over the television for nothing. He only jived well with very specific personalities like Jaz's. Those he didn't jive with full on hated him. "So?"

"Well, it's kind of a long shot, but maybe someone broke into the parlor and contaminated our supplies to get back at Garrett. I mean, it's gonna look pretty bad if anyone finds out that someone died after getting a tattoo from his shop. Maybe someone is trying to get revenge by ruining his business." Jaz hadn't considered this; she'd been so focused on putting her own mind at ease and clearing Annie name that she hadn't thought about Garrett and what role he could've played in the incident. It wasn't *completely* outside of the realm of possibility. "I mean, his client that night didn't seem to like him very much."

"Client?"

"Yeah. This big guy was getting a tattoo on his ring finger. I saw him when Rosamie and I were leaving. He was with a really pretty girl, but he looked," Annie trailed off, trying to find the words to describe what she saw. "He either looked suspicious or pissed off. I couldn't really tell. He was staring Garrett down like they were about to fight."

"Did this guy look stupid rich, by any chance?"

"Well, not in his appearance, but there was a Porsch parked outside the parlor. I assume it belonged to the client, so maybe? Why? Do you know him?"

"Not very well." *So Jessica asked Garrett to do their engagement tattoos. Like that's not gonna rub it in the poor guys face.* "But based on what I know, I don't think the guy would bother with trying to ruin Garrett's business. At least not like that. It would be more like 'my father will hear about this' and stuff like that. Leaving bad reviews and telling everyone he knows to avoid Garrett's shop. I don't think he would get his hands dirty by breaking in and sabotaging the supplies. I don't even think he would bother to pay someone else to do it for him."

Annie still looked worried. "I know this is asking a lot and you might get arrested again, but can you take a look around the parlor? Garrett told me that he closed up for a while given the circumstances. Maybe if you take a look around while no one else is there, you'll be able to see something the police and Garrett missed."

Jaz sighed. This one night in jail made her want to table her investigation all together. It may have not been terribly uncomfortable, but the atmosphere alone was bad enough. If she had to keep going back every time she got caught investigating, the NYPD would eventually lose their patience and make her arrest even worse. "Do you mind if I think about it, Annie? It's not that I don't want to help—"

"No, I get it," Annie reassured. "I wouldn't want to risk it either if I were in your shoes." As much as Annie tried to pretend she was okay, Jaz could see the tears pricking at the corner of her eyes. "Thank you for trying."

Right as Jaz reached out to comfort her late niece's girlfriend, a police officer approached the cell. "Jasmine Dilan?" Jaz stood up, answering to the name. The cop pulled out a set of keys and unlocked the cells heavy, barred door. "You're free to go."

Jaz and Annie furrowed their brows as they looked at each other and the cop. "Why?" Jaz asked.

"Someone's paid your bail."

"So, have we finally reached the moment where we think 'this has gone too far'?" Garrett asked. It was only a little after five in the morning, so Jaz and her best friend had to wait on the subway deck longer than they usually had to. The slow wait time and limited trains to certain locations was one of the reasons why Jaz rarely stayed out past midnight.

When Jaz didn't immediately answer, Garrett sighed and pinched the bridge of his nose. "Jaz. I just bailed you out of jail. How is that not enough for you?"

"It's not me that it's not enough for. It's my brain," Jaz stated tiredly.

"What the fuck are you talking about?"

"As much as I want to let this all go, my mind keeps bringing those nightmares. I just feel that if I don't figure out the truth, the nightmares won't stop and I'll never be able to sleep again."

"Jaz—" Garrett cut himself off. She knew what he wanted to say, but he thought better of it; telling Jaz that it was all in her head wasn't going to make her want to listen to him or even talk to him. She would just close herself off from him, thinking that she was burdening him. "Jaz, it will all be okay. You have to trust the police to do this."

"But what if they're wrong?"

"Jaz, they're professionals, and from what little I've seen, no one on Rosamie's case seems crooked. I think it will all be fine. You, on the other had, are not. And you won't be if this keeps up."

"What are you talking about?"

"Jaz," Garrett's tone took a serious, lecturing tone. "I know you're drinking again." Jaz's eyes went wide as she looked at Garrett. Jaz couldn't tell if the shame was turning her face red or white. "Oh, don't look at me like that. Don't you remember? Three days ago, when Annie got arrested, you sent me to your place to pack an overnight bag so that you could stay with me. There was a full and unopened bottle of mouthwash in the bathroom. After I got the call from the police this morning, I decided to do the same thing." Jaz wondered why Garrett had a duffle bag with him when he picked her up. "I'm just supposed to believe that half of the bottle has disappeared in three days because you suddenly became anal about your teeth?"

Jaz dropped her head into her hands, not knowing what to say or do. The sight of her shame and helplessness seemed to soften Garrett's tone with her. He took a seat next to her and took his volume down, out of respect for her privacy. "Jaz. Tell me the truth. Have you talked to your counselor since Rosamie passed away?" Jaz shook her head, refusing to look at him. "What about AA?" Jaz shook her head again.

Garrett nodded again and dug into his pocket. "You should've told me," he said as he handed her a coin. Jaz recognized it on sight; it was a sponsorship coin. Jaz finally looked Garrett in the eye. There was something in his eyes that she couldn't put her finger on; it wasn't quite sadness or sorrow. But it was something deep. "You're going back. Tonight. And I'll go with you."

Jaz didn't know what else to say. There was nothing she *could* say. She knew well what commitment Garrett was making for her. Her parents and her sister had made the same commitment when she turned twenty-one. It was a commitment that was not made lightly by anyone, and it should never be taken for granted. Jaz's head fell on Garrett's shoulder. Garrett wrapped an arm around her shoulders and didn't release her until their train arrived. Then, once they were settled on some seats, the two friends took the same position as they sped through New York's Underground.

21

PAINFUL ENDINGS

J AZ STOMPED DOWN THE sidewalk. Why couldn't Garrett wait for
her? It would've made a lot more sense than going to his parlor
and leaving her a note to go there and meet him as soon as possible. In
fact, why couldn't they just stay at his place if he needed to talk to her
as badly as he said he did? He owed her big time.

Jaz was just starting to think of the lunch her friend could buy her
when she arrived at *Venom Art.* She opened the door, and hesitated
there when she heard the buzzing of a tattoo pen. Didn't Annie say
that Garrett had shut the shop down until further notice because of
everything that had happened? Who was he tattooing this early in the
morning anyways? At first, Jaz took a seat in the waiting room, trying

to be polite even in her confusion and hoping that the appointment would be over soon. After five minutes, her patience had worn too thin. Asking her to come all that way and then making her wait was just flat-out rude.

"Hey, Garrett!" Jaz called as she stomped into the back of the shop. How could he work in such a dim room? Jaz could barely see across a room. Did all of the lights go out at the same time?

Jaz's heart stopped. Through the darkness, Jaz could see the familiar form of Rosamie on the tattoo table. Tears streaked her mascara down her face and over the strip of duct tape over her mouth. Garrett didn't even flinch at Jaz's angry voice or Rosamie's muffled screams; he continued carving into the girls back, unphased.

"Garrett! Garrett, stop!" Was he deaf, or was he just ignoring her? It didn't matter. She just needed to get him to stop. Jaz stomped up to Garrett, grabbed him by the shoulder and yanked him away from her niece. "Stop!"

The grab made Garrett spin around in his stool. No. It wasn't Garrett; it was his clothes, his tattoos, and even his hair and beard, but it wasn't his face. It was the face of the old man with black eyes. It looked like he was wearing a costume and some very convincing wigs, but it was him. "Tsk, tsk, tsk. Patience is a virtue, kitten, You'll get your turn soon enough." The menace in his voice was punctuated when he spun around and slammed the tattoo pen into Rosamie's back, right where her heart was. The black ink mixed with her red blood and sprayed everywhere.

Jaz sat up and was immediately comforted by the familiar sight of Garrett's bedroom, which was well lit by the early February morning light. Sweat poured off her head and onto the sheets beneath her. As she caught her breath, she remembered how she got there. The moment that they arrived at Garrett's apartment, Garrett immediately

sent Jaz to his bedroom, relinquishing his bed to her for the night. Jaz
had been so exhausted by what had happened that day that she didn't
argue and fell asleep almost as soon as her head hit the pillow. Looking
at the clock, she had only gotten about two or three hours of sleep.

Once Jaz was calm again, she slipped out of the bed and tiptoed
out to the living room. Looking around, Jaz found that Garrett was
nowhere to be found. The only trace he left behind was a note.

Jaz,

*Had to run an errand. Be back soon. Get something to eat and make
yourself at home. You know how to turn on the TV.*

Garrett

An errand? At half past eight in the morning? Jaz's eyes immediately
fell to the liquor cabinet. It was unlocked and completely empty. *So
that's what he's doing. He really is dedicated to helping me, isn't he?* It
was comforting to see what a friend was willing to do for her.

Jaz decided to take her time that morning and made herself a nice
breakfast of fried eggs and bacon with hot sauce and buttery toast. Jaz
hadn't spoiled herself in such a way for a long time.

Once breakfast was ready, Jaz took a seat on the couch and turned
on the TV. She chewed her eggs as she flipped through the channel,
looking for something to watch. As she got into the news channels,
she asked herself, "Do I really want to hear about how fucked up the
world is this early in the morning after everything I've been through?"
Though her original reaction was "No", she remembered that an elec-
tion was coming up. As the daughter of an immigrant, Jaz had heard all
her life that it was her duty to stay informed about what is happening

in the country and in the world so that she could do her civic duty and make an educated vote so that she could do her part to save the world. "Fine, dad," she thought to herself. "I guess looking at the local news is better than nothing." Picking up the remote, Jaz short-cutted to channel four and got comfortable on the couch, continuing to eat her breakfast as the newscasters started telling her and the rest of New York about the current new stories.

Continuing with a breaking story. We have finally identified the victim that passed away at the Viprus Club. Franklin Kennedy, the youngest sone of the New York Kennedy socialites, was celebrating his pending nuptials with a bachelor party at the club. According to eye-witness testimony, everything was perfectly normal until Kennedy started feeling poorly in the middle of the night. An ambulance was called when Kennedy suddenly started having a seizure. While the hospital and the family have not made any statements regarding the man's death, the EMTs who transported him have informed us that he died on the journey to the hospital. He was only thirty-eight and is survived by his fiancé, Jessica Price.

Jaz dropped her entire plate of breakfast onto the nice hardwood floors of Garrett's apartment. She didn't change into warmer clothes that weren't pajamas. She just grabbed her coat and shoes and rushed out of the apartment.

As she was rushing through the hallways of the building, Jaz speed dialed Detective Moore and got his voicemail. "Detective! I think there's something you're going to want to talk to me about. Meet me at *Venom Art*, Garrett Weber's tattoo parlor. It's where you arrested Annie. Please hurry. This is important."

22

THE SMOKING TAIL

THE CITY WAS ODDLY quiet as Jaz made her way to *Venom Art.* The cold New York air seemed still, almost like the world was holding its breath. For what, only God knew.

As ominous as the quiet was, it allowed Jaz to keep her wits about her; everywhere she went, she surveyed for any sign that she was going to cross paths with Garrett. Though it also worried her that Garrett would have an easier time finding her as well. She took advantage of any way to hide on the way as she could. She switched which side of the subway train she sat on several times, trying to keep her back to the platforms, in case Garrett was standing on any one of them. The few people who shared her same car didn't confront Jaz about her behavior. They did, however, get off the train as fast as they could. Some of them probably got off at a stop that wasn't there just to avoid Jaz.

During her sprint to the subway station, Jaz used her smartphone to search for ways to identify snake venom. The results managed to come up before Jaz arrived at the station and descended into the Wi-Fi-less tunnels beneath the city that never slept. Jaz used the ride to look at the results and study them. Based on the pictures, venom was supposed to look like whatever Bruno Griffin gave her; clear, yellow liquid with only slightly thicker consistency than water. This was what she needed to find.

When Jaz finally arrived at the tattoo parlor, she did as Annie told her and opened a compartment in the base of the little scorpion statue near the door. Sure enough, there was a spare set of keys that allowed Jaz to roll up the grate and unlock the parlor door. Jaz decided it was best to keep the blinds down and the lights off to not tip anyone off. She only had the dim glow of daylight that came through the blinds to illuminate the place. Koki the Scorpion was still in her tank by the front desk, and she was very still. Was she dead? Asleep? Or was she waiting for something? Even though the scorpion would hardly do anything to rat her out, Jaz still felt the need to move quietly to not wake or upset Koki.

As Jaz moved into the back of the parlor, she needed to get her phone out to use its built-in flashlight. Had this place always been so creepy? Or was it just because it was dark and she was alone? Jaz shook off her shivers and pushed forward into the back office where Garrett kept all the files and legal documents for the shop, as well as his personal belongings when he was working.

The office was not locked, and the only reason Jaz could think of for that is because either Garrett didn't feel the need to lock it when he was the only employee, or the drastic recent changes led to him forgetting to secure the place. Tiptoeing into the office, Jaz had to wonder how Garrett ever got his taxes done with the mess that he kept the office in. Stacks of papers were everywhere, and there was no rhyme or reason to the stacks: one paper would be a bank statement; the next five would be work orders for issues at the shop; then there would be 3 shops copies of receipts for tattoos that were bought by customers

All the receipts statements, however, caught Jaz's eyes; between Garrett's need of an apprentice and the incredibly expensive apartment he rented, Jaz had come to understand that business was going very well for him. The receipts told a very different story. There were only a handful of them from the past month, and judging by what the customers were charged, they weren't very big projects. In fact, they were very minimal much like Jessica and Frank's engagement tattoos. Based on the number of receipts and the amount of them, Jaz could only conclude that Garrett hadn't even made half of what she made in the last month. Yet, he could afford that fancy ass apartment. Where was the money come from?

Ten-thousand-dollars; that's what that tiny little bottle of venom she got from Bruno has cost. Ten-thousand-dollars for barely an ounce of venom. *Judging from his look and attitude, I can't think that Bruno gets the venom out of snakes himself. He must have to get it from someone else and pay them a portion of what he receives from customers.* Even if someone shady like Bruno only gave a venom collector twenty percent of what he made, that would be enough to pay Garrett's rent. *God, I hope I'm wrong about this.*

Leaving the paperwork in their piles, Jaz started looking all over the office for anything that even remotely resembled snake venom. It was a little hard to look through the office between al the piles of paper and the weird junk that Garrett had collected for whatever reason: a metal tea strainer was screwed to a piece of scrap wood, and then was connected to some kind of battery. *The man has never drunk tea in his life, and he doesn't own a fucking car. What the fuck would he need this stuff?* Jaz shook her head, trying to focus on the task at hand. "Snake venom. You're looking for snake venom."

Jaz did as thorough of a search as she could, knowing that she only had a limited time before Detective Moore would show up. That was assuming Garrett didn't get there first. In that short but as thorough as possible search, Jaz found nothing that even remotely resembled snake venom. All she did find was some hygiene supplies that Garrett kept on hand just in case: deodorant; toothpaste with a brush; an unmarked bottle that was white and creamy like some generic man's shampoo. She couldn't tell if she was relieved or disappointed. On the one hand, it cleared her best friend's name. On the other hand, it was another dead end in the investigation, and she was out of ideas.

Now I have to call the detective and let him know that it was a false alarm. I can't imagine he'll be too happy about that. Jaz walked toward the front of the shop as she pulled out her phone and pulled up the detective's phone number in her contacts. As she hit the call button and held the phone up to her ear, preparing for the scolding she was going to get, Jaz's eyes fell on Koki, still in her cage waiting like a patient predator.

Wait a minute.

"Hello? Ms. Dilan? I just got your message. Is everything okay?" The detective's voice held a genuine worry in it.

"Detective, can I ask you a question about the case?" Jaz never took her eyes off of Koki the scorpion.

The detective's worry dissolved with a sigh. "You can but understand that I may not be able to answer you."

"Do we know what kind of venom killed Rosamie."

"I believe I told you that the toxicology report takes six weeks. We won't know for sure until then." The detective seemed a little annoyed that he had to repeat himself, but he didn't complain.

"Has the coroner made any guesses?"

"Bails said that it's impossible to guess venom by sight unless we see what kind of wound, they came from. If there were two punctures, we'd be able to determine that it was a snake bite. Since the venom was dispensed in an unconventional way, however, the report is the only clue we have."

"What about side-effects? Can they tell us anything?"

"Bails says that most venoms have very similar side-effects, save for one or two differences on the list."

"So scorpion venom and snake venom work in similar ways, right?"

"Bails never said that specifically and I'm no medical expert, but I would assume so. Ms. Dilan, what is this about? What is going on?"

"Detective Moore, I need you to come to *Venom Art* as quickly as possible. I think there's a theory we haven't considered."

"Can't you tell me about this theory on the phone."

"No time. Besides, some things need to be seen for themselves. Get here quickly."

"Ms. Dilan! Wai—" Jaz hung up in the middle of the detective's last statement.

Running back to the office, Jaz launched into the desk chair in front of the office computer. Turning it on, she was greeted with a login screen that said, "Hello, Garrett!" right above a bar where a four-digit passcode needed to be entered. *What would his passcode be?* It didn't take long for the answer to become obvious. 1116; Jessica's birthday. *That's how he always remembered.*

The passcode permitted Jaz into the computer, revealing Garrett's oddly empty desktop. *There should be like twenty spreadsheets on here for the business.* Instead, there were only a few files. One was a photo gallery file, simply titled "Jess". Opening the file, Jaz saw thousands of familiar pictures of Jess and Garrett that had been posted on social media while they were dating. *He must've never been able to bring himself to delete them.* As Jaz scrolled through the photos, however, some unfamiliar ones started to stand out to her. Part of why they stood out was because they were different in composition from the familiar ones. The familiar ones were like your typical boyfriend-girlfriend-dating photos: selfies of the two of them; pictures of the two of them that had been taken by other people; pictures of just Jess that had been taken by Garrett, and everything in between.

But the new pictures were just of Jess, and they were from a distance. Based on how she wasn't looking at the camera, it seemed that Jessica didn't know that she was being photographed. And there were thousands of pictures in the same location on the same day, showing how Jess walked down the street. If the pictures had been compiled into a flip book, it would've made a short, but smooth movie of Jess walking down the street. There were a bunch of other sets of pictures that were very similar, showing almost every moment and every aspect of Jessica's life: where she got her hair and nails done; where she shopped; even her presumably first date with Frank was included in the pictures. There were also a bunch of pictures that would've made good money on the revenge porn section of PorChive.

Jaz didn't know how to feel as she looked at these pictures. Her long-standing friendship with Garrett made her pity him, but her life experiences made her disgusted by him. And then there was the part of her that felt guilt; *How could I let it get this bad? How did I not notice?*

Finally, Jaz had to close the folder; it was too disturbing to continue to look through any longer. She needed to find something—anything that would clear Garrett's name. She clicked on the first file she saw.

That file ended up being an archive of emails between Garrett and some company Jaz had never heard of.

To: employment@CobraTechInc.com

From: VenomArt@gmail.com

To Whom It May Concern,

A mutual friend has suggested I contact you about a job opportunity with your company. I find myself in need of a part-time job, and I think that I would fit in well with your company.

It is my understanding that you need a distributor for some ink. I am happy to say that I have a direct contact with someone who makes such ink. Their name is Koki, and I can meet up with them every three weeks or so to receive more product. This way, I can keep your steadily stocked up, and replenish your supplies when it's needed.

I would love to speak with you more about the possibility of joining the company. Please feel free to contact me at any time. Or you can come to my shop if you wish to meet in person if you prefer.

Garrett Webber
3/14/19

Garrett's shop address followed his signature. *That's only a month after Jess dumped him.* The next message was from almost a month after that.

Mr. Weber

It was wonderful to finally meet you in person last month. I apologize that it has taken us so long to give you an answer. I'm afraid our Human Resources department has been having difficulties lately, since we have recently transferred to a new software.

I'm happy to tell you that we have decided that you would be a perfect fit in our company as a distributor. I'll be dropping off a contract in person in the next few days. Understand that as an up-and-coming technical company, we must employ the use of contracts to keep our projects confidential until they are ready to be revealed to the world. We have experienced many issues with employees not being held by contract who have leaked information to our competitors like Griffin Enterprises. I hope you'll understand our need for security.

Speaking of our competitors, I should warn you that they have many spies who are trying to constantly infiltrate us and steal our secrets. If you're approached by anyone who shows an abnormal amount of interest in your work with us, please let us know immediately so that we can take proper action against them. After all, your safety is as much of a priority to us as our confidentiality is.

I look forward to working with you in the future.

Kellam Delacriox
CEO of Cobra Tech Inc.

Griffin Enterprises? As in Bruno Griffin? The black market venom dealer? Jaz clicked open the web browser on the computer and typed CobraTechInc.com into the url bar.

SORRY!
This website is currently down for maintenance. Please come back later.

Jaz type "Griffin Enterprises" into the url bar, hoping that a web search would provide some results. Sure enough, the first non-advertisement result was for GriffinEnterprises.com. However, clicking on that link led to the same maintenance page that Cobra Tech had. *Fuck.*

Maybe his bookmarks with have some clues. Jaz pulled down the tab that provided a list of Garrett's favorited pages, looking through them. After seeing a lot of digital art pieces that other artists created, Jaz realized that there was an old computer, and the tabs hadn't been cleaned up in a while. *Maybe the bottom tabs will be more recent.* Jaz scrolled all the way down to the bottom of the favorites tab. The last two pages that were saved were for those Griffin Enterprises and Cobra Tech Industries pages that were being worked on. The one right above those pages had a disturbing title. It was an article written by a biology professor at the University of Arizona, and it was called "How To Milk A Scorpion".

Even as Jaz clicked on the link, she kept praying that this wasn't what she thought it was. The step-by-step process of the article came with pictures that dashed those prayers. This professor needed to collect a lot of scorpion venom for experiments. To do so, he had to shock and agitate the arachnid to get it to expel the venom from its table. He did this by connecting a metal tea strainer to the positive notch of a battery. The negative end was connected to a pair of forceps which were used to hold the scorpion by its tail so that the creature could sting the collect. Every time the professor set the scorpion on the tea strainer the circuit would be complete. This gave the scorpion enough of a shock to expel the venom without hurting it. The professor then used a capillary tube to collect the venom bit by bit, much like how pediatric phlebotomists used capillary tubes to collect blood after they pricked a child's finger. It took a lot of patience, because the venom would only come out in tiny droplets and it took three weeks for a scorpion to replenish its venom, but this article showed that even an amateur could collect a fair amount of milky venom from any scorpion.

Looking at the final picture in the step-by-step process made Jaz's heart sink; the picture of a full vile of white, creamy venom was very familiar. Numb with dread, she stood up from the desk and walked up to the table where Garrett kept his personal hygiene supplies. Her eyes fell to the unlabeled shampoo bottle; the color in it was identical to the color of the venom in the picture from the article. Jaz picked up the bottle bringing it closer to her face so that she could examine it. At a closer look, there was no way this was shampoo; it was too watery, and judging from the residue inside, there had initially been more in the bottle that had recently been taken out. Not much. Not even an ounce, but if Bruno was right, an ounce was more than enough to kill any one person.

"I'm sorry, Jaz." Jaz's heart stopped and her body froze, and Garrett's voice came from the doorway of the office.

There was a long silence as two best friends stared at one another, both knowing the truth of the tragedy that had recently struck their lives. Jaz could see the guilt in Garrett's eyes, even though he couldn't even look into hers. Jaz had no clue what her own face looked like; she was feeling too many things to know which emotions were coming through.

Garrett was the first to speak. "What gave me away?"

As emotionless as she could, Jaz said, "Frank's death was on the news this morning, and Annie told me that he and Jess were here that night. Apparently, she could tell that you two weren't getting along. That's when I realized that Rosamie was never the target."

Garrett scoffed. "Why would we?"

"What happened?"

Garrett started scratching the back of his head in the way that men did when they felt awkward or didn't know what to say. "I think I distracted Annie while she was getting her ink for Rosamie, and I kinda talked to her while I was preparing mine. I guess she accidentally grabbed my ink and I grabbed one of hers."

"'You guess'?" The anger Jaz felt was much more obvious in her tone now.

"It was a stupid mistake."

Jaz couldn't hold herself back anymore. "It was stupid to try to kill anyone in the first place!"

"I had to Jaz! He took Jessica away from me!"

"No, you didn't. You could've realized that she is a shallow gold-digger who was never good enough for you and you could've let her go!"

The shame in Garrett's eyes and face evaporated and gave way to injured rage. "Don't you dare talk about her that way."

"It's the truth, Garrett! She was only with you because you were a little rebellion! A way for her to shock her friends and family! She always knew she was going to dump you because you were never going to be rich enough for her!"

"But now I am! Now, I can afford to give her the life she wants; a beautiful apartment just for us and anything she could ever want. Now I can make her happy."

"By selling Koki's venom on the black market? You're making money off of criminals killing and hurting other people. Innocent people like Rosamie."

Garrett scoffed. "Jaz, I know she was your niece so of course you loved her, but 'innocent' she was not." Apparently, Garrett didn't see the rage in Jaz's eyes because he continued to list off the reasons why Rosamie was a bad person. "I mean, she was clearly drunk off her ass that night, and I've lost count of how many stories you've told me about her flirting with the line even when she wasn't living with you. I mean, I agree that some of the laws here and in Washington are way too strict, but how many times have you called her a pain in the ass after she moved in?"

Garrett didn't stand a chance against the pale, clenched fist that hurtled into his face. The punch was so hard that it knocked him straight into the wall behind him. Blood started leaking out of his nose into the mustache part of his patchy goatee, and his pompadour hair had flopped out of its gelled, sculpted state from the force of the impact. Garrett had only seen Jaz get into a few fights in the time that they had known each other, but he had always said, "Remind me never to piss you off" after each one of those few fights. Apparently, those reminders never got through.

Jaz stood over her best friend, her dark hair with red ombre going wild with the invisible electricity in the air. Her dark brown eyes looked red in the darkness of the parlor. Her heavy eye make-up was starting to stream from the hot tears that tumbled out of her eyes. "Do you have ANY idea what you've put me through?"

"I'm sorry, Jaz—" Garrett was cut off by the fist coming back at him, jamming right into his open jaw. The bruise started to spread beneath that patch facial hair.

"Do you have any idea what you've done to me?!"

"Jaz—" This time, Jaz's tennis shoes clad foot jammed into Garrett's cut, knocking the air out of him and making it impossible for him to continue to speak.

"How could you do this to me?!" Jaz kept hitting and kicking and punching Garrett and he struggled to breath, speak, protect himself, and make a run for it. He never got far and had to take every strike. "You're the reason why I haven't been able to sleep all week! You're the reason why I've been having nightmares!"

The only reason why Jaz stopped hitting Garrett was because a thought occurred to her that reignited the tired parts of her anger. "You knew. You've known since the police arrested Annie. You've known what happened this whole time. And you were just going to let Annie take the blame for your bullshit."

Garrett managed to cough out, "I thought she'd be okay; there's no evidence against her other than the timing."

Jaz grabbed Garrett by the t-shirt collar and yanked him to his knees, forcing his bruised and battered face to look at her. "Why didn't you come forward? Why didn't you tell the truth?"

"Jessica will want nothing to do with me if I—" Jaz cut him off again with an uppercut punch right to the jaw. The force of the impact was so hard that it made him snap his teeth together audibly, not unlike a turtle or an alligator.

"Jessica. Jessica, Jessica, Jessica. You're willing to kill people, work for the black market, and let other people take the blame for your actions all for a fake-ass bitch like her. Wake up! She never loved you!

You killed Frank and Rosamie for nothing! What are you going to do now?! Kill me?! Your best friend?! Just to be with her?!"

Garrett's silence was unnerving. He wasn't making any more excuses or begging her to stop. Jaz had come to learn that Garrett was having his best ideas (or worst ideas, depending upon your point of view) when he was dead silent. "If I have to, yes." Garrett's knee shot out, slamming right into one of Jaz's knees. The strike was enough to bring Jaz to her knees as she hissed in pain.

"I'm sorry, Jaz." That apology was enough to bring Jaz's gaze up. Garrett managed to stumble to his feet, and now he was armed with a syringe that was full of the same milky liquid he had gotten from Koki. Jaz barely had enough time to grip Garrett's armed hand and extend her arms so that Garrett couldn't get too close when he lunged at her.

The force of the lunge was enough to knock Jaz onto her back with Garrett on top of her. It was a power struggle as Jaz dug her nails into Garrett's wrist, trying to keep the syringe away from her skin. Her other arm was bent into his neck, trying to deter his attacks so that he could avoid his windpipe being crushed. They weren't gonna last long like that; Jaz's early anger and ferocity had weakened her, but her strikes had done the same to Garrett. This fight was going to end fast, but it was anyone's guess who was going to win.

"NYPD! FREEZE!" As a familiar and authoritative voice called out to the two fighting friends, three strong points of white light hit them and blinded them, making them freeze.

Garrett only froze for a moment, however, before he tried to scramble to his feet. Knowing he was trying to make a run for it, Jaz jammed her knee right into his groin as hard as she could from her prone position. While it wasn't the hardest kick, it was just strong enough from the right angle to take Garrett to the ground in the fetal position.

Ignoring his groans of pain, Jaz called out, "Detective Moore!"

The detective answered by approaching her carefully. His gun with a flashlight on top was still out but it wasn't trained on her. The other officers didn't dare to move; they didn't approach, back up, or lower their weapons. "Are you alright, Ms. Dilan?"

"I'm fine, but he killed Rosamie and Franklin Kennedy. Garrett did it. The proof is in his office, on his computer, and in his hand."

"I assume you mean this." Pointing his gun to the ground, the detective pulled out a handkerchief and picked up the syringe that Garrett had dropped when he hit the ground after Jaz kicked him right where it hurts. "Things are not looking good for you, Mr. Weber." The detective passed the syringe back so that one of the four officers could bag it for evidence. Once the syringe was safely sealed away into the plastic, the detective stood up and pulled out a pair of handcuffs from his trench coat pocket. He approached the curled-up Garrett and yanked his hands away from his bruised crotch and behind his back. "Garrett Webber, you're arrested for the attempted murder of Jasmine Dilan and for suspicion in the murders of Rosamie Dylan and Franklin Kennedy." Garrett was in too much pain to fight, even when Detective Moore pulled him to his feet and shoved him into the grasp of two more officers. "Get him out of here."

As the two officers escorted Garrett away, the two remaining ones made their way into the officer to look for the evidence that Jaz mentioned. Detective Moore knelt down next to Jaz and asked, "Are you alright Ms. Dilan?"

"Detective Moore?"

"Yes? I'm here."

"Can you just call me Jaz?"

"I think I can do that, Jaz." Without warning, Jaz crumbled into tears, the shock of the events of the week finally hitting her all at once. The detective removed his trench coat and wrapped it around Jaz's shoulders. "What did I tell you about going out in the cold in just your pajamas?" For some reason, the joke was enough to make Jaz smile for a moment, though the tears never stopped. Detective Moore wrapped his arms around Jaz, embracing her until she could compose herself again.

23

FORGING A NEW PATH

Two week later, Jaz found herself at Newark Airport, waiting for her flight to Seattle. Rosamie's body had, finally, been released from the coroner and sent to Rubylyne in preparation for the funeral. Even though the coroner had still not confirmed if the venom that Garrett had was the venom that killed Rosamie, an interrogation and a look under the microscope made the NYPD confident that they had a strong case against Garrett. Garret refused to make a confession, but the fact that the police saw him trying to kill Jaz made it possible for them to keep him locked up while they gathered evidence. Eventually, the charges were increased when they found out that he was working with the black market. However, the NYPD were considering a plea deal with Garrett; if he lead them to those he worked with, they would only sentence him to fifty years without parole instead of life.

Considering he would be in his eighties before that day would come, Jaz was perfectly okay with Garrett getting less time if it meant that people like Bruno were off the street. It wouldn't make much of a difference in the fight against the black market, but they had to take the wins where they could.

TVs all over the airport were covering Garrett's story. Of course, those news stories focused on how he killed Frank and didn't bother to mention Rosamie. As Annie had pointed out, "Rosamie and I are minors so they probably couldn't even mention us by name if they wanted to". *Maybe it's for the better. I don't know if I want to make the national news.*

Jessica, on the other hand, was relishing the TV time. Every opportunity she was given, she was interviewed by the press and did a good job of condemning Garrett and his actions. Of course, Jaz was pretty sure that most of her anger stemmed from the fact that she missed out on a family fortune and influence. That may have been harsh at first, but when Jessica's TV interviews started displaying her new boyfriend, who was literally a carbon copy of Frank, Jaz was justified in her pessimism

Jaz has just found a seat near her gate that wasn't near a TV that played Jessica at full volume when he phone buzzed with a new text message.

Annie
Did you get through security okay?

Yeah. It's fucking crazy, but I got to the airport early enough.

Good. Have a good flight. I wish I could go with you.

So do I. You deserve to be there.

Isa and some other guys at the support group are gonna hold a potluck in Rosamie's memory. I'll say goodbye then.

Ok. Be safe. NO DRINKING.

Believe me, I may NEVER drink again, even when I'm legal. Thank you. And thank you for hiring me. It's a lot of weight off my mind.

Hey, I know you're a hard worker. And besides, after that amazing tattoo you gave me, how could I NOT hire you?

Jaz rubbed her shoulder, covered in the rose line art that Rosamie had recently designed for her. The color could be added once the initial line art healed up. Even so, the lines alone were gorgeous.

Annie
My pleasure. I love the one that you gave me too. Have a good flight.

Will do. See you when I get back.

Right as Jaz went to put her phone away, a new text message came in.

Detective Moore

Jaz. It's Josiah Moore from the NYPD. I asked about you at your shop and Annie told me that you're on your way to attend your niece's funeral. Do you have a moment to call me?

Jaz furrowed her brows, worried about what the detective needed to talk to her about. *I better call him now.* Hitting the phone button and holding the phone up to her ear, Jaz waited as the phone rang until Josiah answered with, "I take it that this is a good time?"

"Yes, Detective. Is something wrong? Has something happened?"

"Everything is perfectly fine, Jaz. I just wanted to check in on you. You had a pretty frightening experience and that can really affect a person."

Jaz sighed, "Detective, I think you know well that I have been through much worse."

"I do, but even so, it would be irresponsible for me to not make sure you and Annie are okay."

"I appreciate your worry, Detective, but I'm actually okay."

"That's good to hear," Josiah said. A long silence fell between them before he asked, "May I ask why Annie isn't going with you? To the funeral, I mean?"

"She's still a little shook up with everything that happened. She's not really sure that she could take a funeral right now. Besides, she thinks that she's not welcome."

"Why would she think that?"

"When they were dating, Rosamie convinced Annie that my sister was homophobic, so she thinks that her being present at the funeral will cause a problem with the family. I tried to tell her that wouldn't happen and that she's welcome, but I'm not sure if she doesn't believe me or if she's just not ready. Know what I mean?"

"I do. I know that feeling all too well. Is she going to be okay by herself?"

"She's spending some time with some friends and I told her to call me if she needed to talk. If I see anything that worries me, would you mind if I let you know? And could you check on her if that's the case?"

"Of course. Not a problem."

The silence fell again. "Is there something you want to say, Detective?"

"Is it that obvious?"

"I can just sense these things. What is it?"

"I wanted to say thank you for your help."

Jaz tried to keep the surprise on her face and out of her voice. "You're welcome."

"But what you did was incredibly stupid and you could've gotten yourself killed. You need to be more careful next time."

"'Next time'?"

"Yeah. Believe it or not, Jaz, you've got the makings of a private detective and I get the distinct feeling this won't be your last case."

"I only did this for Rosamie, Annie, and myself. I needed to put my own mind at ease. I'm going to let you do the investigating from now on."

"That's too bad. You have a knack for it. Well, if you change your mind, I've emailed you a link that has a list of steps. That has all the information you need to know if you want to become a private investigator."

Before Jaz could asked anymore questions, a voice came over the nearby intercom and said, "Attention Passengers: Constitution Flight 2057 to Seattle is now boarding at gate 25."

"I have to go, Detective. My flight is boarding."

"Alright, Jaz. Have a good flight and give my condolences to your family."

"I will. Thank you for all your help, Detective."

"My pleasure. Goodbye, Jaz."

"Goodbye, Detective." Jaz hung up and got into the line by her gate, and used her phone to open up the information that Detective Moore had emailed to her.

KENNEDY KILLER CAUGHT

Ethan Turner

Garrett Weber, 37, has just pleaded guilty to the hired murder of Franklin Kennedy, the youngest son of the New York socialite family.

According to the NYPD, the tattoo artist murderer took a plea deal that resulted in a lighter sentence in exchange for helping them. Weber only got fifty years without parole as opposed to life in prison when he passed information about New York's Black Market and identified people that he worked with as an underground distributor of scorpion venom. According to the court, Weber used his connections to kill

Kennedy, telling those he worked with that Kennedy was a competing dealer and had to be "taken care of" to protect their sales.

Bruno Griffin and Kellam Delacroix, the CEOs of two competing tech companies, are just two of the names that Weber provided to the NYPD as being part of the New York Black Market. While no one can say much, Detective Josiah Moore has confirmed that the NYPD are in the process of building a case against Griffin and Delacriox. Both CEOs have refused to comment, as have their lawyers and their companies' representatives.

The death of Kennedy is not the only crime that Weber has pleaded guilty of. He has also confessed to the murder of another person, the attempted murder of a third person, and the stalking and harassment of Jessica Price, Franklin Kennedy's fiancé. When asked about the case against Weber, Price said, "He deserves the death penalty for what he's done. He has ruined my life, and I am filing a restraining order again him as we speak."

Price's statement seems to not be far from the truth. Investigations have shown that Weber's motivations for killing Kennedy can be linked to her, and Weber and Price used to date before she became engaged to Kennedy. No word, however, on how Wbere's other two victims play into this story.

The police have refused to identify Weber's other murder victim, claiming that they were a minor and, as such, the name cannot be released without the permission of the family, which has not been given. The attempted murder victim has been named as Jasmine Dilan. Little is known about Dilan, as she has refused to interview or comment on the trial. Research shows that she is a tattoo artist in New York, but her shop is currently closed until further notice.

The gray-haired, spectacled man looked out of place in the cafeteria of the Federal Detention Center, SeaTac. His fellow inmates were what the world would describe as "hardened criminals" who had ended up there for any number of reasons; gang initiations, grand theft auto, manslaughter, and everything in between. None of them took pleasure in reading things like the New York Times like he did. Yet, no one bothered him as he read during the sanctioned lunch hour. As overflowing as the jail was, he got a table all to himself; all the other inmates were more than willing to squeeze each other in if it meant that they didn't have to share a table with him.

As he was reading the frontpage story of his favorite paper, his wrinkled face wrinkled even more as his thin mouth curled into a smile. Jasmine Dilan. That was a name he'd not heard in years, and yet he thought about her every day. He found it delightfully ironic that she had become a tattoo artist. Perhaps he deserved some credit in her path to success. She owed him a debt of gratitude.

"Soon."

THE END

K ELSEY ANNE LOVELADY WAS born in Billings, Montana and grew up in Bozeman. At fifteen her family moved to Shawnee Mission, Kansas. She stayed there from her Junior year of high school up until she graduated from Johnson County Community College with her Associate of Arts Degree in Arts and Science. She graduated from the University of Wyoming with her B.F.A. in Musical Theatre and her Minor in Writing. She published her first book, "STAFROGED: Orion" on the day she graduated, and is in the process of rewriting it. She has also dabbled in writing for the theatre with her 10-Minute Play "How Are You?", which was produced by the True Troupe of Cheyenne as part of their 2019 Wrights of

Wyoming Playwrighting Festival.

Kelsey also writes for the online literary magazines "In The Pantheon" and "In the Crescent"

She can be reached at: loveladynovels@gmail.com

Kelsey Anne Lovelady on Patreon

Kelsey Anne Lovelady on Facebook

Kelsey Anne Lovelady on YouTube

@KelseyALovelady on Twitter

Lovelady Novels on Tumblr

KelseyAnneLovelady on Instagram

Kelsey Anne Lovelady on Goodreads

Adrestia on In The Pantheon

Namid Cook on In the Crescent

STAY TUNED FOR KELSEY'S NEXT BOOK

"INDIFFERENT"

COMING NOVEMBER 2022

CPSIA information can be obtained
at www.ICGtesting.com
Printed in the USA
BVHW031208021022
648495BV00002B/8